DUE DATE

WELL SUITED

STACI HART

Cover design by **Quirky Bird**

Photography by **Perrywinkle Photography**

Editing by **Jovana Shirley, Unforeseen Editing**

Book design by **Inkstain Design Studio**

WELL
SUITED

To those who aren't sure if love is real:
Love believes enough for the both you.

PROLOGUE

THEO

THAT NIGHT

"Hello, Theodore."

A very serious, very stern, utterly stunning woman stood before me with her hand jutted out and a determined set to her chin, which was tipped up so she could look me square in the eye.

The only thing I hated worse than blind dates was the use of my full name. But from her lips, I was disarmed and unexpectedly charmed by the formality, as if she were meeting a colleague or a second cousin, twice removed, not a date. I had a feeling the context didn't matter. She'd greet everyone with the same businesslike matter-of-factness and firmness of hand.

Six sets of curious eyes—her friends and my twin brother—watched on as I took her offered hand. But rather than shake it as she'd intended, I turned it over and brushed the soft skin and delicate bones with my lips.

At the flash of simultaneous heat and aversion behind her steely eyes, my smile tilted higher.

"Nice to meet you, Katherine."

Her palm, which had bloomed with a cool sweat, disappeared in a snap of motion. Wide, full lips the color of a stoplight flattened.

"That's how the flu spreads, you know," she said, wiping the back of her hand on her dress.

I fought the urge to laugh, saying instead, "I'd hate to be the cause of senseless virus-spreading. I'm sorry."

She gave me a single curt nod. "You're forgiven. And I hope you like to dance," she said.

For a split second, I imagined turning her around the dance floor at the swing club we were heading to.

"I do." My smile hadn't budged.

"And I hope you don't mind me leading."

At that, my smile liquefied, brows drawing together. My mouth opened, then closed again when I could find no clever response. Only a string of questions.

"Katherine and I usually dance together," Amelia, my brother's wife, offered helpfully, which answered at least three-quarters of my questions.

"Some people say I have control issues," Katherine added with a shrug.

Amelia laughed. "It keeps us from getting hit on, too."

"They think we're lesbians," Katherine clarified clinically.

Tommy burst into laughter, looking down into Amelia's face with disbelief.

"Oh, don't look at me like that," Amelia said. "Pretending to be a lesbian is easier than talking to strange men. Even when she kissed me in front of a hundred people."

Tommy's laughter stopped dead. "I thought you'd never been kissed."

Amelia rolled her eyes. "That didn't count. There wasn't even any tongue."

A single *Ha!* shot out of Katherine.

The conversation shifted, and when we all had drinks in hand, Katherine's friend Val raised her glass and toasted. But I wasn't listening.

I was watching the girl with the stiff spine and dark hair, the girl who smelled like anticipation and fresh, clean soap. Her eyes weren't on me.

But mine were on her.

We sipped our drinks, chatted easily, the camaraderie clear between the group, all bound together by the four girls. Rin, the tall Asian with a gentle smile and soft laugh. Val, the short, curvy one with freckles smattered across her nose and wild, curly hair. Amelia, my brother's fake wife, the fairy with platinum hair and cornflower-blue eyes. And Katherine, the starched, serious girl who was to be my date, and who I'd decided I'd make smile before the night was through.

It seemed a herculean task. But I always loved a good challenge.

Out the door we went, piling into cabs to head to the swing club. We loaded in with Val and her boyfriend, the conversation flowing between the three of them. But I spent the ride in observation, cataloging everything about her. Her hair, glossy and dark, bangs cut in a precise line. Her dress, tailored with an exactness that accentuated the curve of her waist, punctuated by a thin belt. Her lips seemed to forever rest in a flat line, even when she was amused. There was no little upturn in the corners, no mirth. When she smiled, her lips stayed together. When she laughed, it was compact, contained.

In fact, everything about her seemed contained, from her small, straight nose to her level shoulders. From her long fingers, wound together smartly and symmetrically in her lap, to her ankles, which crossed demurely. Her smile. Her eyes. The truth of her, I imagined, was locked down somewhere between her ears and never let out.

And I wanted to pick the lock.

We breezed past the line and straight to the bouncer, who shook hands with Val's boyfriend. He seemed to know everyone except me and Tommy, and eyed us both with suspicion and warning as we passed.

It was like stepping back in time. Swing music filled the ballroom from corner to velvet corner, from parquet to elegantly tiled ceiling, strung with hanging Edison bulbs at varying heights. They cast a golden light on the dance floor, which was a sea of bouncing heads, dotted with the occasional flip of skirts and saddle shoes.

We wound our way into the club, everyone hand in hand, except Katherine and me. That was, until she saw the dance floor.

And that was the beginning of my end.

Her face opened up, her smile wide and bright, her eyes joyous and brows high, the emotion transforming her. The vision hit me in the chest.

When she snagged my hand and towed me toward the parquet, that twist in my chest deepened. Tightened. Simmered and crackled. I followed her willingly.

I chased the fleeting thought that I'd follow her anywhere.

She pulled me to a stop and turned to face me, her smile smaller but undeniable, her arm out to the side, palm posed in wait for mine.

"All right, are you ready?" she asked.

I slipped my hand into hers despite that it was extended to the wrong side. Everything was backward. My hand that should have gone on her waist hesitated.

I frowned.

"Put it on my shoulder," she offered helpfully.

I did as I'd been told. My hand swallowed the curve.

My frown deepened.

"Okay," she said with authority, "let me show you how to triple-step."

I kept my smile put away. Just after my mom had been diagnosed with Parkinson's, Tommy and I had taken classes with her to cross it off her bucket list before she lost mobility. But I held my tongue and did as Katherine guided, appreciating the feel of her hand on my waist and the sound of her voice as she taught me something I already knew.

The backward stance was difficult enough, but when she tried to put me in a sweetheart hold—my back to her front, her arms around my waist—she couldn't get her arms over my head, which was over a foot above hers.

She let me go with her face pinched in frustration and a sigh on her pretty lips. "Well, that does it. You're going to have to lead."

"Oh, thank God," I said with a sigh and a smirk, reversing our hands.

I took off, spinning her out and bouncing her around to the bopping beat of the music. Her face shot open like a starting gate, her black lashes shuttering as she blinked her shock away.

And then she laughed.

The sound was open, lilting and musical, a complete juxtaposition to everything about her. It was free, untethered, floating around us to twist together with the jazz music like its own song.

I should have realized right then that I was doomed, damned. But the novelty of her, the unexpected intrigue, the sheer sight and smell of her were too alluring to resist. I couldn't tell you exactly why. Only that something in her and something in me sparked like a knife against flint.

I wondered briefly which was whom, deciding I was the flint.

Struck.

As I zipped her around the dance floor, she shifted, softened. Changed. I didn't let up, too surprised by whatever was happening between us to willingly speak.

You see, I didn't date—not in the relationship way at least. There were girls, plenty of girls—perks of my brother's firm spot in the public eye—but I hadn't *dated* in years. I was too busy keeping my brother out of trouble and taking care of my mom to have time or energy left over for a girlfriend.

I was too busy to be lonely. And that companionship hadn't ever been missed. Not until that moment on the dance floor.

The music slowed, and her body pressed against mine. She fit into my arms with a click that I felt somewhere in the vicinity of my ribs.

I didn't know what it was. All I knew was that I had no intention of ignoring it.

Her cheeks were flushed, her eyes bright and sharp. She was breathless, and the look in her eyes left me feeling it was only in part from the dancing.

"Why didn't you tell me you danced?" she asked in all seriousness.

I shrugged one shoulder. "You didn't ask."

An upward curl of her lips. "How presumptuous of me."

"Can't say I blame you, Kate."

The curl reversed into a frown. "My name is Katherine, with a K. Not Kate. Not Katie or Kat. *Katherine.*"

"With a K," I echoed.

"Yes. I dislike nicknames."

"Your friends have nicknames."

Her brows flicked together. "Those are their names—Rin and Val. It's how they were introduced to me."

"By that rule, you should call me Theo."

"I dislike nicknames," she said again, her voice a notch lower and her brows a millimeter closer.

I chuckled. "I won't make you defend your code, *Katherine.* I only wondered. What is it you do?"

"I'm a librarian at the New York Public Library."

"A librarian," I said, enlightened as a couple of Katherine-shaped puzzle pieces snapped together.

Her eyes narrowed. "Please, don't make any pornographic librarian jokes. I don't find them amusing."

This time when I laughed, it was a full, deep rumble. "Anything you want, Kate."

"Katherine," she corrected. "You're a wonderful dancer. Much better than me, and I've been coming here for months."

"I've got something to confess," I said, lowering my lips to angle for her ear. "Tommy and I had lessons."

"Oh." The word was full of air and breath as equally as it was contained.

When I straightened up and looked down into her face, her brow quirked like she was puzzling me out. Difference was, I knew how to school my face. When struck with the unexpected, it seemed that Katherine did not.

"Why do you smell so good?" she asked. "Is it your cologne?"

I considered for a split second what she could possibly be smelling. "I don't wear cologne."

She leaned in, tilting her chin higher so she could get her nose as close to my neck as possible. Her hand slipped into my lapel and fisted as she took a deep inhale. A little hum followed that sent a hot pulse through me.

"You smell so nice," she murmured. "I don't recall ever noticing how a man smells. Not a pleasant smell at least."

I wasn't sure what to say, staring into the face of this amusing creature, so brash and strange and lovely.

She spoke first, "Our brains are incredible machines. They know when to open and close gates for pheromones, how to detect chemosignals from another human and make decisions based on them. Adrenaline. Oxytocin. Dopamine. Before we know anything about each other, there's a level of compatibility that can be determined simply by smell."

"Well then, I'm even more flattered."

She didn't acknowledge what I'd said, just continued as I swayed with her under the golden light of the Edison bulbs. "Everything we feel can be equated to a chemical reaction. Lust, for instance, is driven by a desire for sexual gratification."

"Kate," I said with a sideways smile and a thumping pulse, "are you coming on to me?"

"Katherine, and maybe. Something about the way you smell, the way you move, makes me salivate. Do you think I smell good, too?"

I would have called the question timid had it not been so unaffected by emotion. "Hmm. Let's see." My hand shifted from her waist and gathered her hair to expose her neck. And I lowered my nose to the column, brushed the silky skin, dragged the tip up to the space behind her jaw, around the curve of muscle to the hollow behind her ear.

She smelled like rain and fresh-cut flowers, like desire and unspoken promises. She smelled like my last meal, like a color I'd never seen before. Like a sense I hadn't known I had was awakened simply by the proximity of my lips to her skin.

Her breath consisted of shallow sips of air. Her fist around my lapel clutched tighter and pulled like she wanted me to wrap myself around her.

I caught her earlobe in my teeth. A shudder trembled through her.

"Good enough to eat," I whispered into the curve of her ear.

"Did you know that lips are the most exposed erogenous zone we possess?" The question was rough and shaky.

I couldn't seem to stop myself from nuzzling her neck, breathing her in. "I might have been able to guess."

Her neck bent, cradling my face to keep it where it was. "Lip contact engages five of twelve total cranial nerves. Every sense is engaged. Electricity is sent between our brains, skin, tongues, lips, back and forth, carrying the signals to relay every feeling."

My lips closed over the tender skin behind her ear, trying to understand how her clinical explanation of kissing was so hot. "Do you want me to kiss you, Kate?"

"Katherine," she breathed. "And yes, I think I do."

I dislodged myself from her, fueled only by the knowledge that if I did, I could kiss her.

But not yet. Not here.

Instead, I cupped her jaw and looked into her eyes. "What do you say we get out of here?"

And with a smile, she answered, "I'd say, lead the way."

We spent the following few minutes saying goodbye to everyone under the guise of me getting her home safely. Without a sideways glance, they sent us on. I found myself surprised. No one had noticed our exchange or whatever zinged between us. Maybe I appeared unassuming, or maybe they doubted Katherine's desire to go home with anyone.

Either way, they were wrong.

We hurried out of the club, slipping silently into a taxi. The second he had his destination—her place, which was slated to be empty all night—I grabbed her around the waist and pulled her across the bench, tucking her into my side with another neat, nearly audible click. She felt it too, leaned into it. Into me.

Anticipation, thick and heady, clung to every molecule between us.

Her face turned to mine, a request for a kiss.

One that I denied.

Instead, I engaged every other avenue of connection. Hooked her knees to sling her legs across my lap. My fingertips tasted the skin of her thigh, slid under the hem of her dress, only high enough to tease. My lips I kept directed to the front window, a testament to my will as her hands cupped my neck, my jaw, tested the consistency of my hair with thirsty fingertips. Her lips—I could feel them across the slim space, her breath humid and sweet—hovered over the tender, tingling skin of my neck, just above my thrumming pulse.

It was a game, a teasing game of control, a momentary denial of the thing we wanted desperately as we reveled in the sweet suspense of restraint.

I touched her in places never considered indecent—the hollow under the ball of her ankle, the tendon behind her knee, the soft space inside her elbow, the dip above her collarbone. Every second that kiss was denied heightened the simmering desire, the strange, unexpected tingling of my lips painful in intensity. She squirmed in my lap, setting another painfully intense sensation beneath her legs with the rise of my cock. It was unmistakable, and for a moment, I feared she'd shift away. But instead, the smallest moan slipped from her, and her thighs—thighs I'd have around my waist or so help me— shifted against my aching length.

And still, I didn't kiss her.

But the desire to consumed every thought.

When the cab stopped, I shoved a wad of cash at the driver before throwing the door open. Her hand was in mine. We trotted up the steps. She unlocked the door with trembling hands. And then we were inside the dark house, the door closing with a snick, shutting out the city and the night outside.

The only sound was her breath and mine in a matched rhythm.

Neither of us moved. The details of her face were obscured in shadows but for her eyes, which caught the ambient moonlight and reflected it back at me.

With a breath deemed to fortify her, she said, "Kiss m—"

She was in my arms, her body soft and supple. And my lips took a taste they would regret.

Because within a single heartbeat, I was addicted.

My universe shrank to the point where our lips melded, exploding in a bang to rival the big one, contained at the tips of our searching tongues. A million nerves fired like starbursts across our lips. And on the fringes in nebulous tendrils were hands, breaths, bodies, heartbeats—all in autonomous sync.

Beyond all reasoning, beyond all sense, some event had come to pass, leaving a deep, thrumming word in my chest. And I wrote that word on her body with fingertips and tongue.

Mine.

The urge was instinct, an impulse, primal in origin and execution. It was, as she'd so studiously pointed out, a matter of science. Of chemicals set in motion by our brains, pumped through our bodies by thundering hearts. But whatever cocktail had been created by the mix of her chemistry and mine was potent and potentially lethal in intensity. And I felt the beginnings of what would become an undeniable fact.

The girl in my arms was no Katherine-with-a-K-not-Katie.

This girl was *Kate.*

This sighing, soft creature, whatever she was, was not who she'd appeared on first glance. She was so much more.

The way I undressed her undid me. The way she tasted consumed me. The way she felt beneath me, around me, stroked the pulse of my very self.

And I didn't care why because *she* was *mine.*

It didn't even cross my mind that I might not be hers.

FIRST
TRIMESTER

DECISIONS, DECISIONS

KATHERINE

5 WEEKS, 1 DAY

I wish I could say that disbelief was the emotion I felt as I held the small plastic stick in fingers I knew to be mine but were utterly unrecognizable. My gaze was fixed on the tiny window where a blue plus sign stared back at me with unflinching clarity.

There was no disbelief, seeing as how I knew exactly when, how, and with whom it'd happened.

When: approximately five weeks ago.

Who: one-night stand.

How: prophylactic malfunction.

If birth control didn't make me an irrational, blubbering mess, my uterus would not be occupied by a zygote.

No, I corrected myself—*not a zygote*. At this stage, it was an embryo and would have a heartbeat, tail, and tiny nubs that would become arms and legs. My photographic memory recalled an image I'd seen in sex ed during junior high of something that looked closer to an extraterrestrial than a baby.

My stomach rolled at the thought. Or at the realization. Or because the surge of hormones was giving me morning sickness. Or, in this instance, afternoon sickness.

I swallowed back my lunch, forcing it down my esophagus where it belonged before shifting my train of thought. If I didn't, I really would vomit.

I inventoried my feelings with the clinical detachment with which I approached everything. Shock was at the top of the list, indicated by my rapid breaths, clammy hands, racing pulse, and the uncommon dizziness that rose and fell in waves. The reason, I quickly deduced, was that an occupied uterus had no place in my current plan, life or otherwise. My dinner plans for sushi were out the window for sure.

I lowered myself to sit on the closed toilet, holding the pregnancy test in dead, foreign hands. My back was ramrod straight, my shoulder blades pulled back, nose in the air sucking oxygen like it would stop me from vomiting. Resisting was beginning to seem futile. I wondered absently how long I could iron-stomach it before I lost my lunch.

The thought made me gag again.

I gripped the reins on my galloping thoughts, pulling them to a halt so I could find the road again.

Because I needed to decide what I was going to do.

I'd always wanted to procreate, assumed that I would. Allotted my future self a single child to appease the instinct to continue my genetics, a sentimental instinct driven by the desire for immortality more than a desire for love. Humans were complex, fascinating creatures, and creating was something I considered an honor. Taking a human life in any form was unfathomable. And I found the thought of giving away a child I'd created beyond comprehension.

The upside to my unforeseen path was that I didn't have to wait to find a suitable mate.

I'd already found one.

Genetically, he was the cream of the crop. As a physical specimen, he was ideal—his musculature a study in symmetry and strength, his height imposing, dominant. He was perfectly masculine, a man who thrived on control and command, and beyond that, he was highly intelligent and resourceful.

Really, I couldn't have handpicked a better genetic pool.

Of course, there was one slight issue.

For the last four-plus weeks, I'd been avoiding him at all costs.

It wasn't because I didn't like him, nor was it because I didn't want to see him again. It was quite the opposite. I liked him so much, I'd immediately distanced myself.

It was better this way, for all of us. That he'd spent one night with me was a fluke. Any more than that, and I'd be pressing my luck. I was built for a lot of things—organization, research, mathematics, pragmatism, to name a few—but relationships was not one of them.

My mind briefly ran over my financials, concluding quickly that my job as a page at the New York Public Library would not suffice to support myself and the embryo. I'd have to move into research, which I had been avoiding—I loved the solitude of shelving books, and trading that for a full day researching any and everything for strangers sounded exhausting. A nanny would be necessary, of course, but who didn't have a nanny in Manhattan?

With a deep breath and a curt nod at my reflection in the bathroom mirror, I decided.

This was the perfect opportunity to achieve a goal, and it seemed silly not to take it simply because it wasn't in my plan. It had landed in my lap. Or, more accurately, my uterus.

With that resolved, I stood, set the pregnancy test on the counter, and got down on my knees to empty my stomach.

I swiped at involuntary tears from my cheeks as I stood and turned to brush my teeth. A rush of irrational sadness arrested me. Because all I truly wanted was to tell my friends. Not for validation, but because they were the people I shared everything with. And the comfort of sharing this with them was something I thought I might need, judging by the unfamiliar twist in my chest.

But they were all gone, living their own lives with their boyfriends and husbands and fiancés. And I was here, alone. I didn't even have Claudius the cat anymore. Amelia had taken him with her when she got married.

I'd text them later and ask them to come over, which I knew they would honor without question. And maybe I'd swing by the shelter and get a cat of my own.

But first, I needed to find Theodore Bane and tell him I was having his baby.

TRANSACTION MALFUNCTION

THEO

"Hello, Theodore."

My shock at finding Katherine Lawson on my stoop, clutching her bag with her chin tilted up to eye me with clinical coolness, happened behind a flat mask of indifference. Primarily because I hadn't seen her in four weeks, five days, and a handful of hours.

Though not for lack of trying. The elusive creature had avoided me with the stealth and skill of a spy on the run.

"Hello, Katherine."

"May I come in? I'd like to discuss our transaction last month."

She used the word *transaction*—which made her sound like either an ATM or a hooker—with the detached objectivity that had amused and intrigued me when we met. *That night.* I felt the tug of my lips on one side, a climbing smile I couldn't have stopped if I wanted to.

Which I didn't.

I shifted out of the way, taking the door with me. "I've been interested in discussing our…transaction for a while."

"Yes, I know," she said as she passed.

I caught the scent of clean, crisp soap, nothing more. No perfume, no makeup, her face as fresh and pretty as I remembered. More so. My memory paled in comparison to the real thing. Chestnut hair, straight and neat, with bangs manicured to a strict line. Her eyes were hazel, an amalgamation of browns and mossy greens, flecked with bursts of blue. Bright eyes, sharp with intelligence and curiosity, dark with the shroud she kept between herself and everyone else.

There was an entire world behind those eyes, locked up and kept from everyone.

But I wasn't everyone.

Her back was straight as an arrow, her shoulders proud and shoulder blades together. But once, I'd seen her soft. Once, I'd heard her sigh. Once, she'd been supple and giving beneath me.

Goddamn it, I hated that she'd blown me off. But as I closed the door and followed her into the entryway, I smirked with smug certainty that I was back in the game.

I stepped into her, reaching to help her out of her coat. "Here, let me."

My breath stirred her hair, and she froze for a nanosecond before relaxing. I even thought I saw a flicker of a smile on her level lips.

Once her coat hung on a hook, we headed into the living room.

"Can I get you something to drink? Scotch on the rocks, right?"

"No, thank you," she said, taking a breath to say something else. But she caught herself, lips closing. She moved to the couch and sat.

I took a seat opposite her, leaning back as I hooked an ankle on my knee and an elbow on the back of the couch. I was the picture of casual impassivity. Inside, I was rubbing my hands together as I mapped out every path to convince her to see me again.

"I'm glad to see you, Kate," I said, still smiling sidelong at her.

"Katherine," she said stiffly. "I don't like nicknames."

"I know, but I do."

Her eyes flicked to the ceiling. But her cheeks belied her annoyance with a rosy flush. "I have something very important to discuss with you, Theodore."

"You're sorry for not calling?"

"No. I didn't call you on purpose," she said as if I didn't know. "Such was our arrangement."

A chuckle hummed in my throat. "Arrangements can be renegotiated."

"That's not why I'm here. During our transaction, there was a malfunction, if you remember."

All levity was gone with a cold, heavy thunk. My heart and stomach do-si-do'd. I swallowed a lump the size of Delaware, and it bobbed back up and to the back of my throat. "I remember."

"Well, I've just confirmed that I'm pregnant."

My lungs emptied like I'd been kicked in the chest and propelled off a cliff. Gravity shifted in a sickening tilt that brought my lunch charging up my esophagus. Pregnant. She was pregnant. The word was nonsense to my brain, a made-up string of syllables with letters pulled from a Scrabble bag.

Her face was as stoic as ever. I thought I might have imagined a flicker of concern or indecision behind her eyes, but it was gone by the time she began to speak again, the speech rehearsed, outlining every detail like a cartographer.

"You were the only man I have had intercourse with in quite some time. There's no question as to whether or not it's yours. After going through my finances and making some cursory plans, I've decided to have the baby and raise it. If you would like to be involved, your assistance would be welcome, but you are not obligated in any way. I am fully capable of raising the embryo on my own. Well," she corrected, "with the help of a nanny. But without your aid."

I blinked.

"I can see that you need a moment to process. Please, take your time."

At that, she sat back, reached into her bag, and returned with a book.

My first thought was that she was absolutely lovely, sitting there on my couch with a book in her long fingers.

My second thought was that my child resided somewhere in the vicinity of her hips.

Stunned was an understatement, though the closest word to describe how I felt. Stunned, like I'd been brained with a Louisville and was lying on the sidewalk, trying to figure out why the horizon was vertical.

"We're having a baby," I mumbled.

"Technically, I'm having a baby. But I appreciate the sentiment."

A disbelieving laugh chuffed out of me. The creature before me tilted her head curiously.

She was without a doubt the most intriguing woman I had ever met. And I'd known scores. Perks of being the twin of a famous author and notorious rake, although since he and Amelia had gotten together, things had slowed down. Frankly, I'd been too busy helping Tommy run his career to date for the last six years. Fuck, sure. But Katherine was the first person in years I'd actually wanted to see again.

And she'd stayed away with annoying determination.

Flashes of that night flickered in my mind, from the stiff shake of her hand to her shock as I whipped her around the dance floor. Spent the night with her, one night. She'd said that was all it'd be.

But when the time had come to walk away, I hadn't found it as easy to follow through as she had. I'd called. Texted. Resorted to running around with Tommy and Amelia in the hopes that we'd bump into her.

I'd been ignored and avoided on all fronts. And now, here she was, sitting in my living room for no reason other than that she was pregnant.

With my baby.

She watched me with those complicated eyes, cool as a cucumber on a sweltering August day—refreshing, crisp and sharp. I untied my tongue, lining up my thoughts so I could deliver them to her with the same clarity and decision as she'd afforded me.

I didn't think she'd agree to what I was about to propose otherwise. Because Katherine Lawson spoke the language of logic.

And that was a language I was familiar with.

"I would like to discuss the nature of my involvement with the baby."

"Embryo," she corrected, closing her book with a nod. "Yes, of course."

I shifted, still trying to collect my wits and words, smoothing my tie as I thought. Her gaze snagged the motion, catching on my hands. Absently, she wet her lips, the tip of her tongue appearing and disappearing.

"I would like to be involved at every level, on all fronts. Doctor's visits and childbirth classes. Baby registry and stroller research. Nanny interviews. Diaper changes. Midnight bottles. I don't want to miss anything, Kate."

She ignored my needling use of her nickname. And really, I should have felt bad for using it. It was just that the woman I'd had that night was not *Katherine with a K, not Katie or Kat*. The girl I'd held in my arms was a soft, sighing Kate, and that was all there was to it.

But the reason the offense had gone ignored was that it seemed it was her turn to be stunned. It was in the slight widening of her eyes, the unnatural stillness of her body. I wasn't sure she was breathing.

"Are you all right?" I asked with a flex of my brows.

She drew a breath that seemed to reanimate her. "Yes. I just expected a different answer."

"You expected me to wish you good luck and send you on your way?"

"Well, yes. It seemed like the easy answer."

"Easy doesn't suit me," I said, shifting back to the details. "I have a proposition to make. Once the baby comes, it's not going to be easy to live separately. Or," I amended, "I should say, it would be much easier *not* to live separately."

Suspicion flickered across her brow. "You suggest we cohabitate?"

I wanted to suggest more than that. But rather than press my luck, I said, "Yes. It makes the most sense."

The corners of her lips dipped in the smallest of frowns. But that was how she seemed to do everything. By increment. "I'd like to think about that offer and discuss it later. I've made enough mammoth decisions today. I think I might need to pace myself."

I smiled, not only because she was endearingly pragmatic, but because she hadn't said no. "Of course."

She took a deep, decisive breath through her nose and nodded once. When she stood, it was to extend her hand. "Thank you for seeing me unannounced, Theodore. And for your offer of help."

I rose to meet her, taking her hand. But rather than shake it, I pulled her closer. "You won't be alone, Kate. I'll be here every step of the way."

There she was, the girl from before. She appeared like a specter with a softening of her eyes, her face, her body, affected by me as I was by her. It was automatic, unwitting, a natural reaction of her body and mine. An instinct. An impulse.

"I don't think we should see each other romantically, Theodore," she whispered. Her eyes said something else entirely.

But I didn't press. Somehow, I'd known this was what she'd say. "Whatever you want, Kate."

"Katherine," she breathed.

"When you call me Theo, I'll call you Katherine."

For a moment, she said nothing, just stared at my lips. "Why do you want to raise a child with a stranger?"

The question simmered in my chest, warm and bubbling and steady. "Because I didn't have a father, and the thought of fathering a child who doesn't know me just isn't something I can live with."

A break in the clouds, a slant of light behind her eyes. Her understanding shone on me like a ray of sunshine.

"That, and I don't feel like you're a stranger at all."

"But I am," she insisted.

I shrugged my shoulder as I slipped a hand into her hair. Her stubborn little jaw rested in the curve of my palm.

"Technically, yes."

"There's no other way but technically."

"Oh, there is. And when you figure it out, I think you'll marry me."

The color rose in her cheeks the split second before she laughed. It was a strange, musical sound from a woman so contained, a sound free and floating. "I don't believe in marriage."

"Don't worry. There's plenty of time to change your mind."

Brighter her cheeks flared, though her eyes were merry, laughing as readily as her lips. "You are presumptuous."

"It's true. But I'm always right. Statistically, it's safe to presume."

With another chuckle, she stepped back. I instantly wished I'd kissed her.

But if I was going to have her for my own, I had the feeling that patience and logic were the only paths to get her.

And I had both in spades.

I was about to reach for her bag in an effort to help her out. But before I could, she listed, shifting in a dangerous tilt that indicated a loss of control.

And with one step and a painful lurch of my heart, I intercepted her before she hit the ground.

LET ME HELP YOU WITH THAT

KATHERINE

"Kate? Kate, wake up."

A big, warm hand on my clammy face. His voice, tight with concern, deep with worry. Something soft under my back—the couch, I realized.

My lids were vault doors, heavy and immovable.

"Katherine," I corrected, a whisper through sticky lips.

A chuckle.

"Oh, thank God." The voice was Amelia's, and the sound wrinkled my brow.

I summoned the strength to crack my eyelids and found three worried faces hovering over me. One was Amelia's, her eyes wide and bright. The other two were mirrors of each other—dark eyes, dark hair, furrowed brows, full lips ticked down in a frown. But Tommy's hair was long and irreverent while Theo's was cropped and contained.

I found I much preferred the latter.

I moved to sit, eliciting arguments from the peanut gallery. But Theo took my arm and helped me up, kneeling at my feet.

"We should get you to the doctor," he said. Worry etched his brow.

I sighed, rolling my neck. "I'm fine. It's just that I've thrown up everything I've eaten. I think my blood sugar is low."

Amelia slid in next to me. "Are you all right? Are you sick?"

"No, I'm pregnant."

Her lashes were flittering wings as she blinked. "You're...I'm sorry. You're what?"

"Pregnant. With Theodore's embryo."

Her mouth opened. Closed again. Opened and hung there. Closed once more. Tommy turned to his brother, and when their eyes met, they had a full conversation without speaking a word.

"The night at the club," Theo said, answering their silent question.

"A baby?" Amelia breathed, her big eyes sparkling with tears.

"Eventually, yes. But right now it looks closer to a Lovecraftian demon than a baby. So, for now, it's just an embryo."

She laughed. "Katherine, it's a baby."

"Amelia, it has a tail."

Another laugh. "I suppose I shouldn't be surprised that you're handling this so well." Her voice softened. "When did you find out?"

There it was again, a twist in my chest that wasn't painful, just a tight ache that seemed to be trying to tell me something, though I couldn't imagine what. "Just a bit ago. I was going to ask you all to come over so I could tell you. I didn't expect for you to find out like this."

She took my hands, her lips smiling. "Oh, Katherine. I'm just... I'm so happy for you."

I smiled back, a cursory flicker of my lips. "Thank you," I said like I was supposed to. Because the truth was, I didn't know how I felt. I just was. *It* just was, when a few hours ago, it wasn't.

I wondered briefly if some emotional fallout would come from the decision. It was likely. And the when and how of it would probably be out of my control. I shifted against my discomfort.

Theo's dark eyes appeared black, the pupil and iris a meld of color so deep, there was no discerning their bounds. His lips, which were wide and lusciously full, frowned.

"Who's staying with you?" he asked with the direct authority of a man about to get something done.

"No one," I answered. "Not anymore. Occasionally, my roommates will stay over, but that's become infrequent now that they're in relationships."

His frown deepened. "I think you should reconsider my suggestion. In fact, I think it should become effective immediately."

"Suggestion?" Tommy asked, a looming column of darkness. The same black eyes, the imposing dark hair, the inky color of his leather jacket, which squeaked as he crossed his arms.

"Theodore suggested that we cohabitate. That it would be easier if we're living in the same space once the baby is born."

At that, Tommy shared another look with his brother. This one held an edge of amusement, judging by the uptick of those devilish lips of theirs.

But it was Amelia who spoke. "I have so many questions, but we're going to talk about that later." It was as close to a warning as Amelia ever gave.

I sighed, already dreading the full focus of her attention when we were alone.

It seemed I had quite a bit of explaining to do.

Theo's jaw was set, his eyes sparking with determination. "You just fainted. What if you'd been alone? What if you'd hit your head or fainted in the shower? I don't think you should be alone, Kate."

Amelia's face swiveled to Theo, her brows arched in surprise.

Another sigh, this one resigned. "I'm not infirmed. I'm pregnant. I doubt I'll faint again."

"There's no way you can know that," he countered deftly.

Amelia nibbled on her lip.

Tommy watched the whole thing with the gears in his brain whirring.

They were all looking at me. And I found myself struggling to argue.

"I appreciate your concern, but really, I'm fine. I should have eaten some crackers after throwing up. As long as I keep my blood sugar in a healthy range, I won't faint again."

Theo ignored my protest completely. "Upstairs are two full master bedrooms and a living area. There's an office, which we can convert to the baby's room. I'm here. My mother is here. Amelia and Tommy are right upstairs. You won't be alone if something happens."

Now it was my turn to frown. The expression felt mighty on my face, though it was little more than a fractional downturn of my lips. "That's a lot of people in one place."

"It's not really one place," Amelia said, instantly excited. "We're in a separate apartment, and Sarah is down here. Really, you should see Theo's floor. You'll have privacy. It's quiet here. You won't be bothered. And I'll be right here, all the time. I hate the idea of you being all alone in the house. You don't even have Claudius anymore."

A single chuckle huffed from my nose. "I was thinking about going by a shelter on my way home."

"A cat won't push a Life Alert button for you," Tommy pointed out. "If you're here, we can all help."

My frown deepened. "I don't need help."

Amelia squeezed my hand. "No, you don't. You can do anything. But wouldn't it be easier—safer—if you weren't alone?"

I had no argument beyond not wanting to live with strangers. The idea of so much change made me uncomfortable. But I considered the embryo. And the fact that I had just fainted. Had Theo not been there, I would have hit my head on the coffee table.

The thought gave me pause.

"I...need more time to consider it," I finally said.

A flash of triumph shot across his face before it smoothed, though his smile remained intact. It was small, higher on one side, cocksure and infallible.

I wondered briefly what his percentage of the time he was right, and estimated by his confidence that it was extraordinarily high.

"I'll take that answer as enough," he said as he stood. When our eyes met, he added, "For now."

I ignored the implication that he'd press me. I didn't like to be pressed. Or coerced. Or told what to do. I appreciated order and rules, but beyond that, I was as steadfast and stubborn as anyone, including Theodore Bane.

"Well, I'm coming home with you," Amelia insisted.

I couldn't even pretend to argue. My relief was instant. "All right," I said, shifting to stand.

All three of them moved to help me at once. But Theo made it first, taking my arm, slipping a hand around my waist. Something in his touch relayed his thoughts—tenderness, affection, protection. And although I rankled at the feeling of being treated as an invalid, there was something deeply comforting about the gesture.

I didn't dislike the sensation at all. In fact, I leaned into it for just a moment.

And then I broke away.

There were things in life that I cherished, upheld as holy gospel—logic, knowledge, and truth. And in that triad, there was no room for such things as sentimentality. Feelings were false, brain chemicals and triggered dendrites. Love wasn't real. It was a series of chemosignals that one became addicted to. Nothing more.

There was no magic to love. Because magic didn't exist.

Not for me.

But partnership did.

And Theodore had already proven himself to be well suited for the job.

To someone more tenderhearted, our meeting would have been called fate. But to me, it was a matter of momentary compatibility. In truth, we could have been compatible for longer than that, which was in large part why I'd avoided seeing him again. The idea that I could find someone to truly be with, who would overlook my multitude of faults, was a theory I didn't want to test. And that I liked Theo very much only deepened my aversion.

The more I liked him, the harder it would be when he realized I was impossible to endure.

And now, I was even more thankful for the distance I'd so astutely placed between us.

Because starting a relationship out of obligation and with a child hanging in the balance was a terrible idea.

And I'd keep reminding myself of that until I convinced myself it was true.

EXEMPLARY SPECIMEN

KATHERINE

"You're *what*?" Val screeched.

It was the closest word I could find for the high-pitched sound that could have come from a bird of prey were it not for syllables. I didn't think raptors had the tongue dexterity to form syllables.

"Pregnant," I said again, though a little slower, just in case she'd actually misheard me. I could never be sure.

Rin blinked. Val gaped. Amelia's arms were folded, her lips a disapproving line.

"I can't believe you told Theo before you told us," she said again.

We sat in our kitchen. Well, I sat. My three roommates stood around the island, staring at me in disbelief.

"Well, no one was here, and his sperm had created the embryo. It doesn't seem that unrealistic that I'd go straight to him."

The three of them gave me a look.

"I was going to text you when I left," I added.

It didn't faze them.

"What are you going to do?" Rin asked, her porcelain face touched with worry and dark hair falling over her shoulders.

My brows flicked together. "Have the baby."

"Alone?" Val's question was dubious. She crossed her arms, leaning the wide curve of her hip on the counter.

I opened my mouth to answer, but Amelia beat me to it.

"Theo wants her to move in with him."

Val's and Rin's faces immediately softened into smiles.

"That's genius," Rin said. "Amelia will be right upstairs, and when the baby comes, Theo will be right there to help."

My frown deepened. "But I'll have to live with strangers. Lots of strangers. I haven't done that since freshman year with you three."

"But wouldn't it be better than you being all by yourself?" Val asked.

"I can't imagine how. I'll go from blissful solitude to reminding Theodore to put the toilet seat down. Everything will change."

"Everything's already going to change," Val pointed out helpfully.

I realized I was pouting and smoothed my face. "So why pile more change on top of the inevitable?"

"She fainted," Amelia blurted, her cheeks flushed and voice high.

I pinned her with a look. She wouldn't meet my eyes.

"She swooned and fainted, and Theo caught her and had time to call us down before she even woke."

Now, they were only concerned.

"Oh my God," Rin breathed, reaching for my hand. "Are you all right?"

"My blood sugar was low," I huffed. "It won't happen again."

"You don't know that," Amelia countered, her little mouth set in a firm line. "She could hurt herself, and no one would be here to help her."

"I'm pregnant, not infirmed."

"I know that," she said, "but it's not just you anymore. You have your embryo to worry about."

My nose wrinkled. She was right, I knew, but I didn't want to move. I wasn't ready for *that* much change.

Rin and Val exchanged a glance.

"Maybe we could move back," Rin said.

Val nibbled her lip. Rin's eyes were wary.

And I shook my head. "Rin, you should live with your fiancé. Court's place is right next to work, and you're about to get married. And Val, you and Sam are just starting out."

"I don't like the thought of you being alone," Val said quietly.

I sighed, trying to release the pressure in my chest, but it did little good.

"Well," Rin started, "you don't have to move in *now*. I mean, the first trimester is kinda dodgy anyway, right? So what if you wait until you get through that? Go to the doctor, confirm all the things, get out of the danger zone."

I perked up, straightening on the stool where I sat at our kitchen island. "I like this idea. I like this idea a lot. Theodore and I could spend the next seven weeks getting used to each other."

"I dunno," Amelia said. "He already seems pretty used to the idea."

This time, it was Val who looked accusatory. "That's another thing. How the hell did you not tell us you slept with *Theo*?"

A hot flush crept across my cheeks. "Because it was a one-time thing."

Val snorted a laugh. "I mean, they say it only takes once, but this is taking it to the extreme."

"He smells good. We have chemistry. When we danced, I knew we would. So we went home together."

They waited for me to finish.

"And that was it," I clarified.

"Oh, that was *not* it," Val said with the roll of her eyes. "How was it?"

For a second, I didn't answer. I hadn't had a wide variety of trysts, but he'd easily topped them all. Another reason to stay away.

If I continued to see him, I would become beholden to him. And if I gave him that power, I would lose control. That possibility scared me even more than the embryo in my uterus.

"It was exemplary," was my answer.

"Why didn't you see him again?" Rin asked gently.

"Starting off a relationship with a one-night stand seems irresponsible."

"Well, now you're starting one off with a baby," Val said.

"There is no relationship," I assured her. "Theodore and I won't be romantically involved."

Now Val was pouting. "Why the heck not?"

"Because I'm also not willing to be with a man simply because he fertilized my egg."

A laugh burst out of Amelia, and she clapped her hand over her mouth.

"What? That's what happened."

"I know, but you sound like you're talking about chickens. He's the father of your child," she reminded me. As if I didn't know.

"There will be too many variables, too many emotions with the baby alone. We can't get our hearts involved on top of that. It would be too messy to untangle."

"Well, you might not have a choice," Amelia said. "I was bound and determined not to fall for my fake husband, and look how that turned out."

"I slept with Theodore once."

"I know, but you never sleep with anybody, so he's obviously special," she argued.

"That's not true. I occasionally sleep with people."

Amelia rolled her eyes. "Biannual one-night stands barely count."

"How so? I sleep with them, don't I?"

"But you don't *like* them."

"I don't *like* Theodore."

Amelia's face was as flat as a pancake. "I saw you two together. You like him."

I shifted on my stool. "No, I don't."

"Yes, you do," she insisted. "And he likes you, too. I'm just saying, it might be harder to resist that than you think."

"I thought you wanted me to move in with him."

"I do. I just also want you to fall in love with him so we can be sisters-in-law."

Rin shook her head. "I still can't figure out how Amelia was the first of us to get married, and Katherine will be the first to have a baby. It's like we're living in Backward Land."

"A baby," Val said, smiling. "It just really hit me. You're gonna have a tiny little baby with tiny little hands and tiny little toes."

"You're gonna get big and round and gorgeous," Amelia added, smiling wistfully.

"I bet it has dark hair, a fuzzy little head," Rin mused.

"Hopefully I don't develop gestational diabetes or anemia. Or preeclampsia," I said. "I have a lot of research to do before my doctor's appointment. I'll need to sign up for childbirth classes and a tour of the hospital. I'd really like to see a female reproductive diagram, too."

"Sign Theo up, too. He said he wanted to go to everything," Amelia reminded.

My frown was back. Because the thought of him suffering through *The Miracle of Life* with me made that twisting ache in my chest tighten again. I'd bet he wouldn't even flinch at the sight of childbirth.

The thought was oddly appealing.

"Well," I started, "I guess I'll accept his offer."

Amelia clapped, her smile bright and bursting at the seams. "I'm going to be right there with you the whole way. Don't worry."

"I'm not worried," I assured her.

And with a healthy dose of research, that would cease to be a lie.

MODERN MAN

THEO

Tommy's smirk sent an urge through me to pop him in the nose.

"Don't look at me like that, asshole," I warned.

"You sly fucking dog. You slept with *Katherine*. I wasn't entirely sure she liked anything outside of the Dewey decimal system and late fees. Never mind you."

"Well, we're both full of surprises. Somehow, you convinced Amelia to marry you."

"And God help us all if she figures out she's too good for me." He sat in an armchair, draped regally on the article of furniture, effectively turning it into a throne. "I need to know how this went down and why the fuck you didn't tell me."

With a sigh, I sat on the couch, leaning to rest my elbows on my knees. "I'm not sure how it went down. She said I smelled good, talked about pheromones. It was the hottest, strangest pickup I'd ever

And in the morning, she informed me that it was a one-time thing and asked me not to tell anyone. I've been hounding her ever since, but she hasn't returned a single call or text. The last thing I thought I'd find when I opened my door was her. And the last thing I thought she'd say was what she said."

Tommy shook his head. "A baby. You're having a baby."

"Technically, she is," I said, repeating her observation. "But yeah. A baby."

"You're gonna be a dad," he noted quietly.

For a moment, we sat under the silent weight of that word. Dad. Father. Something we had never known and had no context for. Something we had always wanted and could never have. And now, I had to fill that role as best I could with nothing to guide me but the idea of what a father *should* be.

I wouldn't fail. I wouldn't let either of them down.

My hand moved to my lips, scrubbed my jaw. "There's more," I admitted.

His head tilted curiously.

I drew a thick breath and let it out. "I like her."

His eyebrow rose, just one.

"I don't know what it was or how it happened. But something happened. Five weeks, she's been avoiding me. Five weeks, I've thought of nothing but her. Last week, Ashley Fairview practically unbuckled my pants in a meeting, and I was completely uninterested. I think Kate broke me."

Now it was disbelief, written all over his face in black Sharpie. "You've been trying to get Ash to pay attention to you for years."

"It's like she could smell that I was off the market. I didn't even realize it myself."

"And I don't know how you're getting away with calling her Kate, but kudos. Though pissing her off probably won't help your cause."

"It's because the girl I took home was no Katherine. I don't know how to explain it, Tommy. She was just…*different*. Softer. Lighter. And anyway, I think she doesn't mind Kate as much as she lets on."

"Well, she calls you Theodore. Ma doesn't even call you Theodore."

I huffed a laugh. "I'll take Theodore over Teddy."

Tommy watched me, puzzled and amused. "The last guy who called you Theodore caught a fat lip."

"I dunno what to tell you, Tommy. I think I *like* it."

"Man," he said with the shake of his head, "you really do like her."

"I know. And now…now she's…God, I can't even say it." I cupped a hand over my eyes and squeezed, pressing my temples, looking for relief. "I've gotta figure out how to get her to move in."

"She's a loner, Theo. She needs space, quiet. Boundaries. You really think her living here is a good idea?"

"She's carrying my baby. Yeah, I think her living here is a good idea. I think it's the *only* idea. I want to know her, and I want her to trust me. I want her to stay, because if she doesn't or if she changes her mind…if she leaves? I don't want to lose the chance to father my child. And I don't want to miss the opportunity to be with Kate."

That eyebrow, which had returned to its resting state, spiked again. "You're gonna trap her into a relationship with a pregnancy? How modern."

"A what?" came a sleepy voice from behind me.

Tommy sighed but didn't say anything. I turned to find our mom shuffling into the room.

My heart climbed up my throat and lodged there.

"Have a good nap, Ma?" I asked, hedging.

"Mmhmm," she hummed, blinking slow as she rounded the couch. "Did I hear someone say pregnant? One of Amelia's friends?"

Tommy and I exchanged a look.

"Yeah," he answered.

I swallowed.

"Which one? The tall one, the curvy one, or the strict one?"

Tommy's smile tilted up on one side. "The strict one."

I shot daggers at him.

"Ha, how about that?" she said as she settled into the couch.

"Ma," I started softly, "there's something I need to tell you."

At that, she chuckled. "Don't tell me it's yours."

My throat clamped shut. Tommy's smirk rose. Ma's face fell.

"Teddy," she warned gently, "I am not as healthy as I used to be. Please don't give your ma a heart attack."

I took her hand in mine, feeling the tremor through every bone in my fingers. "We got together once, a few weeks ago. She was just here to tell me the news."

Her eyes widened, her free hand moving to her lips. For a moment, I watched her as her eyes filled with tears. Her lips were hidden behind her fingers, her face pinched with emotion.

Dread crept over me.

She'd be angry with me. Furious for being irresponsible. Upset for bringing a child into a home that wasn't stable, that wasn't filled with love. Because she knew that pain after being abandoned by my father.

We all knew that pain.

I'd loaded a dozen arguments, all the ways I'd make it right, all the things I'd do to make sure that history wouldn't repeat itself. I wouldn't abandon Katherine, and I wouldn't abandon my kid. And I'd make sure she knew it.

I'd do everything in my power to make my mother proud.

When her hand fell away, it wasn't anger I found.

Her smile hit me square in the heart.

"Oh, Teddy. You're gonna be such a good dad."

I found myself in her arms, hanging on to her with relief and gladness. "I'm gonna take care of her, Ma."

"I know you will, honey. I know you will." She didn't let go until I did. "You've been taking care of us since always. I put too much on you when your dad left, let you take on too much."

"Don't do that, Ma," I said quietly. "I wanted to help. The thought of you having to do any more than you already were woulda killed me. Plus, I like folding laundry."

"And cooking," Tommy added helpfully.

Ma cupped my cheek, her eyes brimming with tears. "You are a giver, honey. The most loyal, the most dependable—"

"Hey," Tommy joked.

She laughed. "Teddy, I know you'll do right by her. I'm just so happy!"

She flung herself into my arms again, and I closed my eyes against my emotion.

I'd been granted a chance to rewrite my past, erase my pain by providing a future for my child.

And that was an opportunity I'd take gladly.

DESTINATIONS & DOORWAYS

KATHERINE

5 WEEKS, 4 DAYS

The squeak of the cart wheel echoing in the expanse of the silent Rose Room was blasphemy.

I cursed Eagan for giving me this one. He'd probably done it on purpose.

My lips flattened, and I picked up my pace. The squeak picked its pace up and its pitch, too. The library patrons looked up from their tomes with accusatory glares.

I decided then to make sure Eagan got stuck on card catalog organization. In addition, I decided to shuffle them before he got started.

My anxiety eased marginally once I was through the room and into a quieter, less traveled part of the library. I wound through mazes of shelves, towering sentinels of knowledge containing countless words, the results of millions of hours of combined work, of strategy and planning, of research and thought.

What lived in these rooms was more valuable than all the riches in the world.

When I pulled to a stop in front of my destination and the squeak ceased, the quiet wrapped around me, a cocoon of sound, heavy and warm. And I took to my task.

Someone had been busy researching Mesopotamia. I had stacks of books about Babylon, Gilgamesh, and Sargon and the Akkadians. Gods and myths, legends that had spawned stories to be retold in religions all across the world. As I shelved a few and wheeled the noisy cart around the corner, I imagined what the reader might have been doing. Writing a paper for school perhaps. Or researching to write a novel. Maybe a fantasy with roots in history. Or, —even more impressive—they'd just wanted to learn for the joy of learning.

I smiled at the prospect. There was nothing I found more appealing than a person who loved to learn.

When I reached my next shelf, my smile faded. Someone had put books back incorrectly. Not only were they in the wrong section of the library—we were in nine hundred, geography and history, and these belonged in the three hundreds under social sciences and folklore—but they were flipped upside down.

Eagan, I'd put money on it. I'd bet he'd set the whole thing up, that lawless bastard.

With a magnificent scowl, I cleaned the shelf up. What Eagan didn't know—and what I'd never tell him—was that fixing the shelf actually sent a shot of dopamine and adrenaline through me.

There was little I enjoyed as much as putting things in their place.

It had been three days since I discovered my uterus was occupied, three days since Theo asked—demanded?—that I move in. He wasn't wrong. I knew it would be easier together than apart, especially with everyone moving on. If things were the way they used to be, maybe it'd be different. Because it used to be me and my friends and no one else. We'd have raised the embryo together.

Don't get me wrong—I was happy for them. They'd all found exemplary men, and the progression was natural. But I found myself unexpectedly mourning the idea of the four of us essentially sharing a baby.

I brushed the thought away and shifted it to reality. Being so deeply alone and pregnant was not ideal. As much as I loved solitude, I was unused to it. Our house had always been full. Someone had always been home. Now it was as silent as a tomb, and as lively as one, too.

But the thought of living with strangers was enough to make me wildly uncomfortable.

As I shelved a book about the Assyrians, I considered the man who would father my child, as I had so many times over the last few days. Really, I'd been thinking about him far longer than that. Since that first night. The only night.

I couldn't say I didn't know what it was about him that struck me. I knew every reason and had cataloged each one in detail and in stone. His physique alone was enough to make a heterosexual woman—*any* heterosexual woman—offer herself up like a filet mignon, stripped and seared and raw in the middle. But when coupled with his quick wit, persistence, and his body chemicals, I was helpless to resist.

Which was the foundation of my problem.

He made me feel reckless. Thoughtless. He robbed me of inhibition and denied me of choice though not by his own design. It was simply a fact that resided in the space between us. The way he kissed me claimed me.

And I wasn't interested in being claimed. Especially by a man who I'd unwittingly given control.

One night had been enough to push my boundaries into spaces

I wasn't comfortable in. In the moment, it felt like relief, release, and for that moment, I unclenched my grip and let go, and I floated away in the currents of him. But when I'd realized I couldn't feel the ground beneath my feet, I'd scrambled to find it again.

And that meant staying away from Theodore Bane like a recovering alcoholic stayed away from Wild Turkey—with willpower, longing, and a touch of regret.

What I needed was a relationship built on equality and partnership. Passion had no place in my life because passion was unpredictable.

My parents, for example, were passionate creatures. They were also the most unpredictable humans I'd ever known. They loved each other—anyone could see that with little more than a glance in their direction—but they were also unstable.

Case in point: they had been married and divorced four times.

To each other.

In their defense, they were never hostile. I had never once seen them fight, not in the traditional sense of the word. They would have discussions in voices somehow both firm and soft. My mother would consult her tarot cards and burn red candles and fall asleep with rose quartz on her chest and sandalwood burning on her nightstand. My father hadn't cut his hair since sometime in the late seventies, and the scent of patchouli clung to him like he exhaled it—the oil used to mask the aroma of cannabis, which he smoked often and in large quantity.

They were gentle, peaceful people who made every decision with their hearts rather than their heads. Mom taught yoga classes. Dad played bass in a cover band. And somehow, their genetic mix had made me. Even though they didn't understand me, they accepted me with all the grace they contained, which was a lot.

But what they *hadn't* given me were the boundaries I so desperately needed. I had no bedtime. I could choose what I wanted for dinner. There were no rules, which, to most kids, would have been some version of heaven.

For me, it was a veritable hell.

So I made my own rules. In bed by ten. Up at six thirty. Meals planned with food groups and nutritional value in mind. If I didn't wash the sheets, they wouldn't have been washed. If I didn't sit Mom down to plan meals and if I didn't physically accompany her to the grocery store, we would have survived on ramen and kombucha. When I was little, we had.

By the time I was twelve, I had a day planner for their schedules. Because if I didn't remind them to be where they needed to be, they'd have been incredibly unsuccessful adults.

Honestly, even their small successes were debatable and largely contingent on me.

Alongside the reversal of dynamic, we just didn't understand each other. I thought they believed me to be just a little different, just a little odd. But to cover their bases, Mom took me to spiritual healers in the hopes they would *fix* me, make me more like them. Read my tea leaves to search for some truth to connect us when we were so deeply separated. Pulled tarot cards for me regularly, which she took for gospel.

I took them for nothing more than a deck of cards with pretty pictures on them.

I believed in what I could see. In science and fact, not faith. Extreme emotions made me uncomfortable and uneasy, and I avoided them at all costs. My parents had them in abundance, and every time one presented itself, it would deplete my emotional resources. They left me drained, left me feeling tired, left me folding in on myself, retreating into my room with music and a book and the still calmness of my sanctuary. Refused emotion in place of logic. Observed rather than participated.

Emotions were exhausting, and I had no practical use for them.

But Theo inspired extreme emotions in me.

My brow furrowed as I wheeled around another shelf, scanning the spines for my destination. I wondered how sharing space with him would end, knowing I had no control over my brain's traitorous chemicals beyond keeping a safe distance. If I couldn't smell him, I wouldn't want him. It seemed fairly simple. I wondered if some essential oil might help, something potent. Like menthol or maybe something stronger. Like gasoline.

He'd accepted my request to stay uninvolved, and I trusted him to uphold that request. I lived my life within the bounds of rules, and if Theo respected that, everything would be fine. We would cohabitate for the sake of our baby. He and I would provide that stability that I'd always wished for as a child, the structure and dependability of consistency. Because in his way, he seemed much more like me than I'd realized on first glance. We wanted the same things.

Which was why we would make an excellent team.

So long as we kept all the riffraff out of the picture.

THAT EVENING, AFTER WORK, I walked toward the subway, in the direction of the Village where Theo lived, just a few streets away from my place. Well, really, it was Amelia's place. Her parents had bought it as an investment property when we were in college, gutted and renovated it, and let us all live there for practically nothing.

I wondered, as I had many, many times, what would happen to the house. Rin was on the Upper East with her fiancé, who was the heir to an obscene fortune and curator at The Met. Val was all but living with Sam a few blocks away, his money not only his, but accrued from his wealthy, intellectual parents. And Amelia was married to a famous writer, the same one who employed Theo, his twin, to run his business for him.

And with me moving in with him, the house would be empty.

I hated the thought of it empty.

As much as I would prefer Theo move in with me, I knew it was impossible. Not only was the property not mine to claim, but Theo helped take care of his mother, who had rapidly progressing Parkinson's. She needed him. And the house I'd lived in for years, I supposed, would return to the hands of Amelia's parents for sale or rental.

The thought made me uncomfortable. But change always did.

And this week seemed to be full of it.

I sighed against my discomfort, flowing west with the stream of people leaving Bryant Park for the subway. My speech had been prepared along with a list of rules and requirements I had. I'd written it longhand, watched each precisely written letter form, and the effect, as anticipated, was committed to memory. But I was uneasy regardless.

I knew my friends and could gauge their reactions in advance. But Theo was largely an enigma to me. I had no idea his thoughts or reactions, no context for how he would accept or reject my requirements. My upper hand was in my steadfast stubbornness, and I knew I could rely on that to maintain my boundaries.

I'd cross my fingers, if I believed in magic.

The subway was packed, the scent of metal and bodies and the combating aromas of various street foods an assault on my senses. But I controlled even those with the help of noise-canceling headphones and a book to use as blinders. I had Vicks in my bag too, just in case the smell was too much.

I was nothing if not prepared.

Jane Eyre was as brilliant as it had been the other eighteen times I read it. It made for excellent subway reading. I knew every word, so nothing was lost, only a replay of events in comforting repetition. By the time I exited the train, Jane was on her way to Thornfield Hall, and my task lay before me.

The declaration of acceptance I was about to give would shift the course of my life almost as deeply as Thornfield Hall would for Jane. It was acknowledgment and action of the imperceptibly magnanimous change that the child would bring. And though I knew it was inevitable, part of me—a large, loud part—wasn't ready.

But I had eight weeks to warm to the idea. With some time and patience, I believed I could do it.

If nothing else, I believed I could *make* myself do it. And that was enough for me.

I stood for a fortifying moment on his stoop, reciting my list once again for good measure. And then I knocked.

The door opened almost immediately, the doorway framing the imposing sight of Theodore Bane.

He was all darkness, from his seemingly black eyes and hair, the cut of his hard jaw and the exactly masculine proportions of his olive face. The only light was behind his eyes, a spark of mirth that found its way into the corner of his mouth as it rose.

"Kate. You came."

My head tilted in confusion. "I told you I would."

A soft chuckle. "So you did. Please, come in."

I detected something in his voice, nerves perhaps. A touch of disbelief, which confounded me. If I said I'd do something, I did it without wavering. I reminded myself he didn't know me, which oddly made me feel both better and worse.

When I passed him, I caught his scent again, crisp and clean and familiar. My salivary glands opened up and let loose.

The door closed behind me, and when my bag was hanging on a hook in the entry, I felt his hands on my shoulders, hooking my jacket to help me out of it.

I swore, I'd know those hands in the dark, a thought that surprised and intrigued me.

"Thank you for seeing me this afternoon," I said as he hung my jacket.

"I'm glad you're here."

The purpose of my visit niggled aggressively at my mind, and so, without pretending pleasantries, I got to it.

"I would like to discuss the arrangement you proposed. After giving it some thought—"

He turned on his heel, his face composed but tight at the edges—his eyes, his lips, his jaw. "Before you say no, hear me out."

I opened my mouth to inform him I wasn't planning on saying no, but I didn't have the chance.

He took me by the arm to guide me into the house, launching into a speech he seemed to have prepared as devoutly as I had mine.

"I know how crazy this all is, no matter how logical it seems. But I want to show you around, let you get a feel for things before you decide. Will you let me?"

I made the mistake of looking up at him as we headed for the stairs, and for a moment, I was caught by surprise. I searched for the line delineating his pupil from his iris, leaning in when I couldn't discern the two. It was exquisite, the velvety black, the bottomless depth. *There*—I caught his pupil dilate, the motion indicating that edge I'd been looking for but couldn't find.

I noted his worry, and the knowledge that this meant so much to him struck me in a soft place in my chest.

"Of course," was the only answer I could give.

Relief softened his face, and up the stairs we went.

"I wanted you to see the setup upstairs. We knew I'd be living with Ma for the foreseeable future, and she insisted I make a separate space for myself. I thought she was crazy. In fact, I've never cooked in my kitchen, not once. My guest bedroom has never been used. But that's a mom for you. They know things."

I made a noncommittal sound.

When we reached the landing, he didn't let my arm go, and I couldn't find it in me to care. It was strong, secure, reliable. Everything in his touch spoke of dependability.

"We can put in a door at the top of the stairs for more privacy. The living room is here, the kitchen over there. My room is there, and your room is back here. Come on, I'll show you."

I took a second to look around as he towed me nervously through his place. The space was open and inviting, the big windows at the back of the house letting in buttery light through sheer curtains. The kitchen was small but cozy with a table for four that boasted a pot brimming with succulents and two place mats. The surfaces were pristine, light and airy without being feminine at all. Everything I saw was neat and orderly, clean and uncluttered.

I found I liked it very much.

We passed a room on the way to the one I would inhabit, which I thought he might be saving for last. I caught a glimpse of a desk and bookshelves and assumed it was his office, which he'd mentioned would become the baby's room.

The place where that baby currently resided did a curious flip at the prospect.

We stepped into the guest room, and I was instantly hit with an uncommon sense of rightness.

My mother would have attributed it to feng shui or the direction of the windows or the placement of the bed in conjunction with the chair and dresser. But I believed it was more than that. It was a flame in my ribs that told me this was a step. This was a doorway. This was tangible movement toward my future.

My throat closed, clamped shut by unfamiliar emotion.

Damn hormones. Damn them all, every one of them.

As I swallowed to try to dislodge the lump in my esophagus, Theo chattered nervously, avoiding eye contact. Every time I tried to speak, he'd cut me off to explain some more as he showed me the space, pointing out its features like a real estate agent. There was no emotion in his explanations, only logic, as if he knew that would be the only applicable argument.

I watched and listened, letting him say what he needed to while I fought my feelings down. He was so concerned, so worried I would say no. I thought about his past. He'd never known his father, and now he was going to become one.

And here I was, the vehicle for his hopes and dreams. I held the power to take all that away from him, and he was afraid I would. He was afraid I'd cut him out, I realized. He was afraid to lose his child.

In that moment, with Theo regaling details about the plumbing, my needs became secondary. My discomfort and apprehension quieted, replaced by concern for him. Because if the tables were turned, I would have the same fears. And I knew right then that I wouldn't be a part of his pain. I'd already decided to move in. But that was the first moment I wasn't afraid of doing it.

"Theodore," I started gently, not trusting my voice.

"Hang on, Kate. One more thing."

The use of my nickname made me sigh, but I found myself smiling despite the annoyance. He was perhaps the only person in the world that could call me Kate and not incite violence.

He snagged my hand and pulled me back into the hallway, pushing open the door to his office.

"And this will be the baby's room. Imagine it, Kate. We'll move the bookshelves, put the crib over there," he said with a gesture to the far wall. "An armchair and footstool there, in the corner, and a changing table here. It's right across the hall from you, but I'll be just on the other side of the house for anything you need. We can take shifts at night so you won't have to do it all alone. We can decorate it however you want, anything you want."

He paused, shifted, stood before me, a pillar of strength and protection. And perhaps it was my delicate state, but I wanted to wrap myself up in the feeling and drift away on its eddies.

"Kate," he said, a single, soft syllable, "I know it's a lot. A little wild, a little insane. But it's not irresponsible. Please, let me do this with you. Please, don't do it alone. I want you both here with me, and I'll do whatever it takes to make it work. I just need you to give me the chance."

Fear flickered behind his black eyes when I finally parted my lips to speak.

"I came over today to say yes," I said with a smile. "I'll move in with you."

The sweetest expression passed across his face, a mixture of relief and elation, though it was contained. *He* was contained, though the latent energy in him reached through the slim space between us. His smile tilted into a smirk, his eyes shining with excitement.

"You let me take you all through the house when you were going to say yes anyway?"

"I tried to tell you, but you wouldn't let me answer."

His laugh was little more than a puff of air. "I'm surprised you didn't force your hand anyway."

I shrugged, though my cheeks warmed. "It was important to you, so it was important to me."

The spark in his eyes smoldered.

But before he could comment, I spoke again. "I have some perimeters though."

He nodded, that smirk ticking higher. "I'd be shocked if you didn't."

"The first is the most relevant—I won't move in until after my first trimester. Once into the second trimester, the odds for complications decrease dramatically. Before we make any major changes, I'd like to be through that statistic."

After a moment of indecision, he said, "All right. Plus, it will give us some time to get to know each other better."

I frowned. Not because he was wrong, but because it sounded suspiciously like dating. "I had the same thought. But I'd like to reiterate that I am not interested in being involved romantically. Things are complicated enough. I'd like to keep them as simple as possible. Introducing too many variables at once will make it impossible to track when issues arise."

"So we're entering into a grand experiment?" he asked without even a hint of heat.

"Not an experiment, but a controlled environment. There's plenty we won't be able to control, so why not keep the boundaries in place where we can?"

"Kate, I'll take you any way I can get you. You tell me the rules, and I will abide by them." His hand slipped around my waist, his body inching closer. "But if you change your mind—"

"I won't," I breathed, not believing the words any more than he seemed to.

"You are an anomaly in my universe, and ignoring that fact is a testament to my devotion. I won't break the rules. But I hope you do. If anything changes, just say the word. Deal?"

My brain fired a thousand nerves at once, the scent of him drawing me closer without my will. My body, it seemed, was beyond my control. He was so close, I had to tip my chin to keep my eyes on his.

I could lose myself in his eyes, like a black hole. He'd stretch me to infinity, and I'd die happy.

Somehow, I found myself. I stepped back. Extended my hand.

Squared my shoulders.

"Deal," I said.

And he took my hand, which disappeared in the expanse of his. He shook it once, then tugged, pulling me into his arms. They wrapped around me like a velvet cage, and for a moment, I closed my eyes and breathed him in. Ignored the musings of his effect on me in exchange for the comfort.

He pressed a kiss into my hair. "It's gonna be good, Kate. You'll see."

And I smiled. Because he didn't need to show me.

I already knew.

BRILLIANTLY BEIGE

THEO

I didn't want to let her go. But I did.

My relief was palpable, settling over me like a balm after days of scratchy nerves.

She'd said yes. When I looked down into her determined little face, I couldn't stop myself from capturing her chin in my thumb and forefinger.

"We have eight weeks to get to know each other before you move in. I have a proposition."

The slightest frown touched her lips, her chin flexing against my thumb. "I haven't finished relaying my rules."

I chuckled and let her go, stepping back to give her space. I hitched a leg on the surface of my desk as I sat. "All right. You first."

She cleared her throat, stretching to her full height. Her back was as straight as a ruler. "I require certain levels of solitude and privacy

If my door is closed, that indicates I am not open to conversation. I'll leave it cracked, if not open, if I'm available."

I nodded, tamping down my smile.

"I would like to share financial burdens as well. My portion of the rent. Groceries. Baby supplies."

"That might prove complicated. First, there is no rent. We can thank Tommy for that. Groceries we buy and have delivered, and I cook our meals. Splitting that up seems unnecessary."

"I'd like to try all the same. Just provide receipts, and I'll do the math. For your approval, of course."

I sighed. "If you insist."

A curt nod. "I insist."

"And baby…supplies—that's also up to you. If it makes you happy, then we'll do that too."

"It would. There are two more things, both of which are difficult to quantify." Her face pinched, as if she were having trouble trying to figure out just what to say. "Regarding our relationship beyond the embryo, I would like to keep certain boundaries in place, as discussed. It's very…difficult to retain balance when you invade my personal space. I believe it's due to your pheromones. They're particularly potent."

I pursed my lips and bit down hard to stifle laughter. Clearing my throat helped. "You smell good, too. I'll admit, it's hard not to invade your personal space. But I'll do my best."

"Thank you. And the other point is the level of our relationship in general. I would like to become friends, Theodore. It would benefit our child and make rearing it easier if we respected one another."

Friends. It sounded blatantly, painfully offensive from her mouth.

"Fair enough," I said rather than agree. Even that tasted sour.

She sighed, smiling her relief.

"Now, it's my turn."

Instantly, she tensed again.

"I would like to agree to seeing each other once per week prior to you moving in. That's eight opportunities to cultivate our... friendship."

"Seven opportunities. The eighth, I'll be moving in."

"I stand corrected. We can decide at a later date, if you'd prefer."

After a split second of consideration, she said, "Yes, let's decide later. I've scheduled my first appointment with the obstetrician in two weeks. Let's begin our weekly meetings then. There, I'll receive a full pelvic exam, and the doctor will locate the embryo's heartbeat. We should have sonogram pictures afterward, too. It'll only look like a staticky blob, but better that than being able to distinguish its tail."

A laugh escaped me. "All right. Let me know the date and time, and I'll make it work. Can we ride together?"

"If you'd like."

"I'd like."

Another perfunctory nod. "All right. As always, it's been a pleasure doing business with you, Theodore."

She didn't offer her hand, which I mourned. But, after her comment about my pheromones and her personal space, I figured it was a precautionary measure.

In fairness, I didn't know how I'd resist her pheromones either. So, I'd give her the distance she'd asked for regardless of how I hated it. Every molecule in my body wanted to invade the eighteen inches of air around her.

But I wouldn't. Not until she asked.

And she'd ask. Once I proved myself, once she figured out how she felt, she'd ask.

Until then, I'd stay thirsty and pray.

"Want to stay for dinner?" I asked, hoping I'd schooled the hope in my voice. "My mom really wants to meet you, and Tommy and

Amelia will be there."

But she shook her head. "I'm sorry, but I've been on my feet all day, and I'd really like to lie down. Plus, I can only eat beige food."

My brow quirked. "Beige food?"

"Yes—mashed potatoes, chicken nuggets, mac and cheese, oatmeal, hashed browns, plain pasta, crackers, bananas, toast, rice. As long as it's beige, it stays exactly where it's supposed to. The second I introduce color, *blort*." She motioned with her hand, indicating an exodus from her mouth.

"The beige diet. Sounds like every toddler's dream."

"I'm a little concerned I'm going to go into carb shock. But I'll take anything over vomiting. There's nothing so exquisitely disgusting and traumatizing as throwing up. And I've done enough of that in the last few days to last me for quite some time."

For a moment, I watched her as she stood straight and proud in my office. Her little nose was up in the air, just enough to make her look discerning, her shoulders square. The effect jutted her breasts out, framed by her arms, her hands clasped in front of her hips.

God, she was pretty without even trying. Her eyes were lined with thick black lashes, her lips curved and wide. She was sensual without realizing, without intention.

Which made her all that much more beautiful.

"Well, I'll be going then," she said. "Thank you again. For…for everything." A flush rose in her cheeks, her eyes suddenly shining. It was emotion, a foreign thing on her stoic face.

"No, thank *you*," I insisted. "For trusting me. For agreeing to something so unorthodox."

A smile, small and delicate. "Well, we aren't really the orthodox type, are we?"

And with a laugh, I agreed.

I escorted her through the house and out the front door, waiting in the doorway to watch her walk away.

Oh, how I hated watching her walk away. But soon, I wouldn't have to.

With a deep sigh, I closed the front door, slipping my hands in the pockets of my slacks. I heard Ma's TV on in her room and was grateful for the privacy she'd afforded Katherine and me. I'd been terrified I'd spook her, run her off for good. But to my absolute shock, she'd come over here just to say yes. I'd thought I'd be chasing her around for months.

Logic and reason for the win.

The doorbell rang, and I paused, glancing over my shoulder. My first thought was of Katherine, the hope that she'd changed her mind and decided to stay paramount.

But instead of Katherine, I found a big-eyed Amelia on my stoop with my smirking brute of a brother behind her.

"How did it go?" she asked, bouncing a little on the balls of her feet.

"She said yes," I answered with a smile too big to be considered anything but a grin.

At that, she shot off her feet in a squeal and into my arms. "Oh, I'm so glad, Theo. I knew she'd come around."

I chuckled and set her down. "Come on in. I need a drink."

They filed in, and I closed the door, beelining for the booze. I poured a scotch for each of us, grabbed them by the rims in one hand, and headed into the living room.

"Well, tell us what happened," Tommy said as he took it. "Melia's been watching out the front window for Katherine to leave for twenty minutes."

She nodded emphatically. "It's true."

I laughed and took a drink. "It went as expected. Better, I guess, since she didn't refuse. She had a list of rules, and I got her to agree to see me once a week so we can get to know each other before she moves in."

"Oh, smart, Theo," Amelia said with an approving nod.

"Thank you." I tipped my glass in her direction before taking a sip. "Her first doctor's appointment is next week. We're going together."

Amelia frowned. "You know they're going to…you know…*check her out*, right?" She waggled her fingers in the direction of her hips.

"I figured that was what she meant when she mentioned a pelvic exam."

"Don't you think that'll be a little weird? You seeing a doctor… you know." Her cheeks were a brilliant shade of red.

"I'm sure they see enough vaginas to be completely desensitized. And I'm quite familiar with hers. I'm not going to miss the opportunity to hear the baby's heartbeat."

At that, her face opened up. "Oh my gosh. The heartbeat?"

I nodded. "We're supposed to get a picture, too."

She pressed her palm to her chest. "Oh, Theo."

Now I was flushed, too. So, naturally, I changed the subject. "She's moving in when she's out of the first trimester, so in a few weeks. She laid out her ground rules. I'm optimistic."

"Think she'll come around?" Tommy asked.

I glanced at Amelia, not sure if she knew how I felt about Katherine.

"She knows," Tommy answered the unspoken question.

I sighed.

"I want to believe the way I feel isn't one-sided. When I touch her, I know it's not. But she's not ready. So, I'll be patient and hope she either learns to trust me or can't fight it anymore. And if not…well, I suppose there are worse things than wanting a woman who doesn't want you back. We're bound together regardless. Do I have a reason to be optimistic about that too, Amelia?"

"You do," she said. "She resisted being friends with us at first. But once she opens that door and lets you in, her loyalty is unwavering. She is one of the most dependable, steadfast, giving people I know. I mean, as long as giving doesn't require hugs. She has a thing about personal space."

I chuckled. "I've heard. In fact, I've been asked to stay out of hers so as not to tempt her with my pheromones."

"That sounds about right. But just…just be patient. I can't say much, but I'll tell you there's hope."

And I took that blessing and let it fuel my resolve.

BLOB

KATHERINE

7 WEEKS, 3 DAYS

The silence in the cold waiting room was broken by the sharp crinkling when my naked ass stuck to the paper under it.

I shifted, my face pinched in a glorious frown as I tried to dislodge the thin, cold liner of the table from my butt. My feet were in stirrups, my bare knees pointed at the dotted ceiling tiles, the gown draped between my legs so my entire vagina wasn't on display.

Theo was thankfully at my shoulder and not sitting in the chair. From there, he probably would have been able to note the anatomy of my vagina in great detail.

I huffed, pushing myself up to sit. "This is silly. I don't know why the nurse made me put my feet in the stirrups when the doctor isn't even here yet." I was so worried about covering my legs, I forgot the back of the gown was wide open.

"Here, let me help you." His fingers brushed the exposed skin of my back with the softest touch.

A riot of goosebumps flared from the spot.

He tied each of the ribbons deftly and in quick succession.

"Thank you," I murmured. "I dislike feeling helpless."

"Something we have in common. But I have to admit, I like being useful."

"Something we have in common," I echoed as he rested his hand on my back in a gesture of comfort for only a second. I was instantly cold when it disappeared.

"Nervous?" he asked.

I shifted to look up at him. He was resplendent in a suit so dark, his eyes looked like shining mahogany, shot with a brown so vibrant, it was nearly red.

"A little," I admitted. "There's a possibility she won't find a heartbeat."

A shadow passed across his face, but before he could speak, a knock sounded on the door. It opened without confirmation.

"Hello, Katherine," Dr. Stout said, extending her hand. Her smile was kind, comforting. The gesture coupled with the firm shake put me instantly at ease.

"Hello," I echoed.

"I'm Dr. Stout," she said to Theo, offering her hand again.

"Theo," he said as he shook it.

"Nice to meet you," she said, taking a seat on the rolling stool. She glanced at my chart on the counter as she pulled on rubber gloves the color of a robin's egg with a creak and a snap. "So it looks like we're nearing seven weeks. How are you feeling?"

"Fine, other than the nausea."

"She's on the beige diet," Theo added helpfully.

"Smart. Carbs, carbs, and more carbs. Keeping your stomach full will help." She rolled over to the stirrups. "All right, let's get your feet up here."

I exchanged a look with Theo, who shifted to move further up the table in a discreet display of respect for my privacy. I reminded myself that at least a dozen people would see my vagina, and all those people saw vaginas for a living. Old news, no big deal.

But if I were being honest, I was more concerned with Theo seeing it than the doctor. There were times and places for a man to see a vagina, and in the presence of a doctor was not my preference on any one of them.

The view was shielded by my gown, which Dr. Stout draped artfully between my legs. The click of the speculum in the quiet room made me wince even more than the cranking of the damn thing to open me up. Theo shifted again, this time to lean on the table next to my head. I looked up at the upside-down image of him.

He smiled and reached for my hand. His was so broad that it easily covered mine, warm against the chill of the room.

"We're looking good," she said, removing the device.

Theo stifled a smile, and I rolled my eyes at him even though I wanted to laugh, too.

"Katherine, I want you to start taking prenatal vitamins. Just any over-the-counter brand will be fine," she said as she stood, reaching for my belly to feel around. She pushed hard enough to make me wince again, dragging her fingers down. Noting my expression, she said, "I'm just checking the height of your uterus. It's in line with your conception date. Now, let's take a listen to that heartbeat."

Theo squeezed my hand, and as much as I hated breaking the personal space rule, his presence was too much of a comfort to lose strictly because of my rules.

The doctor wheeled over a machine with a wand hooked on the side. Not the magical kind that turned on lights or called Death Eaters, but the kind you had to lubricate to get it to do its job.

Although cold, it was preferable to the speculum. The sonogram machine came to life in a wave of white noise, the screen static. There was nothing but empty gray.

My lungs burned. I realized I wasn't breathing, but I couldn't seem to force my lungs open. My ribs were locked down tight.

In a burst of sound, a heartbeat filled the room, fast and fluttering. It sounded like it was underwater, the *bow, bow, bow* of a pulse through amniotic fluid.

My throat closed, and an unfamiliar sting nipped at my nose, the corners of my eyes, the weight in my chest.

That sound was the sound of my child. In my body was a baby, tail and appendage nubs and all. There was a person growing inside of me, which I had known all along. But the unexpected reaction to that sweetest of sounds was the instant connection, the complete and undeniable realness of the fact.

I looked up at Theo, at the softness of his face, the depths of his dark eyes, shining with emotion. But he didn't speak, and for that, I was glad. Because no words could have possibly explained the complexity of the moment.

He smoothed my hair, pressed a kiss to my crown, kept holding my hand. The doctor turned the screen a bit, angling it toward us as she manipulated the tools she needed to take a picture and some measurements with the help of a little yellow cursor.

She pointed at the screen, a sea of gray static with a little white blob in the middle. "And there's your baby."

Theo and I simultaneously leaned in, squinting at the screen.

She chuckled. "I know it doesn't look like much, but we'll do another one at your next appointment, and it'll look a little closer to what you might expect."

The machine whirred, spitting out a strip of pictures, which she tore off and handed over.

"Do you have any questions for me?"

I did. I actually had a massive list of questions I'd accrued over the last week and a half. But when she handed me the sonogram pictures, my mind was empty of even one.

"No, thank you," I murmured, my eyes on the little blob on the shiny paper.

"All right. Well, if you think of anything, just call. Why don't you go ahead and get dressed, and I'll go get you your information packet and welcome kit."

We didn't answer, and she left the room without waiting for us to.

The door clicked shut. I sat. Theo sat next to me. And for a moment, we stared down at the pictures in silence.

"That's our baby, Kate," he said reverently, brushing the blob with the pad of his big index finger.

"Its heartbeat is so fast. It's so small. Defenseless. Dependent on me." I hushed, not by choice. My throat wouldn't open again.

He shifted. Brushed my hair over my shoulder. His fingers absently trailed down my shoulder blade and down the back of my arm.

"Katherine, look at me."

I broke my stare, lifted my eyes, felt something shift in my chest when I looked into his irises.

His face was tight with emotion and certainty that brooked no argument.

"Your body knows exactly what to do. *You* know exactly what to do. And if you need to be reminded, I'm right here. I'm not going anywhere, Kate."

I believed every word, trusted every syllable. And beyond reason, I found myself leaning into him.

His hand slipped into my hair, the line of my jaw resting in his palm. Those black eyes shifted to my lips, which tingled, parted and aching.

Kiss me, kiss me, kiss me, went my heartbeat.

My hand rested on his chest, fingertips hooking his lapel.

His lips inched closer, his breath sweet and hot.

I closed my eyes.

But the connection never came.

Not from his lips at least.

The fabric of his suit coat brushed my lips, and my eyes shot open in surprise. His arm wound around me, and his lips pressed hard against my forehead. I was crushed to him, held in his arms where I stayed for a stunned, disoriented moment.

"Come on," he said, his voice gravelly and raw. "Let's get you dressed."

And so I did, cursing my hormones and rules in equal measure.

EMOTIONALLY BENDY

KATHERINE

A collective *aww* echoed in the kitchen.

The three heads of my roommates were pressed together like the fates over the sonogram picture.

Val, Rin, and Amelia had been waiting for me when I walked in the door feeling shaken and unsure—two feelings that brought me enough distress to have me questioning everything, even my breakfast choice, which sat sour in my stomach.

I sat at the island in the kitchen across from the three of them, hands clammy and clasped in my lap.

"It's just a little bean," Rin cooed. "So cute."

"It doesn't even have a face," I noted.

They gave me simultaneous flat looks.

"What? It doesn't."

"But it will," Amelia said.

I sniffed rather than respond.

"How did it go? How'd Theo take it all?" Val asked.

"Better than I did. I blame the hormones. I felt very…emotional. Sentimental." I said it like they were filthy words.

Rin chuckled. "Well, you *are* having a baby."

"I know. My hormones are unstable."

"I mean, that's one explanation," Val joked.

"It's the only explanation," I corrected. "Afterward, I almost kissed him."

They shared a look, which I ignored.

"I'm uncomfortable with the lack of control over my emotions at present. In fact, I'm reconsidering my decision to move in with him. If it wasn't for his equal stake in the embryo, I would probably change my mind."

They spoke all at once, echoing their dissent.

I held up a hand to stop them. Partly because the sudden noise combined with the stress of the day and the fact that I'd run out of purse crackers had me feeling woozy.

"I didn't say I was going to. I just need to remind myself why I'm doing this. I'm sacrificing so much. My body. My emotions. My privacy. I'm opening my life, my *self*, to another person. Two, I suppose, including the embryo."

Val frowned. "Okay. Unload it, Katherine. What are you afraid of?"

There was an emotion under layers of emotion, one that had been whispering and gurgling beneath the bedrock of my will. And, with her question, it bubbled up and sprang into my veins in a cold rush.

It was panic, I realized distantly.

I drew a deep breath. "I don't know how to live with anyone other than you. I don't even know how to *talk* to anyone other than you. And now, I'm moving in with a man I barely know, one who I want to kiss me again. And he absolutely cannot kiss me again. I've lost enough control without giving in to *that*."

Rin's face was tight with worry. "But why not? You clearly like each other very much."

"Because I don't trust myself to make decisions about things like that right now. It's too complex. I don't like complex in anything except puzzles. Things are already… *messy*. And messy makes me feel crazy. I feel crazy. Am I crazy?"

Amelia reached for my hand. "You're not crazy, Katherine," she assured me. "This is just going to be hard on you. I think we all knew it would be."

Tears stung my eyes, and I fumed, sniffling and swallowing and choking them down. "It all feels like a mistake," I admitted with a shaky voice.

"Do you really feel that way?" Rin asked.

I sighed, my breath trembling. "I don't know. And I hate that I don't know."

Val watched me for a moment. "Let me pose a scenario. What would have happened if you hadn't found a heartbeat today at the doctor? Would you feel better or worse?"

I flipped back to that moment just before we'd heard the sound that affected me so. The fear. The worry. It was as fresh as it had been then. And the elation on hearing the thrumming pulse was undeniably my answer.

"Worse. Much worse."

Val nodded, though her lips smiled small. "Then you know this is the right thing. It's just not going to be easy."

My shoulders fell, my body curling in on itself. My hand shifted absently to my belly. "There has to be a way to make it more bearable."

"Of course there is," Rin said with a smile of her own. "With rules. Lists. Research. Planning."

The mention of my favorite things lifted my spirits marginally.

"What about the unpredictable? What about *him*?"

"Well, you have rules with him, right?" Val asked.

"Yes, but today I wanted to betray them. We were sitting there in the doctor's office with my naked ass stuck to the exam table, and I wanted him to kiss me. I thought he was going to, too. But then… well, he didn't, and that was somehow infinitely worse than if he had."

"Maybe you need to bone him out of your system," Val offered.

My jaw clenched, lips flattening. "That will only make things worse."

One of her brows climbed. "Oh, really? Because I seem to remember you offering *us* that advice at one point or another."

My brows knitted together so tight, they almost touched. "That was different."

"How so?" she countered. "Seems to me that your body knows something your brain hasn't figured out yet. So give in to those hormones and pheromones and whatever other *mones* you're a slave to. Put rules on it if you're afraid of getting attached. Give in *and* get control."

The sense she made annoyed me. "Well, for starters, none of you were pregnant and living with the father. Who, might I add, is a veritable stranger. There are too many red flags to count."

"I'm just saying, I think you should consider it. You're into him. So, scratch the itch. Put rules on the whole thing to make yourself feel better. You're having a baby. You're moving in with him. Do you really think you can resist?"

"After today, no. That's my problem."

"Then figure out how to have your proverbial Theo cake and eat it, too."

For a moment, I let myself wonder if it were possible. Maybe there *was* a way to control it, some perimeters I could establish to help keep myself safe from losing emotional control.

It was too much to even consider.

"One thing at a time," I said definitively. "First, the embryo. So far, everything is on track. I hate that I was overwhelmed by today. But there was something about hearing and seeing and the reality of it all that caught me off guard. I think that's really my fear—this is only the beginning of events that will catch me off guard. I need a contingency plan."

Amelia perked up. "I can help with that. One of the things my therapist had me do to overcome my anxiety in public was to recite the ABCs."

I frowned. "The alphabet?"

"No—acknowledge, breathe, and connect. Acknowledge what's making you anxious, breathe through it, and connect."

"Connect with what?"

She shrugged. "Anything. The ground, something solid, or with yourself and the acknowledgment. It's almost acceptance. But really, labeling the thing itself is sometimes enough. For instance, when Theo gets in your space, acknowledge the fact that you want to ride him like a cowgirl."

Laughter burst out of Val. "Or a reverse cowgirl, if you're feeling sassy."

"I hate that there's logic in what you're saying. I really do." I tried to smooth the pout off my face, but it didn't work.

"How's your research coming?" Rin asked, changing the subject like the saint she was. "I saw the stack." She nodded to the shelf next to the couch in the living room, which was stuffed haphazardly with the top-rated books on pregnancy and early childhood.

"It's going well. I've gotten through four already, and I have notes. I'm annoyed that I didn't ask the doctor any of my questions. I'd prepared them specifically for the appointment."

"Why didn't you?" Amelia asked.

"Because I'd just heard the baby's heartbeat, and I had the

sonogram in my hand. It took everything I had not to cry, never mind recall the questions I had." I shook my head. "I don't even recognize myself. I have lost all control over my thoughts and emotions, and I hate it. I hate it so much." My voice was raw again, my emotions surging in an epic flail and flex of power.

Traitors.

Rin said softly, gently, "But that's life. That's living. That's growing, Katherine. Even how you feel right now will change. It's fluid, and sometimes, it's unpredictable. There's only one way to survive."

I met her eyes, silently begging her for the answer.

"You have to find a way to be flexible."

My eyes narrowed.

"Hear me out," Rin started. "There's never just one way to get from one point to another, right?"

"Debatable. The shortest distance between two points is a line."

She gave me a look. "Let's say you want to go from work to home. There's one route that's the fastest, sure. But what if the subway station is closed?"

"Why would the subway station be closed?"

Rin waved a hand. "Doesn't matter. It's hypothetical."

I frowned. "I've never seen a closed station."

Val sighed. "There was an accident on the tracks, and none of the trains are running."

My frown eased. "Okay. Continue."

"So," Rin said, "how would you get home?"

"Probably a taxi. I could walk to a different station, depending on where the accident was and if the other lines were up. Or a bus. I could take a bus."

"There you go. Flexible. It's about problem solving in the moment rather than depending on a single plan. You were flexible on finding out you were pregnant."

I considered that for a moment. "Huh."

"It's accepting what has happened and making a new plan. Really, it's more efficient this way, if you think about it. You don't waste time worrying or planning for things that might or might not happen. You allow things to happen as they come," Rin said.

"Flexible," I muttered.

Val chimed in with a waggle of her brows. "I bet you were *super* flexible when Theo took you home."

"And look at what that got me. Knocked up."

Val shrugged. "Maybe being flexible with Theo again will get you something even better than a baby."

"It's not *Let's Make a Deal*. I'm not picking behind one of three doors for a prize."

"I mean, you kinda are," she insisted.

"Anyway," Rin said with a pointed look in Val's direction, "just problem solve in the moment. Take a minute to weigh out the outcomes and consequences. And then, jump."

Val lit up. "Jump. Be brave." She reached into her bag at her feet, returning with her red lipstick. "Once upon a time, we all four went to Sephora and left with tubes of red lipstick and a pact to be brave. We've held up our end. Now it's your turn."

I stared at the lipstick, not wanting to meet her eyes.

"We do so solemnly swear," she recited, "to use this shiny little tube of power to inspire braveness, boldness, and courage. We promise to jump when it's scary, to stand tall when we want to hide, to scream our truth instead of whisper our fears. May we be mistresses of our destinies, and to hell with anyone who tries to tell us otherwise."

Hear, hear, Amelia and Rin chimed, smiling.

Val handed me her lipstick with all the hope and faith in the world written in her smile. "Be the mistress of your destiny."

I took the shiny tube, staring at my stretched-out reflection on the metal surface. It was as disorienting and distorted as I felt. But her words rang true. They were etched on my heart and had been since we first uttered them.

"I don't trust myself," I admitted.

"Well, that's why we're here," Val said. "And so is Theo. Lean on us. We won't let you down."

I squirmed against the discomfort of being reliant on others. I had always been self-sufficient, and now…well, I couldn't even choose what I wanted for lunch without potentially crying. I could count the number of times I'd ever cried on two hands, and seven-tenths of those had happened since I peed on that damnable stick.

And then there was the matter of Theo.

I'd wanted him to kiss me today. I wanted him to kiss me right freaking now. I wanted to throw my rules and rationality out the window.

And though I knew it was a horrible, potentially catastrophic idea, a sizable percentage of me didn't care.

IF I HAVE MY WAY

THEO

8 WEEKS, 6 DAYS

My office was silent but for the scratch of my pen in my checkbook.

Pay to the order of John Banowski in the amount of Ten Thousand and 00 cents.

The scribble of the pen as I signed. The rip-crack of perforated paper tearing.

It had been nearly six years since John Banowski first showed up on my doorstep with an open palm and a smile to rival the devil himself.

I couldn't call him my father. I couldn't call him anything but a waste of skin.

Six years ago, Tommy had broken out, hit number one on the *New York Today* bestseller list. A week later, the doorbell rang to reveal the man who'd abandoned us twenty years ago. It didn't matter that I barely remembered him from my childhood—at least not as much as I remembered his absence. The second I'd opened the door, I knew exactly who he was. His height alone was the first clue—few people could look me straight in the eye other than Tommy. Dark hair, the same jaw I saw in the mirror every morning, a smirk that was mine.

Thank God Tommy and Ma hadn't been home. I couldn't imagine what his showing up twenty years late would have done to Ma. And Tommy...well, I probably wouldn't have been able to stop him from disfiguring John if I'd tried to. Which I wouldn't have.

Especially when he asked for money.

Demanded really.

You see, when Tommy had gotten his first book deal, we'd sat down and made a series of decisions. Ma had just been diagnosed with Parkinson's, and the last thing either of us wanted to do was expose her to the media. So we came up with an elaborate plan to smoke-screen our lives, to create an image for him. We changed our last names, covered up our meager beginnings in the Bronx, started fresh. And Tommy'd made a deal to fake date a famous actress in the months leading up to his first book release.

Six years ago, John Banowski stood on my stoop, noting with calculated precision all the things we'd done so much to hide. The front we'd developed to keep her safe from the public eye had been endangered with the help of a medical bill that had made its way to him.

He and Ma had never gotten divorced.

Hard to divorce someone you couldn't find.

Of course, at the time, she couldn't afford to divorce him, and then the prospect just drifted away. That bill was his leverage. His knowledge was a foot in the door. He knew we'd made the whole story about Tommy up, and he'd be the first to take it to the media.

Unless I paid him.

And with that bill in hand, he'd explained the ways he would systematically take us down.

So, for six years, I had been writing a monthly personal check to keep Tommy and Ma safe from John Banowski's designs. No one was to know. If Ma or Tommy found out, the deal was off.

I'd do everything in my power to keep him away from them. Especially Ma. Tommy would kill him. Ma would just be devastated.

It was so much easier to bear my past when I could pretend he never existed. That was one thing I had been sure of the second I shared air with the opportunistic trash pile. And it was a comfort I was determined to keep intact for my family.

We hadn't spoken a word since he showed up that day so many years ago. And as long as his checks came on time, I figured we wouldn't.

Which was exactly how I preferred it.

The financial burden wasn't a burden at all. Tommy paid me half a million a year to be his assistant, manager, and publicist, and I had no bills to speak of. The house had been paid for in cash, and Tommy took care of the utilities. Well, I took care of them. With his credit card. I didn't go out, didn't go on vacation, didn't own a car—what's the point in New York?—didn't do much of anything other than work and take care of Ma.

My only luxuries were my suits. Gorgeous custom suits, closets of suits, a sea of black and white and gray. My affinity for well-tailored suits could be traced back to my teens. We'd been running wild in the neighborhood—one of the guys we ran with had the big idea to vandalize all the bus stop ads, which, at the time, primarily featured Paris Hilton in a bikini with a hamburger the size of her head in her pretty little hand.

But then we came to a stop devoid of bikinis or hip bones or the come-hither stares of a hotel heiress.

It was an ad for TAG Heuer smack in the middle of Mount Eden, which on its own should have had an ad exec fired—nobody in fifty blocks could afford a TAG. But there he was, some good-looking guy in a suit that made him look like somebody. Somebody in a place full of working-class nobodies. He had dark hair like me, dark eyes like mine, his jaw set in determination, like he was about to make a million-dollar deal. The dim shade of my form reflected off the scratched-up, foggy plastic casing, superimposing me onto him.

And that was when I'd known. Someday, I'd own a suit like that. Someday, I'd be somebody.

I'd kept that promise to myself along with all the rest of them. Once I decided to do something, I did it. Once I declared I'd go after something, I got it.

It was a knack of mine.

I stuffed the lone check in an envelope and hastily addressed it, leaving his first name off—less questions if, for some reason, it was returned. And when it was done, I slipped it into my inside coat pocket and headed downstairs.

Ma was in the kitchen, shuffling around the island with a plate in her hand. I frowned at her.

"I was just coming to get you lunch," I said, taking the plate.

"I figured, but I don't mind doin' it myself."

"Well, I do. Come on. Come sit down."

She sighed but let me take her arm and deposit her on a barstool at the island. "How's your day, honey?"

"Fine," I answered noncommittally as I pulled containers out of the fridge with prepped food. "What have you been doin'?" The Bronx slipped, as it sometimes did around her.

"Readin' a book Amelia gave me. It's about a girl who time travels to Ireland during the rebellion. I think I've cried through half of it."

I shook my head. "That's why I read nonfiction. Last thing I need is for a book to make me cry."

At that, she laughed. "Please, when have you ever cried? I'm not convinced you have working tear ducts."

I chuckled, plating her food and turning for the microwave.

"I mean it. Even Tommy cried when he broke his arm that time at the basketball court."

"Ah, the great trashcan escape of '02," I said with a smile and a shake of my head.

"Couldn't blame him for crying. I almost fainted at the sight of his arm bent in the wrong direction. But you? You dislocated your shoulder riding your bike through that drainage tunnel and didn't shed a tear. Never seen anything like it."

I shrugged. "Didn't hurt that bad."

She made a derisive noise. "That's a bald-faced lie, and you know it."

"Didn't hurt bad enough to cry."

She sighed again, smirking as she changed the subject. "How's Katherine feeling?"

"Seems to be okay. I'm meeting her for lunch tomorrow."

At that, she smiled, a wily expression that sparked a glint in her eye. "Oh?"

"Trust me, it's not that glamorous."

"Oh," she said as her face fell. "Still not interested?"

Now it was my turn to sigh. "I told her I'd follow her rules, so I will. I'll respect the hell outta her boundaries. I'll respect them so good, she'll be wishing I disrespected them."

A laugh. "I hope she comes around."

"Me too."

"Think you'll end up together?"

"If I have anything to do with it, I sure do. It'd be different if she refused me because she didn't want me. But she does. I can feel it. She almost kissed me at the doc's office. But that's just the thing. We're like magnets trying to get at each other through a sheet of plastic— not enough to stop the pull, but just enough to keep us apart."

"Think you'll get married?"

I snorted a laugh. "I'd settle for a kiss. Anything past that... well, I don't even want to think about it until that door opens up. It's currently locked tight."

"Dead-bolt tight?"

"Nah, but she's left the chain on."

She smiled. "She's strict, huh?"

"Rules make her feel safe. She likes control, and she's in the middle of something she's got no control over. Throw me in the mix?" I shrugged a shoulder. "Anyway, I have an unending well of patience." I watched her for a second. "What'd you bring up marriage for?"

"Oh, I dunno. Nothin' more than that I know you, and the fact that she's carrying your baby probably makes you feel a certain... obligation."

I frowned as the microwave beeped. "That's not why I want her, Ma."

"That's not what I meant."

I gave her a look and handed her the plate.

"Well, that's not exactly what I meant. It's just that you have your own set of rules. I figured it bothered you not to have her locked down and the baby along with her."

"I knew the second I saw her that she was special. Different. I'm playing for keeps. But she doesn't do this, Ma. She doesn't even date, never mind cohabitate or have babies with somebody. A stranger, no less."

"Can't say I blame her. Didn't quite work out for me," she said lightly, as if it were a joke.

But it didn't feel like a joke at all. Not to me.

"It's not your fault you ended up yoked to a son of a bitch."

One of her dark brows rose with her lips. "Oh? Whose fault would it be then, Teddy?"

"His." A single definitive word that held decades of indignation.

She sighed, the sound weary with years of regret. "I shoulda been smarter. I shoulda known better. Everybody knew Johnny was trouble, but I thought he loved me."

"Because he told you he did. But he didn't end up showing it."

"Sometimes I wonder why he married me. Why not just sleep with me and leave the door open to walk out of when he was through? Why promise me forever? And the only thing I can think is that he *did* love me. He was just too messed up to love me the way I loved him."

My jaw clenched tight enough to pop. I didn't want to think about him as anything but a lazy piece of shit who never did right by anybody. But I doubted she was wrong. I didn't know how anybody could know her and not love her. But I didn't know how anybody could leave her like that.

A flash of fear bolted through me. Was Katherine too *Katherine* to ever choose me? It wasn't a possibility I could fathom. I felt sure if I followed the rules, checked all the boxes, waited patiently, she'd come around.

But what if she didn't?

That answer was too much to fathom. So I packed it away and relit the brazier of hope in my chest.

If I had my way, we'd have our happy ending. I was gonna marry that girl one day. Someday.

But for starters, I'd happily settle for a kiss.

"I've been thinking a lot about that lately," she started, pushing her food around her plate with her fork.

"About what?"

"Your father."

A burst of adrenaline ripped through me. The check in my pocket felt like it was on fire. "What about him?"

"I think I want to file divorce papers."

A frown, mighty in intensity, weighted my face. "Ma, that's crazy.

You know you'd have to see him, right?"

"I know. But it's been twenty years. He couldn't affect me after all this time."

I gave her a look.

She gave me one back. "I've been bound to him for too long."

"But why now, Ma? Where'd this come from?"

"I've been thinking about it for years. Since he left. I couldn't have done it back then, but now... well, now I can. But I need your help."

Thunder and lightning rolled through my chest. "He could take everything you have."

"You know as well as I do I've got nothing that isn't Tommy's. There's nothing for him to take."

"But whatever you *do* have, he'll take it."

Her face bent in sorrow and pain. "I don't understand why you're mad. I thought you'd want this. Teddy, I thought you'd understand. I don't want to end my days married to that man." The words choked off.

The sight of her face falling quieted the storm in my rib cage, filling me with dread and remorse.

I moved to her side, pulled her into a hug, and said the only thing I could. "It's all right, Ma. If this is what you want, I'll do whatever I can to help."

"Thank you," she said into my chest, her trembling hands hanging on to me with all her strength, which wasn't much.

God help that son of a bitch if he hurt her again. And God help us all if he showed up here to make trouble.

Because all of this meant my secret wouldn't stay quiet much longer. The second John got served, he'd come straight to me and make demands. Demands and threats.

So long as he kept his mouth shut, I'd keep paying him.

And so long as he stayed away, his nose would stay unbroken.

PREPOSITIONAL PROPOSITIONS

KATHERINE

The Rose Room was dark and empty, lit only by the lamps dotting the long work tables, casting soft, quiet light on the planes and angles of Theo's face. His smile was sideways and touched with heat I felt through my suit dress.

"I've outlined the merits of the top three convertible cribs and compared their features in a bar graph." He gestured to the foam board on a stand I hadn't seen until just then.

I was so hot for him, I started sweating.

His suit was black as pitch, brilliantly tailored, squaring his broad shoulders and hugging the curves of his biceps.

I stripped off my suit coat and rose from my seat. "Tell me more."

His eyes were molten as I hitched my skirt so I could climb onto

A shudder of pleasure rolled down my back as I crawled toward him.

"Organized by safety ratings." He stood, slipping his hand into my hair. "Categorized by price." His lips inched closer, setting fire to every nerve in my body. "Lowest to highest," he whispered, the words bouncing off my lips before covering my mouth with his.

I was a superabundance of sensation, a seismograph charting an eight-point-nine. I was hot and cold all over, but the vast majority of feeling concentrated in two places—the seam of our lips and the aching point where my thighs met.

It was wrong, being in the library like this. And we couldn't be together, shouldn't be together. The danger of it all—not only for getting caught, but to myself, to my heart—zinged between us, the desperation in our kiss hot and thick.

We were instantly naked, my back warming the hard table, his body heavy on mine. His hand brushed my sex without knowledge of how it was possible with his hips flush against mine. My legs wound around his narrow waist, his skin hot and soft over the hard mass of his muscles.

He broke the kiss and looked down into my face. And as he slipped into me, filled me up, he breathed the word, *"Come."*

My eyes shot open with my lungs, the gasp noisy and desperate in the quiet of my bedroom. I groaned into my pillow, my lids fluttering, hips grinding into my mattress as I did just as he'd commanded, my orgasm shuddering through me, body clenching around nothing.

A sigh as it ebbed, my heart slowing. And my brain had only one question.

What the fuck was that?

The answer was, of course, simple. I'd had my first wet dream.

I'd read a lot about increased libido in pregnant women but assumed that was constrained to actual physical acts, not lucid dreams that ended in a real, actual orgasm.

I flipped onto my back, flushed and disoriented and sated. Well, other than that my poor vagina had been empty when I came. I decided there was little so unsatisfying. Even a measly finger would have been better than *nothing.*

The sense of loss that Theo wasn't actually there overwhelmed me. My mind echoed what he'd said to me weeks ago.

Say the word.

All I had to do was say the word, and he *would* be in my bed, giving me real, super-full, super-hot orgasms. The temptation was alluring, especially with the memory of his dream-kiss and his dream-body and his dream-peen fresh and real in my mind.

I huffed, flinging my covers off and slipping out of bed with a mighty pout on my face.

I couldn't say the word. Because it wouldn't be so simple as hot beef and exchange of bodily fluids. Especially not if he came bearing spreadsheets.

With sharp snaps, I made my stupid bed. Brushed my stupid teeth and my stupid hair. Stood in front of my stupid closet and picked out a stupid outfit, telling myself as I zipped up my pencil skirt and slipped my feet into heels that I only wanted to look professional at work for the sake of my promotion. No, I didn't pick up my tube of red lipstick with the moniker Hot Mama printed on the bottom because Theo was coming to meet me for lunch. I just felt like a little self-care in the way of looking pretty.

It had nothing to do with Theo or the hope that he'd be wearing a suit or the dream I'd had where he nailed me on a library table.

Because saying the word wasn't an option. Saying the word would mean complicating an already complicated situation. It would mean giving up, giving in. Stepping into something that would inevitably blow up in my face. Because if I knew one thing, it was that I had no idea how to date Theo.

No matter how badly dream-me wanted it to be true, real-me's job was to be smarter than that.

Spreadsheets or not.

THEO

I trotted up the library steps, passing between twin lions standing sentinel to guard the knowledge inside.

My smile was immovable.

A week had passed since the doctor's appointment, and we hadn't seen each other, per her rules, damn them. But we'd texted. Quite a bit actually. What had begun as a request for our next meeting started a string of conversation that occupied far more time than either of us had intended and both seemed to enjoy. I'd started to look forward to texts with random pregnancy facts at unexpected intervals and updates on her day. Like the realization that folic acid made her more nauseated and the subsequent discovery that Flintstones vitamins would work in their stead. Or that rice had become a staple of every meal she consumed.

Even breakfast. She'd taken to eating a bowl topped with canned diced tomatoes.

I shuddered at the thought.

It was why I'd gone out of my way to make a lunch today that would appease Katherine's digestive gods.

I'd discovered my joy of cooking gradually and against my will. Once we moved to the Village with Ma, it became my responsibility to feed us. Tommy was busy writing and being social, and Ma couldn't quite manage it anymore. So I started planning meals. Following cooking blogs. Downloading apps to help me find recipes. And a couple of years in, I'd realized I loved it, looked forward to it.

There was something supremely satisfying about literally putting dinner on the table. I enjoyed making a meal out of a pile of ingredients. I found the assembly and care it took to complete a meal the most tangibly productive part of my day.

When presented with the problem of Katherine's particular tastes, I accepted the challenge with all the determination of Tom Brady at the Super Bowl, less the whiny crybaby entitlement and bad wardrobe.

Once inside the library, I scanned the entry for her, setting down the soft cooler so I could text her.

I'm here. You ready?

Let me just grab my bag. Meet me at the desk.

I scooped up the cooler and headed that way, the spring in my step unmissable.

I couldn't help it. I'd been waiting a week to see her. And the last time I'd seen her, I'd almost kissed her.

Stupid, necessary rules, trying my patience and will at every turn. My respect for them was the only reason I hadn't kissed her breathless in the doctor's office. I swore I could hear her begging me—with her eyes, with her lips—and when she'd closed her eyes in anticipation, I'd almost caved and given her what she'd asked for.

It was at the very last second that I'd caught myself. I still wished I hadn't, but I was glad I had.

Because she had to make the next move. If I pushed, she'd spook, and I'd lose my shot.

As I approached the desk, the man behind the counter glanced up, his eyes immediately narrowing when he saw me.

He wasn't tall, nor was he short. Wasn't quite handsome, but wasn't homely either. He was perfectly average, from top to toe and everywhere in between. But he eyeballed me like I'd come to confiscate the family farm.

I looked down at him—an instance where my imposing height came in handy. A zip of adrenaline burst through me as I read defense on his end, remnants of the biological training of my youth due to the countless fights Tommy had dragged me into.

I was smiling, but I wouldn't call it a friendly smile.

"Can I help you?" he asked impatiently.

"Just waiting on Katherine," I answered. "Do you know her… Eagan?" That was the name on his little metal name tag. Made me wonder how many black eyes he'd gotten. It'd have been plenty if he'd grown up in the Bronx.

"There are benches over there," he said in an attempt to dismiss me.

"Sure are. But Kate told me to meet her here."

His suspicious eyes narrowed a tick more. "Nobody calls her Kate."

I leaned in a little, smirking. "I do."

He huffed, rearranging a stack of books in front of him without purpose. "You're blocking the desk."

I glanced dramatically over my shoulder. "Funny, don't see anyone who needs anything from you. What exactly do you do here? Head of card stamping?" I flicked the date stamp resting on the pad, and it teetered before righting itself.

He snatched it, setting it out of my reach. "Don't touch my stamp."

"How long have you known Kate?"

"None of your business. What are you even doing here?"

"I made her lunch," I said, holding up the cooler in display.

"So, what is this, a date? Katherine doesn't date either."

"Maybe not you," I said lightly.

Katherine rounded the desk, her step faltering when she saw me. She slipped from the stoic Katherine to flushing Kate in the span of a heartbeat.

I shifted, reaching for her elbow for fear she might fall. "Steady there. You all right?"

"Yes, thank you," she answered breathlessly before stepping back. She smoothed her pencil skirt, adjusting her cardigan after.

She looked lovely as always, but today, she'd stepped it up. Shades of black, including pumps, her hair dark and curled rather than straight, as I'd seen it before. The only color was the ruby red of her cardigan, the flush of her cheeks, and her crimson lips.

I hadn't seen her in lipstick since that first night at the club. And the sight of her wearing it again set a deep groan sighing silently in my rib cage.

"Be back in half an hour," Eagan barked.

She gave him a look that would make any man's blood run cold and said in a steely voice, "Have I ever been late?" He opened his mouth to speak, but she said, "Of course not," turning away from him to take my arm. "I'm starving. Where should we eat?"

I didn't even pretend to contain my smugness, smiling at Eagan the Angry Egghead before turning us toward the exit.

"I was thinking we could sit by the fountain. Will you be warm enough without a coat?"

"Oh, yes. It's nice out today, don't you think? I'm glad to be out of coat weather. I thought winter would never end."

"Punxsutawney Phil ruined us all."

She frowned. "He's a groundhog. He can't determine the weather."

"Tell that to the good people of Punxsutawney."

She chuckled, keeping her hand in the crook of my elbow as we headed down the stairs and toward the fountain in Bryant Park.

"Did you know the lions were carved in Tennessee pink marble? LaGuardia named them Patience and Fortitude."

I smiled, amused. "I didn't know that. What else?"

She paused, the interlude marked by the sound of her heels on the steps. "The light posts over there"—she pointed toward 6th— "were designed by Tiffany Studios."

"The jeweler?"

Katherine laughed at my apparent idiocy. "No, as in the makers of Tiffany lamps. They're beautiful, cast in bronze. You should take a look at them sometime."

"Not now?"

"No. I only have half an hour, remember?"

"Ah, as the illustrious Eagan reminded you."

I glanced down to gauge her reaction and was pleased to find her scowling.

"He's the worst."

I huffed a laugh, surprised by her generalization.

"I mean it. He's the actual worst. He's constantly trying to piss me off. Effectively, I might add. We can't stand each other."

"Oh, I don't know about that. *I* think Eagan has a little crush on you."

Her head swiveled to glare at me. "That's ludicrous."

I gave her a look right back. "It's not at all. I'd be willing to bet you're the hottest librarian in the public library system."

Her cheeks flushed—whether it was from the compliment or fury, I couldn't know. Maybe both.

"That…well, that makes no sense," she sputtered, snapping her eyes back to the path. "He's horrible. Rude. Constantly making my life difficult."

"Playground rules. Boys who pull your pigtails like you."

"Boys who pull *my* pigtails get black eyes."

Laughter spilled out of me. "Why, Kate, I never expected you'd resort to violence."

"When it comes to Eagan, always. He's the exception to my every rule."

For a split second, I envied him that.

We reached the fountain, but the chairs and tables were all taken. I worried she'd balk at eating anywhere else, but without a word, she hopped up on the ledge of the fountain and demurely crossed her ankles.

She was a vision in black and red, the city stretching up behind her, the fountain bubbling sweetly at her back. Her lips, so red and inviting, curled up at the very edges, a smile rare and generally hard won. But she offered it to me without my having to do a thing.

I took that feather and stuck it proudly in my metaphorical cap.

I sat next to her, putting the cooler between us. Preventative measures and all that.

"Is there an occasion today that has you dressed up?"

"Only this."

I glanced over to find her smiling still, something unspoken behind her alluring irises. It was unlike her to keep anything close to the vest.

But by my grand powers of deduction, there was no other meaning to take.

She'd dressed up for me.

"Thank you for meeting me for lunch like this, Theodore. I know it's not very long."

I unpacked the containers one by one. "Like I said, Kate—any way I can get you." I didn't wait for a response, just popped the lid off her lunch and handed it over.

She took it curiously, peering inside.

"Marinated grilled chicken, lime rice, and a kale and spinach salad with edamame, shredded carrots, and sesame-soy dressing. It's beige—with the exception of the salad—and it has your staple rice and plenty of protein. The salad is high in folic acid."

Katherine glanced up, her expression closed but for the inquisitive look in her eyes.

"It's good for the baby's brain development."

"It is. I've added spinach to my beige diet for that reason." She glanced back at her lunch, her cheeks flushed again. "What a thoughtful meal. I can't believe you cooked all this for me."

I shrugged, busying myself with bottles of water and cutlery to avoid her eyes. "It was nothing really. I enjoy cooking. I made enough to feed Ma, too. I used to cook for Tommy, but now Amelia's taken over my gig. Although I almost always cook the four of us dinner."

"I've never quite understood it," she admitted. "Cooking, even eating sometimes, feels like a chore. Filling my body with fuel. It's a necessity, not a pleasure."

"Well, now I have a new goal in life."

Her head tilted.

"To turn your refueling into a pleasure."

She chuckled, forking a bite of salad. Her face was down, her lips smiling. She seemed almost shy.

It was incredibly attractive.

And the sight gave me bravado I should have ignored. But I didn't.

"How about our next meeting?" I asked. "Dinner at my place?"

She paused, fork mid-motion. A spinach leaf fell off the prongs and back into her dish. "I'd like that."

I smiled, taking another bite.

Externally, I was calm and contained, eating lunch with a pretty girl in the park. Internally, I was in the middle of a touchdown dance in the end zone.

But there was a flag on the play. Nothing was certain.

I had no idea what the hell had changed since last week, but whatever the catalyst was, it struck a match of hope in my chest. We were going to have dinner in the privacy of my apartment. And today, she'd dressed up just for me. She'd painted her lips crimson even though I had a feeling lipstick probably bothered her. She'd worn heels, one of which had fallen off the back of her foot and dangled by her toes. She didn't even seem to notice.

This version of her was an in-between—not quite Katherine, not quite Kate, but a hybrid of the two. And she'd agreed to come over for dinner. It'd be good practice. I'd have to keep my hands to myself when she moved in. Better to start building up my immunity now. Otherwise, I'd never be able to keep my promise.

She hummed her approval as she chewed. "I have to admit," she said when she'd swallowed, "I wasn't sure about the salad. Kale offends my senses on almost every level."

"When I used to wait tables at a seafood restaurant, it was nothing more than an inedible garnish on which to place a lemon."

"That's a use I can support. Well, that and this salad." She took another bite and moaned. "So good. I haven't eaten a real meal in so long, I almost forgot what food tasted like."

I frowned. "Does the nausea last the whole time?"

"No. By the time we're living together, it should have subsided. Hopefully, at least."

She said it so casually, without hesitation. *Living together.* I brushed the impulse to read into it away.

"I'll plan a feast to commemorate. Cakes and pies and steaks and vegetables. Not a single thing on the table will be beige."

Her brow quirked. "Can we have fries?"

I laughed. "Anything you want, Kate."

"Thank you, Theodore." She fished around in her container for more food. "I'm surprised you waited tables. I can't quite picture you as restaurant staff."

"Oh? I definitely was. Tommy bartended—way more money in it, but drunk people drive me nuts. He'd tap-dance around and entertain them, eat up the attention. I would have ended up laying them out or pitching them out the front door."

She assessed me, head tilted. "I think it's the suit. You look very... serious. Adult. I can't even seem to imagine you young."

"I'll have to break out Ma's albums for you. Tommy and I were wiry teens, tall and skinny and full of attitude. Well, Tommy at least. I just had to back his attitude up with a couple of spare fists."

"I can't imagine that either. You're too civilized for brute force."

Another laugh, this one a little too loud, the volume broken by my surprise. "You've met my brother, right?"

Her brow quirked. "Of course I have. You were there when I met him."

"What I meant," I said on a laugh, "is that he's savage. He runs strictly on emotion, ruled by his heart. And all that's done is lead him straight into trouble. It's always been that way. He possesses a moral compass that cannot be swayed."

"So do you."

"True," I conceded, "but the difference is that I think. Plan. Calculate. Act and react based on outcomes and consequences. Tommy doesn't think a step ahead—he's caught in the moment. I, on the other hand, don't make many moves without thinking five steps down the line. But when we were kids, there was nothing to do but back him up. Hell, even now I back him up. At least now I get paid for it with more than a fat lip."

Something hot burned behind her eyes like flickering embers. "Without a plan, I'm generally immobilized. I think everything through before taking a step as well. It's why I've had difficulty coming to grips with so much change so fast."

The simple honesty of her admission struck me. I lowered my container, resting it on my lap, waiting for her to continue.

"I'm having trouble with the uncertainty of all this. How do you plan for something you have so little control over?"

"You can't," I answered plainly, gently. "All you can do is plan for what you know. Make contingency plans. And above all else, be flexible."

The embers in her eyes flared at that. "I'm trying to learn that. Flexibility. It's not easy for me."

"Me either," I admitted, "but surviving my life and my brother has instilled that in me by conditioning."

She nodded, pausing to think. And those thoughts were so loud, I could almost hear them. "Then I have another proposition."

My heart lurched, sensing something I hadn't anticipated. "I'm all ears."

I expected her to argue the idiom, but she didn't. She seemed too nervous to point out the impossibility of being comprised solely of ears.

"You are, by your own admission, somewhat of an expert at adapting to the unforeseen, and I am inept. I'd like to propose that you take the lead on decisions."

I stared at her, unblinking. "Do you think that's something you'll actually be able to do? Let me lead?"

"Well, you did it so well at the club," she joked wryly.

"It's true, I did. But this is different."

"I'm not saying it won't come without its fair share of discussion. I need to be convinced. But you're very convincing."

I chuffed a laugh. "You're not wrong there either. But I'm not sure if you really want to give me absolute power."

"It wouldn't be absolute. You're right, there's no way I could do that. But I'd like to open the lines of communication. I need input that's logical and flexible and in opposition of my own. Because currently—and I'm guessing that for some time to come—I am emotional in ways I don't know how to manage. I can't untangle emotion from reason, and it's been…difficult for me. And so, I'm wondering, can you help me?"

Her eyes were wide with uncertainty and open with earnestness. This woman who was so composed by law was vulnerable, laid out at my feet with her underbelly up. The weight of her request wasn't lost on me.

And I had every intention of upholding the promise I made when I said, "Anything you want, Kate."

She smiled, those transmutable eyes softening with relief.

"But first, finish your salad."

When she laughed and scooped up a bite, I was no less than a king among men. Because she'd given me power, given me a modicum of control over a kingdom I'd do anything to rule.

And I wouldn't waste the chance.

SCIENTIFIC METHOD

KATHERINE

9 WEEKS, 4 DAYS

A week later, I was at Theo's door, anxiously waiting just like I'd been since I saw him last.

We were just a few short weeks from our cohabitation date, which seemed to be approaching with a speed I wasn't comfortable with but had no choice but to endure.

The only comfort was Theo.

Our lunch in the park had been another relationship step on a staircase that rivaled a Mayan temple. Agreement to dinner. The idea had struck me like a thunderbolt the second he said flexibility—a word I'd been trying to embrace. I could have him help me make all these decisions with logic and reason since my meter was busted.

Picking out a stroller-car-seat combo was one thing. But being rational about where I lived, how to change, how to assimilate to life with him … well, that was more than I could handle at present.

The truth was, I could use someone stable and rational to help me make decisions, and Theo was the prime candidate.

The downside was that I'd have to be frank with him about everything.

Everything, including my feelings regarding *him*.

Because I had a lot of feelings about him, and I hadn't the slightest idea how to handle them.

They were irrational, the whole lot of them, betraying my original plan to remove myself from the situation entirely. Now I had no choice. And that put me in a precarious place, one I was hoping he could save me from.

I only had to tell him.

He answered the door with a smile. The spice and smell of cooking meat hit me in a wave that had me salivating.

Well, it was either that or the sight of Theo.

I always forgot how tall he was until in his presence, the height of him impressive and commanding, casting a shadow that all else fell under. It was a quiet magnetism, the draw of him inexplicable. He wasn't wearing a suit and tie as he normally did, which was lamentable but for the fact that he still wore a tailored shirt and slacks. But rather than the strict neatness he usually possessed, his shirtsleeves were cuffed at his elbows, and the button at his throat was undone. One revealed wide wrists and broad forearms, corded with muscle. The other exposed the soft hollow of his throat and the angular knot of his Adam's apple.

Both were undeniably masculine. The impulse to press my lips to that delicate hollow surprised and disarmed me.

"Hello, Theodore."

His smile widened. "Hi, Kate. Come on in."

He shifted out of the way, and I entered, passing through the ghost of his scent, which overrode dinner by miles.

"Hope you're hungry."

"I am. Thank you for having me."

"Thanks for indulging me. I told you—it's my new mission in life to make refueling a pleasure."

I laughed, but the sound was tight, nervous.

Theo glanced at me, but the look was comforting even though I caught a glimpse of recognition and worry in his eyes.

"My mom's just in the living room," he said quietly. "Are you sure you still want to meet her?"

I nodded once, trying to be discreet as I wiped my sweaty palms on my thighs. His eyes flicked to the motion, but he offered me a warm smile.

I both appreciated his perceptiveness and loathed how it exposed me.

"All right," he said, laying a large, reassuring hand on the small of my back. "You're lovely, as always, Kate. I really am glad you came."

"Me too," I said, which was only partly a lie.

I was glad to be there, and I was glad to be on the threshold of telling him how I felt about him. It was eating me alive to keep the words bottled up. I wasn't a particularly successful bottler of things. I typically said what I felt, when I felt it, which was its own problem.

It actually hadn't been until recently that I realized not everyone was interested in my opinion, on top of the realization that I didn't actually *have* to say what was in my head the moment a thought entered it.

But I was *not* glad for the anxious feeling snaking through my guts at the prospect of coming clean with Theo. Or with meeting his mother.

Mostly because I didn't give a very good first impression.

I was, from my cursory research and observation, generally taken as abrasive, too forward, and cold. My friends were all warm, with soft faces and pleasant smiles, gentle natures and breezy attitudes. Well, Val was closer to running hot than warm, with a penchant for saying what she felt that ran as deep as my own impulses. The difference was that she was funny and charming about it, where I was just blatant and harsh.

The present issue being that I wanted Theo's mother to like me. I wanted that very much.

The entryway opened up to the living room, and sitting on the modern, low-backed couch was Sarah.

She shifted, picking herself up to stand with far more effort than it would have were she healthy. Theo rushed to her side, cupping her elbow and offering his hand for support, which she took gratefully.

I stopped on one side of the coffee table, unsure of where to stand or how to greet her. Rather than make a wrong move, I waited where I was with a practiced smile on my face. I hoped it looked more natural than it felt.

Theo helped her around the table—I batted away the guilt that she would go to trouble for me—and they came to a stop in front of me. She was beautiful, though small, frail, especially next to the vitality of her son. They had the same thick black hair, and her eyes matched her boys'—unfathomably dark and deep. Her smile felt like a hug. And, since I didn't particularly like being hugged, my preference for her warm smile was easy and welcome. I wanted to wrap myself up in that smile and live there.

"Katherine. It's good to finally meet you, honey." Her voice wavered, her hand trembling as she extended it.

I didn't miss that Theo held on to her.

I took her hand and clasped my free hand to the back of hers, enveloping it like I'd seen Amelia and Rin do. Val was a hugger. I wasn't quite ready for that though.

"Hello, Sarah. I'm glad to meet you, too." I paused, feeling like I should say something else but unsure as to what.

"Come sit with me for a minute before dinner?" she asked hopefully.

"Of course," I answered, composing a list of topics in my mind to carry the conversation as I followed them back to the couch.

"So, Teddy tells me you're a librarian," she said as she settled in. "I bet it's a real treat, being around books all day. I love the smell of old books."

"Me too," I admitted. "And it is a treat. I'm a page, which means I shelve books all day. I don't think I've ever done anything so immediately satisfying as putting things where they belong for a living."

"Does it bother you to be alone all day? I'd probably be talking to myself a couple hours in like a crazy person."

"Oh, no—the solitude suits me, always has. My parents thought I was odd for preferring books and the comfort of my room to playing outside or making friends."

She chuckled. "Depends on the kid. Tommy and Teddy were always outside, and they had about a hundred friends. It coulda been thirty degrees and snowing, and they'd be too busy scheming places to sled with their gang to be cold."

Theo's face was alight with adoration as he watched over his mother. "There was a hill in Mount Eden, and if we got it before it was plowed, we could sled down the sidewalk on a cardboard box fast enough to give you whiplash."

"Especially when you hit a trash can," she added.

Theo smirked. "Tommy lost a tooth. One of many."

"A third of what he's got left is porcelain," Sarah said with a laugh.

"I've never broken a bone," was all I could think to say.

"No, you?" Theo teased. "I was sure you played field hockey."

My brows drew together in confusion. "Whatever would make you think that?"

He laughed. "Call it a hunch."

"Contact sports make me uncomfortable. Why would you willingly do something that might injure you? I've never understood."

"That's because you've never played. Or broken anything. It's almost always worth it." I must have looked unconvinced because he added, "The adrenaline high. Really, the risk is half the fun."

Sarah laughed. "I'm with you, Katherine. I'd much rather be reading than risking my neck for a rush. But my boys...well, they were always out for trouble."

"I'd suspect it's their testosterone production. It makes males much more aggressive and willing to take risks. It also makes them more competitive. Considering their muscle mass and density of hair, I'd say theirs is quite high."

This time when Sarah laughed, it was with surprise and what I thought might be a touch of discomfort. I was glad I'd stopped myself before mentioning sexual capacity.

"I'm sorry," I said, feeling myself flush. "I have a photographic memory and sometimes recite facts when I'm nervous."

Theo's face softened.

Sarah's warmed. "Oh, honey, don't be nervous. You're already a part of our family. There's nothin' you need to do to hang on to that spot. It's yours."

My ribs were a vise, tight around my lungs. "Thank you," I said quietly, automatically.

"Don't ever be afraid to speak your mind to me," she said. "Not about anything, testosterone or otherwise. Anyway, I don't mean to intrude on your night." She shifted, bracing herself on the arm of the couch so she could stand. Theo helped her up. "I'll leave you two to dinner. I've got a date with a serial killer."

I blinked, my lips flattening.

She caught my expression and smiled. "Netflix. The Ted Bundy documentary."

"Oh, of course," I said with a sigh.

Sarah smiled up at Theo. "I like her."

He shot me a pleased glance. "Me too."

Damn him. Damned hormones. Damned heart, pitter-pattering without my consent.

"I hope we have a chance to get together before you move in, Katherine," Sarah said. "And if not, I'm looking forward to more facts and less nerves."

"So am I. It's a pleasure to meet you."

They shuffled past.

"I'll be back in a second," Theo said.

And so, I sat and waited as he helped Sarah to her room.

My palms were a swampy mess, my body reacting to the stress and anxiety of meeting the most important person in Theo's life. The grandmother to my embryo. My future roommate.

The room swam for a moment, the pressure in my brain dimming my vision. I laid my head back, closed my eyes, tried to breathe while unsuccessfully attempting to avoid hyper-focusing on every symptom of my apparent swoon.

"Kate?"

His worried voice forced a crack in my eyelids.

"I'm fine," I assured him, my voice watery.

"You're gray. When did you eat last?"

"Mmm, I had some purse crackers on my way here."

He knelt at my feet, his face frowning and authoritative. "I mean a real meal."

"I had rice and tomatoes for lunch."

"That does not constitute lunch. No protein."

"Does too. A cup of rice has four-point-three grams of protein."

He huffed, rolling his eyes as he stood, extending his hand. "That is not enough protein. Case in point." He gestured to me when I didn't accept his palm.

I sighed. "The thought of meat made my stomach turn. I haven't thrown up in days, and I don't want to start now."

"Come on, Kate. Let me feed you." When I didn't take his hand, a smile tugged at his lips. "I'll pick you up and carry you in three... two..."

I grabbed his hand with a huff, and he pulled me to stand.

For a moment, he kept holding my hand as we walked toward the stairs. But he let me go.

I sighed, wishing he hadn't.

Once we reached the top of the stairs, the delectable scent of dinner and the sweet sounds of music slipped over me. The atmosphere was inviting and warm, settling my nerves. It felt homey, cozy, the rooms lit only by lamps and the soft overhead kitchen lighting.

"Dinner's ready," he said, walking to the oven, snagging an oven mitt on his way. "Have a seat."

I did as I'd been told, choosing one of the two places set up at the table. It was lovely really—fresh flowers in a low vase, salad plate on top of the dinner plate. Water in wine glasses. Cloth napkins set with cutlery. The salad and dinner forks were even in the correct order.

His attention to detail made him infinitely more attractive.

I watched him from my seat, unfolding my napkin to lay it in my lap. With great care, he transferred food from the casserole dish to a tray and bowl. As he walked over with them, he had a proud, mildly smug smile on his face.

I peered into the dishes when he set them down and turned for the fridge.

On the dish sat a row of gently breaded chicken breasts dotted with green herbs and surrounded by steaming cauliflower. The bowl brimmed with hand-cut fries that smelled like garlic and salt and carbs.

Everything was beige.

Inexplicably, the realization made me want to cry.

I glanced down to my lap, pretending to arrange my napkin so I didn't have to look up at him. Because he'd see my emotion and know exactly how I felt.

He always did. He saw straight through me.

With anyone else, I would have been averse to the point of ending a relationship. But with him, I only felt understood.

It was so rare, to feel understood.

Theo appeared in my periphery, but I didn't look up as he set down the salad and took his seat.

"I hope you like the salad. The soy dressing wouldn't have gone with this, so I made a spinach and strawberry salad with balsamic."

"It's ... it's perfect," I said, swallowing hard and forcing a smile as a weak attempt to recover. "You always seem to know just what to do. It's unnerving."

He chuckled, placing his napkin in his lap. "I was going for charming."

"Oh, it's charming. It's ... difficult for me when I'm caught off guard. Especially right now." I reached for the servingware to dish myself some chicken and cauliflower.

At that, a hint of a frown passed across his lips. "I'm sorry, Kate. I don't want to make you uncomfortable."

"No, that's not what I mean." I kept my eyes on my hands, dishing myself some fries. "You've done everything right. Better than right because you anticipate what I need before I know I need it."

"Well, I've been doing that for Tommy for years. It's the first line of my job description," he joked.

Our hands moved around each other, anticipating what the other would reach for and systematically making the rounds on the food. It was a dance of efficiency. I wondered if it would be like this when the baby came, imagined us double-teaming a diaper change, moving around each other with such effortless grace.

We were, without thought or intention, an excellent team.

"It's no wonder you're very good at your job," I said, picking up my fork to dig into my salad. I speared a strawberry and sliver of parmesan and took a bite, moaning when it hit my tongue.

He was so handsome when he smiled. It honestly wasn't fathomable how a man like him could be interested in a woman like me. I wasn't the kind of girl who handsome, successful, charming men wooed. But beyond all logic and reason, here I sat, across the table from one of said men, with a curated beige dinner, complete with folic acid, for the girl he'd gotten pregnant on a one-night stand.

Maybe it was only the baby. He'd made this food not to make *me* happy, but to provide sustenance for his child. He'd fed me folic acid for fetal brain development, not to impress me.

But then I thought back to that night, that first night. And the remembrance of the connection we'd made long before a baby was in the picture had me turned around again.

And that was the most difficult thing of all to parse—logic and reason did not apply here. And without those two systems to count on, I was hobbled.

I took another bite of my salad, unable to redirect my thoughts. And for a moment, we ate in silence but for the music playing from an unseen source. And Theo didn't press. He just ate, occasionally catching my eye or smiling at me. The lack of conversation was companionable, comfortable, terribly natural. And I took the moment to collect myself.

We were halfway through our main course when my blood sugar had normalized along with my heart rate and emotions. For the moment at least. I drew upon my reserves of collectiveness and set down my fork.

He looked up, saw my expression, and sobered, setting down his fork too. "You okay, Kate?"

"I'm much better than okay, Theodore." My hands, which were damp, clutched my napkin in my lap. "I'm nervous and unsure, but you have taken care of me in ways I couldn't have known you would and for reasons I can't quite understand."

"Well, I like taking care of people. Especially you."

I sighed. "When you say things like that, I don't know what to do."

His eyes cast down, and he nodded guiltily. "I'm sorry. I know you asked me not to come on to you, but it's not intentional. It's just honest. I tend to say how I feel, when I feel it."

"I do, too," I said. "And that's what makes it so disarming—your honesty. I asked you to help me last week. Because I'm unable to untangle my feelings and look at things objectively. Especially when it comes to you."

Flint struck behind his eyes, sparking a flame of hope that reached nothing but his irises.

"It's become abundantly clear that the chemistry and compatibility between us isn't something we can avoid. And so, I'd like to propose we discuss alternatives."

"And what kind of alternatives do you have in mind?"

"I'm not exactly sure, which is why I'd like to discuss them. As decided, I would like to defer to you."

Silence, noisy with his unspoken thoughts. "All right," he said quietly. "Let's start with more information. How exactly do you feel about me?"

I considered the question. There were too many answers. "I don't know where to begin."

"With the good. For my ego."

With a long pause and a healthy helping of discomfort, I took a breath and let loose. "I don't know how it's possible that you continually do everything right. You do exactly what I would do but with more…panache. You have respected my wishes. You've done everything I asked. You've stayed away, and I'm starting to hate it."

He stilled.

"I don't understand my feelings, and I don't understand why I can't keep them in check. I don't know why I want you to touch me or kiss me. I don't understand how you make me want things I've decided I didn't want. I don't like feeling like I can't control myself, and it's why I avoided you in the first place. And I should have known I couldn't fight biology, but when coupled with your behavior, I can't imagine how I'm supposed to stop it. I don't think I want you to stay away anymore, Theo."

For a moment, he said nothing. His face, which I scanned for answers, was locked down but for those smoldering eyes of his.

"Okay. Now tell me the bad."

I took a shaky breath. "I'm not prepared to enter into a relationship. I don't know how, and things between us are too complicated. There's no way to determine what's a real connection and what is circumstantial. Or hormone-fueled."

"What are you afraid will happen?" he asked quietly.

"I'm afraid I'll hurt you. Or that I'll get hurt. That we'll ruin our positive relationship by confusing things. Because I'm growing more and more convinced that we'll need each other. And can we successfully raise our child together if we part ways damaging each other? If things end badly because we made poor choices or weren't as compatible as we'd thought, is it possible to remain amicable for the sake of our child? If we live together and *are* together and separate, how can we still be peaceful and productive?" I shook my head, tried to soothe the ache in my chest with a breath. "Like I said—it's just too complicated."

When he didn't say anything, I kept explaining, overcome by

nerves regarding his reaction once he *did* speak.

"I can't sort it out on my own. I need your input. I trust you. Because I know you want what's best for us and our embryo."

"Baby."

My head tilted. "Baby?"

"Baby. It has arms and fingers and toes now."

"See?" I said with an exasperated wave of my hand in his direction. "It's things like this. You remembered what I said weeks ago about the baby not being a baby until it had arms and legs. You remember everything. You are thoughtful and giving. Every word, every detail has meaning. The dinner you made for me. The care you give. It attracts me beyond strictly chemicals."

"Then who's to say a relationship wouldn't work?"

A hot flush bloomed up my neck, to my cheeks. "Who's to say it would? There are too many variables to track. And I don't know if the risk is wise for our future."

Something in him lit up, though his face was still calm and composed. He straightened up and leaned forward, resting his broad forearm on the table.

"So, an experiment is in order. With controlled variables."

I straightened up myself. "I'm listening."

"I've wanted you from the moment you wiped my kiss off the back of your hand."

A short burst of laughter bubbled out of me.

"You ignored me for almost five weeks. And every single day, I thought about you. I think I can safely say I want you just as badly as you want me. More maybe. I understand your fears, and they're real. And I understand the quandary. Our relationship, by accidental default, is happening backward. The rules don't apply, and the stakes are high. So, let's experiment. Rather than introduce all variables at once, let's introduce them in increments."

Hope sprang. "This is a brilliant idea. Where do you suggest we start?"

His sideways smile rose on one side. "Where *we* started."

My eyes widened. My lips parted to speak, but he cut me off.

"Before you say no, consider a few things. Our chemistry, as you mentioned, is overwhelming at best, maddening at worst. By exercising those urges, it's possible we might empty the tank of desire."

The way he said *possible* made me feel like he'd perhaps chosen that word for my benefit. The word held an undercurrent of patronization, as if he knew the tank of desire was bottomless.

But the logic didn't escape me.

"And, if it doesn't, then we can make a plan for more incremental steps."

"Like dates," I offered, my mind whirring as it composed a list. "Public displays of affection. Cuddling. Sleeping in the same bed."

"Exactly. We can start where *we* started. Scratch the itch. See if we get it out of our systems. And if not, then we can add one thing at a time to determine long-term compatibility."

"Take it slow by taking it fast," I mused. "Normally, I would disagree, but in our instance, I think it might work."

That smolder in his eyes was now all over his face, and the full effect would have wobbled my knees if I'd been standing. As it was, it simply made me sweat.

Last time I'd seen that look, I'd gotten myself pregnant.

"All right," I said. "I'm deferring to you. When should we start?"

"Right fucking now," he said, standing, pushing back his chair, and tossing his napkin onto his plate in the same motion.

I laughed, flustered and amused. But he didn't stop, eating up the space between us, his eyes locked on mine and smirk firmly in place as he grabbed my chair and turned it with me still in the seat.

I yelped, still laughing until I couldn't laugh anymore.

Because he was kissing me.

God, was he kissing me, his lips bruising and determined and relieved and demanding. He kissed me like he'd been dreaming of kissing me his whole life, like he'd recounted it in a thousand ways, and now that it was upon him, his restraint was gone. Wild and hot, his breath noisy from his nose, his hands roaming my hair, my face, my thigh.

I broke the kiss, unable to catch my breath, my lips parted and panting. He didn't miss a beat, burying his face in my neck.

My arms wound around his neck, my fingers skimming the close crop of his hair and sliding into the thick, dark locks on top.

"Rules," I whispered. "We need rules."

"Tell me," he said between kisses.

My eyelids were too heavy to keep open. I sighed. "Once a week. No sleeping in the same bed."

"Mmm," was his answer.

"No dating. No kissing and no touching, except for our itch-scratching. We—*oh*!" He nibbled my ear, and for a second, I couldn't speak. "We need a signal. A … a sign."

He broke away, leaning back, his eyes black and lust-drunk. "I have one rule. It can double as the signal."

"What?" I said breathlessly.

Theo reached for my face, cupped my jaw, and ran a thumb across my bottom lip, his eyes following the motion. "Wear this lipstick. I want you in it when we … scratch. And that'll be my cue."

I smiled, shifting to extend my hand. "Deal."

But he kissed me instead.

And I found I preferred it to a handshake without question.

THE ITCH

KATHERINE

D inner was forgotten, the final straw drawn when he picked me up and carried me like a savage toward his bedroom. There was one brief moment when I noted that I had no reservations, not a single one. And then I couldn't be bothered to care.

He laid me down in his bed with gentle care, breaking the kiss to smile down at me. He hovered over me, his forearm planted next to my head, his thigh slipping between mine. And my hands had a mind of their own, roaming down the crisp cotton of his shirt toward his belt, tugging the tails from his waistband.

His lips crushed mine in the same moment my fingers grazed the tight skin of his abs. His pants hung from his narrow hips almost without touching them, the incongruity of the ridges of his body with the sleek lines of his slacks a study in opposites. His clothes were that of a man who had a meeting to attend or a private jet to catch or a business to run. His body was that of a man whose only job was to bale hay or chop wood or run a marathon.

A wealth of muscles hid under the clean lines of his suit, rolling, corded, tight muscles, exposed little by little as I unfastened each pearly button. My fingertips were thirsty to map the topography of every one. He was the only man I'd ever been with who had a body like this. Muscles, sure, on occasion. But never *this*. His was the body of an athlete in the shell of a businessman, and I wondered as my hands skimmed the discs of his pecs and across small, tight nipples what his motivation was.

His hand gripped my thigh, forcing it far wider than necessary to fit his hips. With a slow grind, he pressed his hard length into me.

Control, I realized. I imagined he liked the control over his body, the exertion of his will against his physical self. I also imagined that he wasn't a halfway sort of man. If he decided to work out, he'd push himself to the limits of his body. And then I suspected he'd push it one step further.

I moaned into his mouth, my hands sliding over his hot skin, up to thickly muscled shoulders, catching his shirt on my wrists to rid him of it. My dress was hitched up to my hips, the black skirt hooked in the bend of my thighs and spread out under me. He sighed as his hand slipped high enough to slide his thumb under the silky black fabric.

My body remembered his, ached for his. I didn't realize just how much I'd been holding back, what I'd been tamping down. I'd tried to box up a tiger in cardboard, and it'd shredded the box the second it had the chance.

I reached for his belt, ready to let something else loose, but his hips backed away with his lips. Down my body he moved, kissing a trail across my neck, my collarbone, my sternum. Broad fingers unbuttoned my shirtdress and untied the sash at my waist, exposing my torso, then my stomach, then my hips completely.

He skimmed the eyelash lace at the edge of my bra, sweeping the curve. My breasts ached, heavy and swollen. My bra barely contained them.

"You always surprise me, Kate," he said just before his lips brushed the swell of the breast currently residing in his palm. His voice was rough, low, rumbling.

"What did I do?" I asked.

"This bra is not at all practical." He smirked, his dark eyes flashing a glance up at me.

"No, but it's pretty and French, and I love it."

"So do I." His fingers hooked the edge and pulled until it rested outside the curve. His skin was hot against mine as he cupped the weight and squeezed, bringing his lips to the tight peak of my nipple.

My lids fluttered closed with the sweep of his tongue, my back arching, hands cradling him to me.

Control, his over mine. And I didn't want it back, not until he'd taken his fill and given me mine.

It was a strange, bodiless sensation—to feel the need to do *nothing*. I didn't have to lead. I didn't have to flip him over and do what I needed to do. I didn't have to put his hands where I wanted them—he knew where they belonged. And that afforded me the luxury of lying boneless beneath him with nothing to think about but what I felt.

And I felt everything.

The slickness of his tongue drawing my aching nipple deeper into his mouth. The weight of his body pressing me into his bed. The contained strength of his hand testing the weight of my breast. His breath, noisy and puffing against my tingling skin.

His free hand hooked my hip, squeezed with savage ownership, slipped into my panties. Fingertips grazed the warm center of me, dipping gently into my flesh, slicking itself before brushing my swollen, aching clit with a simultaneous flick of his tongue against my nipple.

I moaned, wriggling under him. My fingers unwound from his hair, moving for his belt again. And this time, I wasn't taking no for an answer.

The metal rattled, my hands rushing to unfasten his pants before diving inside. I found him hot and hard and heavy, the tip weeping and slick. My thumb slid across it, spreading the bead across the velvety skin of his crown, fingering the ridge, the notch, the slit.

Impatient. I was impatient, the tiger let loose and unable to be caged again. I mewled my frustration, shifting to get my hips closer to his, but with his mouth still paying homage to my breast, he was too far away.

He wanted to take his time. It was clear in the way he teased me, slipping nothing more than the tip of his finger into the heat of my body. He tried to move, tried to take his lips to the place where my thighs met.

But that was not what I wanted there.

He chuckled against my breast when I urged him up my body again.

"If I only get you once a week, I intend to enjoy you fully, Kate."

I groaned, rolling my hips to force his finger deeper, but I was denied once again.

"We didn't decide how many orgasms of yours I get every week." He circled my clit with his thumb, dipping that teasing finger in again.

"As many as you want," I breathed, the sound touched with a hint of something I could only call a whine.

"Well, in that case—" He slid his finger into me, all the way to the knuckle.

I flexed into him with a groan that started deep in my chest and hung in the air for a long, heavy moment. He squeezed. I squirmed.

Because it wasn't enough. I'd thought it would be. But nothing would be enough, not until he did what I truly wanted.

"Fuck me, Theo," I whispered.

His entire body reacted, tightening and curling around me, in me. His pants were gone with barely a shift. Then my panties. My dress was shucked off my arms, then my bra in a blur between kisses. And then we were naked, a hot tangle of arms and legs, hips and lips locked together. We rolled once, putting me on top of him, my hair falling around us like a curtain, filtering the golden lamplight. The kiss didn't stop, not until I backed toward his crown, fitting the tip of him at my core.

In a flash of motion, I was underneath him again, legs spread far enough to ache. I couldn't protest, couldn't tell him I wasn't able to come like this. His lips gave me no quarter, bruising and brash. And his hand slipped between us to guide his cock to the threshold of my body.

With a forceful flex of his hips, he thrust into me, the kiss breaking with my gasp. But only for a second. His hand slid to my neck as he pulled out, grasping my jaw with splayed fingers. He kissed me again as he slammed into me hard enough to jostle my breasts.

I was pinned beneath him, held in place by his rocking hips, his hand on my jaw, his lips against mine, unable to move and unable to care. With every thrust, his body rolled, slow and deliberate, pressing and releasing my aching clit with every motion. A series of motions, faster, then slower, the rhythm building with the heat of my body. I was combustible, the pressure setting a tingling across my skin, burning in my chest, shrinking my awareness to the orgasm rising within me.

I was helpless against it. Against him.

Control.

Mine was gone completely.

I came with a thundering rush, a stopping and starting of my body that shook every atom, every molecule that I was composed of. It was blinding, the intensity stopping time and space in my brain, stretching out a moment of both disconnect and awareness, of release and relief.

I realized only on the fringes of consciousness when he came, the slap of skin rising, and at the apex was a moan so deeply masculine, so powerfully possessive, my body squeezed, tightening around him as he swelled inside of me.

Thrust and throb, slower and slower, our consciousness returning by breath, by heartbeat, by kiss on slow, deep kiss. I was surrounded by him, caged by his body with blissful submission. They were two words I'd never have set next to one another. Submission and dominance had delivered me an orgasm that taught me something very important.

My sexual experiences paled in comparison to what Theo could give me.

He kissed me slowly, one hand framing my face, the other in my hair, his body braced by his forearm bracketing me in. I was surrounded, helplessly, hopelessly sated and slack.

A heavy sigh left me by way of my nose—my lips were otherwise occupied.

He broke the kiss, eyes smoldering and lips sideways. I didn't realize I was smiling back until his thumb grazed my bottom lip.

"You're beautiful, Kate."

"So are you," I said, my gaze tracing the hard lines of his nose and lips and jaw for confirmation.

His face tilted as he inspected mine. "I'd say our experiment is off to a good start."

"Agreed. I've never had an orgasm like that."

His brows flexed. "How exactly do you mean?"

"In both intensity and position. I wasn't aware that I *could* have one any way but with me on top."

The smug expression on his face had me shaking my head at him, but I was still smiling. Smiling and blushing with feverish heat.

"You know, flattery will get you everywhere," he said.

"But I mean it. That was impressive enough to outshine any man I've slept with."

"I'd like to find every one of them and tell them a thing or two."

"Like how to be better in bed?"

"No—how stupid they were not to fuck you right when they had the chance. Because now, you're mine."

I opened my mouth to argue, but he kissed me before I could.

By the time he was through, I'd forgotten what I was going to say. I didn't think I could have told you my address in the moment.

"Now," he said, moving down my body with that ridiculous smile on his face, "if you'll excuse me, I have to collect enough orgasms to last me a week."

I laughed, sliding my hands into his hair as he kissed down my body. For a lingering moment, he paused over my stomach, his hand trailing across the flat, skimming the skin under my belly button, his lips tender, pressing to the place over where our baby resided with reverence. But then he moved on, taking his time somewhere else, collecting his dues, as promised.

SECOND TRIMESTER

BATSIGNAL

KATHERINE

13 WEEKS, 1 DAY

The click of hangers on my new-to-me closet rack was a tick of a metronome that matched the beat of electronic music playing from my portable speaker.

The contents of my closet were mostly black—skirts and dresses, pants and blouses and sweaters. Black was easy—everything matched. Every once in a while, if I was feeling adventurous, I'd throw in a little color, and I *did* have some dresses I'd bought on impulse while shopping with my friends. But mostly, I wore them to the club to dance, and even those were essentially neutral. The most risqué color I owned was red, which I'd defaulted to more and more lately.

Theo liked the red. And anytime I was rewarded with The Look, it reinforced the decision to wear it.

It fascinated me, the way I wanted him. Relationships were so often a source of depletion, a drain. A commitment. But with Theo

I never felt exhausted the way I did with most people. With him, I actually felt *replenished*.

It staggered me to recognize the fact. I hadn't known spending time with someone could actually fill me up rather than just draw on my emotional energy, of which I had very little. So I hoarded what I had and thus kept to myself. My friends, of course, were an exception, but I had low limits, and we'd been friends so long, they never took it personally if I bowed out of anything—plans, dinner, even sharing air in the living room—which afforded me the freedom to honor what I needed, when I needed it.

But with Theo, I found my situation reversed—not only did I feel recharged, but I craved *more*.

It was, I believed, because he placed no demands on me. And so, I felt safe in his presence, knowing he wouldn't withdrawal from my emotional piggy bank, only deposit.

And against all odds, I was *excited* to be moving in. Moving in meant more Theo time, and more Theo time meant more refilling my tank with his affection.

I frowned. Was I refilling his tank, too? Was I taking without giving? He seemed to be content, but I only saw what he chose to show me.

I made it a point to ensure I was repaying him. Somehow, I'd find a way.

My attention drifted back to the closet in my new room. It was almost the same size as the one at home, which made organizing easy enough. When I scanned the spread, I frowned again, pulling a blouse out of line to flip so it was facing the right way. I noted with a content sigh that all the hangers were evenly spaced and in perfect order.

I consulted the checklist I'd written out yesterday, which now only existed in my mind. Every word was clear as day—I could see the words being formed as I'd written them down. It was the only way

I could remember anything lately.

Pregnancy brain was a real thing, and I'd been afflicted.

Clothes were put away in the closet and drawers, although I had to reconfigure my plans for the dresser. On opening the top right drawer, where my underwear was slated to go, I found it full.

Full of black French lace and a note: *I see London, I see France. Couldn't resist. Hope they fit.*

I thumbed through the frippery with my throat all tight and my eyes stinging like I was going to cry. Over panties, of all things.

Really, pregnancy was for the birds, if birds were mammals.

Per my list, my next task was the bathroom, and I headed that way, feeling oddly cheerful. My stress over moving had been dissuaded largely by the prospect of Theo's steady presence and the simple joy of organizing and cataloging my belongings. I enjoyed the methodical order, the action soothing in its own right.

And surprisingly, the change didn't feel like so much of a change as I'd thought it would.

Maybe it was because I'd been spending so much time here and with Theo. I'd slowly started moving things over after our first step into the grand experiment, which had been a tremendous idea. I applauded myself for deferring to Theo, the relief of not having to decide everything on my own palpable and welcome. His approach was rational, and the exercise of our attraction had in some ways worn us out, like walking a hyperactive dog. The walk would start with a tugging of the leash and end with us panting and splayed out like starfish.

And for a day or two, we'd both be sated. But by the end of the week, we'd be chomping and wild-eyed and slobbering for each other again.

Despite the compounding desire, the rules were effective, comfortable. They gave me exactly what I wanted and needed in a reasonable increment, keeping a level of distance between us that we apparently needed.

I shuddered to think of what would have happened if we'd allowed ourselves to act on every impulse. I suspected I'd have been living here by default—I didn't think we could stay away from each other. I couldn't have, not with The Look and that body and those lips always smirking at me. Not with his brain matching mine, point for point, and not with the way he took care of me, cared for me. Respected me.

Little did I know that respect could set fireworks off in my pants.

I finished lining up shampoo bottles and moved on to the box labeled *Bathroom Cabinets* in neat, tidy marker, the letters uppercase and masculine. Theo's. Every stroke was certain, confident, deliberate, just like him.

I knelt to pick up the box, and as I stood, Theo walked in. His face immediately twisted into a chastising scowl, and before I was all the way up, he snatched it from me.

I folded my arms, scowling right back at him. "I'm not an invalid."

"I know you're not, but the doctor said no more than ten pounds. This is more than ten pounds." He set the box on the bathroom counter.

"I walked home with more than ten pounds of groceries yesterday and lived to tell the tale."

That earned me narrow eyes and a flex of his jaw that was almost more enticing than The Look. "It's like you want to get in trouble."

"You are not the boss of me, Theodore Bane."

He rolled his eyes and folded his arms too, but he was smiling small. "Who could ever *make* you do anything?"

"Oh, you seem to do quite well. You convinced me to move here, didn't you?"

That smile hitched a little higher on one side. "And to sleep with me."

"To be fair, I opened that conversation."

Step one of The Look hit his eyes, triggering the doubling of my heart rate.

He took a step that breached my personal space. "And I closed it."

I laughed, resisting the urge to reach for him. "Well, it *was* a good idea."

"It was, wasn't it?"

"Thank you, by the way. For the lingerie."

"Don't mention it."

I laughed nervously as he came closer, close enough to feel the heat of his body and smell his soap. "That's funny. Unmentionables."

A smirk. "Tried them on yet?"

"N-no. Not yet." I backed into the counter, grasping the edge.

"Mmm," he hummed. "I'd like to know how they fit. By the way, it's been nearly a week," he said as if I hadn't been counting. His eyes were on my lips, the anticipation firing nerves across mine, setting them tingling.

"It has."

His tongue swept his bottom lip, drawing it into his mouth. "It's been a *long* week."

"It has," I breathed. *Kiss me. Kiss me. KISS ME, DAMMIT.*

But instead, he took a step back, the look on his face smug and teasing, though under it, I saw his restraint. "Good thing we have rules, Kate. Otherwise, I'd lock that door and fuck you right here on the counter."

He turned, reaching for another box from the floor, probably so I wouldn't do it myself. And I stood there, hanging on to the countertop with white knuckles, trying to put my face back together as a burst of imagery of him banging me right here, right now, grabbed my brain's steering wheel and drove it away like a getaway car.

Theo ripped the box open with his bare hands, the pop and snap of packing tape shockingly masculine. It made me think of him ripping other things. Like panties.

The research I'd done indicated my libido might be heightened because of hormones, which I'd found to be undeniably, frustratingly true. But when he did things like ripping boxes apart and hauling furniture and cooking and smelling like a goddamn man feast and such, it magnified all that sexual frustration by a thousand times.

I sighed, releasing the countertop and turning for the box he'd so unceremoniously ripped from my hands.

He reached into his box, unloading its contents neatly onto the counter, changing the subject to dinner. And I half listened, my eyes occasionally darting to his hands, which were massive and broad, remembering all the things those hands could do, reminiscing about how they felt on my body.

And he was oblivious, going on about the menu as I fantasized about him over cotton balls and Q-tips.

He wouldn't kiss me because he was following the rules like the gentleman he was.

Bastard.

I realized belatedly that he was watching me as if he was waiting on an answer to an unheard question.

"I'm sorry, I wasn't listening," I admitted. "What did you say?"

A smile, sideways and sly. "I said, I was surprised to find you listening to electronic music. I figured you for a Tchaikovsky type of girl."

"I like electronic music. It sounds like math."

A laugh. "What were you thinking about just now?"

"The very long week," I answered.

"Well, you know how to put an end to it."

"I do, but we still have two more days until it's officially been a week. We'd be breaking the rules."

"Some people say rules are meant to be broken." He picked up the empty box, ripping the bottom tape to break it down.

"Those people are philistines and monsters. Rules are meant to keep people safe and bring order. Without order, it's anarchy. Mayhem. Just think—if I broke the rules now, what would stop me from breaking them again?"

"That's kinda what I'm hoping for, if I'm being honest."

I found myself chuckling simply because I wanted to break the rules just as badly as he seemed to want me to. We'd had a total of four hook-ups, including the first. And each one had gotten progressively more difficult to ignore or forget. I'd hoped I would get the urge out of my system, but instead, I wanted to slither over to him and slide my hands into his pants so I could—

"Kate, did you hear me?"

I straightened up, busying myself with putting things away. "I was daydreaming again. What was that you said?"

"Just that I love that you love rules, that they give you what you want. And then I asked if you've always been this way."

"Always," I said without hesitation. "Stuffed animals were lined up biggest to smallest, left to right, back to front. For Christmas, I usually asked for things like drawer organizers and closet organizers and, well, really any kind or organizers."

"Spice organizers?"

"Oh, yes. And Tupperware organizers. Those little racks that sort your pot and pan lids? The kind that hang over the back of the cabinet door?" I shuddered in pleasure.

He laughed. "We have those."

"You would," I said with a smile. "I love when things are tidy. When everything has a place. Chaos and I are not friends."

"I'd imagine not. But you have the uncanny ability to bend almost anything to your will, Tupperware lids or otherwise. Chaos stands no chance against you."

Another box was emptied, the rip of tape sending that *other* shudder down my back, the one he seemed to trigger so often. And now we'd be living together, without space or the distance of time to keep all my feelings at bay.

I should have been worried, but I wasn't. Not beyond a fluttering of concern that was gone as soon as it appeared.

Maybe the rules weren't gospel. Maybe we could redefine them. Two days seemed like an eternity to wait.

I wanted him to kiss me, and I wanted him to kiss me now.

I wanted him to do more than that.

And I knew how to make him.

All it would take was a little tube of red lipstick.

THEO

The kitchen was lively, the room full of congruent noise—music playing, Amelia and Ma chatting, the pan in front of me sizzling.

Tommy leaned against the counter next to the stove, facing me with a smirk and his arms folded across his chest. "I cannot fucking believe you got her to move in."

I huffed a laugh. "I cannot fucking believe you ever doubted me. It's like you've never seen me go after something I want."

He shook his head, amused. "Katherine Lawson and my brother. It's both baffling and perfect. How's she doing with the actual move-in? Amelia's been trying to give her space, but she's been crawling out of her skin all day about it."

"She seems fine. I was prepared for some grumping around or maybe an argument. But earlier, she laughed out loud at a stupid joke I made *and* smiled. With teeth."

"Only you could have that effect on her. Amelia can barely get her to smile, and they've been best friends for almost a decade."

I shrugged, pushing the chicken and sauce around the skillet. "What can I say? I speak fluent Katherine."

"I don't know how you do it, man. There's no way I could just sit and wait. Once I figured out it was Amelia, there was nothing I could do but go after her."

"That's because you're a doer, and I'm a thinker. You charge in, and I strategize. Truth is, if I'd gone after her hard, she would have shut down."

"Oh, come on. You know you want to lock her down."

"Maybe I do. Slow and steady and all that."

The curl of his lips was my first warning. "You bust out your wedding scrapbook yet?"

I glared at him, flicking a look over my shoulder toward the stairs. "Shut the fuck up."

"Pick out any fancy centerpieces?"

"Do you want to eat teeth for dinner? Because that can be arranged."

He laughed, saying too loud, "You had that stack of wedding magazines under your bed like they were *Playboys*. I swear, you looked less guilty when I caught you jacking off than you did when I caught you looking at flower arrangements in *Modern Bride*."

"I was twelve, asshole."

He shrugged. "No twelve-year-old boy should know what pound paper he wants for his wedding invitations."

"Listen, I've got the end game in mind, but I can't run in, guns blazing. I've got to come at her sideways. The entire operation is dependent on my ability to be still and quiet while I wait. One sudden move, and she'll bolt. The rules are the only thing keeping us together, and even at that, I've only got her once a week for a few hours. The rest of the time, we're…well, we're just friends, I guess. I've gotta survive the in-between without touching her. It's maddening."

"How long you think she'll hold out now that she's living here? Think she'll be able to keep it to once a week when you're in each other's space like this?"

"Katherine has the willpower of a honey badger. Once she decides something, no cobra or wasp hive could deter her. I'll assume nothing."

His eyes flicked to the stairs, and whatever he saw there made his smirk climb on one side. "Oh, I dunno. I think you could maybe assume a thing or two."

My brows quirked at him, and I turned to follow his line of sight.

Katherine had just reached the bottom of the stairs, her eyes down and hand on the rail. When she looked up, it was straight at me.

She was gorgeous. Her skin was luminous, pale and glowing, her dark hair twisted up in a neat knot on top of her head. Her eyes were framed by the line of her bangs, long enough to cover parts of her brows. And those eyes were amalgamated, a blend of colors, wide and bright and sparking with energy and wit.

Her lips, smiling in sensual challenge, were red as a stoplight. My heart skidded to a halt at their command.

It was my own fault, I realized as she ignored me, heading for the table to sit with Amelia and Ma.

I'd teased her this afternoon, all afternoon. She'd been begging me to touch her, kiss her, without saying a word. And I'd made sure to push her to the edge of the line she'd drawn just to leave her there, panting.

The ball was firmly in her court. But that didn't mean I couldn't use whatever methods of coercion were at my disposal to lure it back into mine.

It *had* been a long week, and judging by Katherine's current display, it seemed we were both at the end of our leashes.

Goddamn, she was so beautiful. And she'd pulled out all the

stops. She never wore her hair up, and the sight of her neck, the column long and creamy white, felt almost pornographic. I wanted to bury my face there and a few other places, like in the V of her dress, which was, by all standards, modest. I wanted to undo the row of tiny buttons down the front and make it immodest. I wanted her shamelessly naked and at my disposal.

Immediately.

But she'd planned this. She had known when she put on a pretty black dress and twisted up her hair and put that damnable lipstick on it would drive me crazy. And that I'd have to endure the sight all through a dinner with my mother.

Clever, clever Katherine.

But two could play at that game.

I cleared my throat and turned back to the skillet, cursing myself when the sauce stuck to the pan.

Tommy just laughed. "Oh, man. Have you got it bad."

"Shut up."

"I'm counting the days until you lose your cool, man."

"Trust me, that should be the least of our concerns. It's her I'm worried about. One wrong move, and the whole thing will fall apart."

He leaned in a little, smiling wide enough to make me want to hit him. "Better lock her down quick then."

"You act like that hasn't been the job all along."

With a laugh, he helped me plate the food, the two of us serving the women in our life. Our mother, who'd given the best years of her life to raise us alone. Tommy's wife, who'd saved him in more ways than one. And Katherine, the one who would extend our family to another generation. The one who'd gotten her hooks in me without intention.

The one I'd have for my own.

Everyone was chatting, getting settled in, and I sat next to

Katherine. She met my eyes, the meaning behind hers clear.

I leaned into her, pressing my cheek to hers as if for a kiss. But instead, I whispered with lips close to the curve of her ear, "I'm gonna fuck you the second this meal is through, Kate."

Her breath caught. My lips brushed her flushed cheek.

And I smiled, smug as all hell as I laid my napkin in my lap.

"Did you get unpacked?" Amelia asked, beaming and upright in her chair.

"I did, thank you. The only thing left to do is organize my bookshelves."

Tommy dished out his dinner. "How do you file them? Amelia's are all by genre, then subgenre, then author."

"By genre and alphabetically by author, and my reference materials are always in Dewey order. It's the only way I can do it without flying into a panic," she answered. "I follow a bunch of bookstagrammers on Instagram, and the ones who organize their shelves by color give me anxiety. Sometimes, I'll zoom in on them just to see how bad it is and have to remind myself not to look. Like when you see something in the road that might be a dead animal—the best thing is to avert your eyes and assume it's a T-shirt." Immediately, she flushed. "I'm sorry. That wasn't appropriate conversation for dinner. I'm…I'm a little nervous."

The admission affected every face at the table, mine most of all. I reached for her hands, which were clutched in her lap. But it was Ma who spoke.

"I, for one, love a good inappropriate conversation," she said as Tommy served her. "With boys like mine, it was inevitable. When they were little, they'd bring bugs to the dinner table and hide rats in shoeboxes in their closets. When they were older, someone was either getting in a fight, getting in trouble from a fight, or had a wound that needed medical attention from a fight."

Laughter rumbled between Tommy and me.

"Ma's a saint," I noted, squeezing Katherine's hands, which disappeared under mine.

She offered me a grateful smile.

"How many boxes of books did *you* have to lug?" Tommy asked me.

"Seven or eight," I answered.

"Thirty-two," he said. "Amelia had *thirty-two* boxes of books. I was sure Katherine would have her beat."

"Oh, these are just the first wave," Katherine assured him. "I have *way* more at home."

Amelia nodded. "It's true. Although she's more of a discerning reader than I am."

Katherine shrugged. "I mostly prefer the classics. There's something familiar and far away about them that appeals to me. I don't enjoy reading much fiction that takes place in contemporary times. Harder to suspend my disbelief, I suppose."

I let her hands go but trailed my fingers across her knuckles, the touch lingering as long as I could. Her fingers relaxed their iron grip on her napkin, smoothing it out.

The conversation drifted around the table as we ate, but my body was attuned to her. I wished we were alone. I wished she'd waited until my mother wasn't in the room to put that fucking lipstick on. I wished I could speed up dinner so I could drag her upstairs and do all the things I'd been thinking about for a week.

We'd spent more than two nights, one week apart, wrapped up in each other, the "no sleeping in the same bed" rule almost moot when she left my place at four in the morning. But, alas, she'd stuck to the rules, and though it took all my power, so had I.

But she couldn't get away from me here.

I wondered if she really would continue to resist. If she'd tire of me. If she'd get me out of her system and call the whole thing off.

Dismiss the phases, throw on the brakes, shake my hand, and put me in my place somewhere in the friendzone.

The only comfort was this: I got the distinct impression that, as planned, the physical contact had made the longing *worse* for her, not better.

I knew it had for me. Difference was, I was prepared.

Judging by the delicate fluttering of her lashes when I hung my arm on the back of her chair, brushing my knuckles against the back of her neck, she had not been prepared at all.

She'd put on that lipstick without understanding that she'd declared war.

I took every opportunity to touch her in the most modest and unassuming of places. And every touch seemed to affect her a little more, tightening the string until she was thrumming, her energy pitched as high as the thinnest guitar string. My thumb on the meat of her palm seemed to set her on fire, my knee brushing the outside of hers under the table quickening her breath.

Like I'd said, it'd been a *long* fucking week.

When the meal was through, Katherine bolted out of her chair, scooping up plates and glasses with the determination of a wide receiver running for the end zone. Into the kitchen she went, hurrying through dishes with the efficiency of a general heading into battle. And when she wiped off the table, she might just as easily have been seconds away from the whistle blowing to signal the end of a never-ending workday.

And with that task done, the whistle did blow, along with the gasket that kept my desire in the steam vent.

She smiled, her cheeks pink and eyes darting to me only once.

"Dinner was lovely. Thank you all for welcoming me. I'm very tired, as growing arms and legs is much harder work than one mightrealize. So I'd like to say goodnight."

Amelia's frown bordered on a pout. "But I haven't seen you all day, and it's only eight thirty."

"I promise, I'll see you tomorrow," she said, stepping into Amelia to give her a stiff hug. "The day has been very exciting, and I'd like to…decompress."

I barely stopped myself from laughing out loud.

Amelia sighed, resigned. "All right. Text me if you change your mind, and I'll come down."

"Thank you," Katherine answered. "Goodnight, Tommy, Sarah." She turned to me. "Theodore, would you mind helping me with something upstairs?"

"Not at all," I said as every nerve in my body jumped in unison.

I was completely composed, and Katherine was trying to be, bless her. But her face was inconspicuous, hinting so blatantly at her actual meaning, it might as well have been a blinking neon sign that said *SEX, PLEASE*.

Tommy and I shared a look, and with a brief goodbye, I followed Katherine up the stairs, shamelessly staring at her ass the whole way.

The second we were clear of the stairs, she turned on her heel and launched herself into my arms.

I locked her there, locked my lips to hers, breathed in the smell of her soap and shampoo and *her*. She smelled like books and paper, like fresh laundry and the gentle sweetness of baby powder.

She smelled like *mine*. The week since I'd held her last was gone with one deep inhale.

Her arms threaded around my neck, mine around her waist, and when I stood straight, I kept ahold of her. Her feet dangled, toes inches from the ground. I knew because they thumped my shins as I hurried toward my bedroom, kicking the door closed behind me.

I'd thought to ask her where she wanted to be, but I couldn't be bothered to break the kiss. So I opted for my room where we'd gone every time, guessing it was best to leave her space her own until she indicated she wished otherwise.

I hummed a sigh as I laid her down, fitted my hips against hers, spent a long moment exploring her mouth, cataloging the feel of her body beneath me, her hands in my hair. The warmth of her. The way she fit against me despite the difference of our height.

When I broke away, it was to trace her face with my gaze. Red lips plumped from the pressure of mine. Lids heavy with desire. Lashes black and luxurious, fanning when she blinked. Her eyes, a kaleidoscope of color, a mosaic of blues and greens, tans and golds, the color quickly fading as the black of her pupils expanded to swallow the sight of me.

I thumbed her bottom lip, finding myself smiling. "That was a dirty trick, Kate."

"Well, I wanted you to kiss me, and you wouldn't."

"You know the rules."

"I wrote the rules."

A laugh hummed behind my closed lips. "You made me sit through dinner with my mother when all I could think about was fucking you." I tsked. "I'm gonna have to get you back for that."

"Please, don't make me wait," she mewled, shifting her hips.

I rolled mine, pressing myself into her. "Oh, it's too late for that. Maybe if you hadn't teased me like you did."

Her thighs parted wider. "But you teased me all day." It was almost a whine, the sound so uncharacteristically needy that I laughed my surprise.

"What kind of man would I be if I didn't follow the rules?"

She sighed. "You're incorrigible, do you know that?"

"It's been said." I looked down my nose at my hand as it traced the V of her neckline. "But you're no better."

At that, those crimson lips of hers curled at the very corners. "It's been said."

Down to the buttons my fingers trailed, a dozen tiny, shiny buttons, rounded on top and marching between her breasts. I popped one out of its loop, trying not to let the feeling of her fingers ruffling the short hairs at my nape distract me.

"I'm gonna take my time, Kate." I unfastened another button. "I'm not giving you what you want until you're begging me for it."

Her bottom lip slipped between her teeth, her hips shifting and rolling against my cock, pressing that spot where she needed me. "If I beg you now, will you give it to me?"

"Not a chance."

I closed my eyes and kissed her, sucked that fat bottom lip into my mouth, pinned it with my teeth, traced it with the tip of my tongue. Melded my lips to hers, angled my face and hers far enough to get deep, tongues tangling, breaths mingling. My determined hand made quick work of those buttons, unfastening them down to the space where her ribs parted ways. Her skin was hot beneath my fingertips, the feel of her breath rasping in and out of her lungs transmitted to me by way of touch. Her breast in my palm, warm and heaving, her nipple peaked and reaching through the delicate lace of her bra—the bra I'd bought, a claim I'd staked.

Stopping the kiss was not an option, no matter how desperately I wanted her naked. Blindly, I unfastened the rest of the buttons, taking my time, teasing every inch of skin once it was exposed until the dress gaped open.

I shifted to stretch my body out next to hers, keeping her hips flat with the help of my thigh nestled between hers.

The touch was gentle, featherlight and teasing. The tip of my finger brushing the tip of her nipple. The slow trace of the curve of her breast. The sweeping line of her rib cage. The gentle swell of her stomach. The hollow of her belly button. Down my thirsty fingertips swept, down to the low flat of her stomach, which had once been soft and giving but now was firm, solid, a layer of protection.

Beyond that space, our baby resided.

It was the impetus to finally break the kiss.

My hand splayed there as my lips tasted her jaw, her neck, the hollow of her throat. Her hand slipped over mine, holding it there as I kissed her breasts, the curving shadow of her areolas peeking out of the delicate black hem. Down her breastbone, down the undeniably feminine curves of her stomach. Down to where our hands rested.

When I moved mine to replace it with my mouth, hers cupped my jaw, her touch delicate, intimate. It was emotion I felt in her fingertips, a physical connection to relay the connection of our hearts, of the life we'd created together.

It overwhelmed me in ways I couldn't understand. I couldn't fathom the depth of it all, the meaning, our future, our past. Who we were and who we would become.

If we should grow together or apart.

But I brushed the thought away. Because I'd known from the moment I first kissed her that this was it. She was it. It was irrational, illogical, and imperative. And that she was pregnant only solidified what I'd only had an impulse of on that night, that first night when everything changed.

She was mine, and I was hers. It was an undeniable fact.

I drew a long breath, one that mingled with the scent of her body, reminding me of the task at my very eager hand.

I cupped her sex, feeling the heat of her through the thin fabric, damp from her desire. The sensation set a hot pulse through me, to the place that wanted to delve into that heat until it was buried.

She was already impatient, wriggling out of her dress while keeping her hips consciously still so as not to deter me, unhooking her bra as I teased the threshold of her body, settling the length of my finger between her swollen lips, pressing my palm to her clit, squeezing to stroke her in both places with one motion.

She hummed, the sound strained and pleading, her free thigh opening up, silently asking me to take her, a request I'd grant.

Though not exactly how she wanted.

I shifted, moving until my torso was settled between her legs, her knees up and thighs resting against my shoulders. Her body was open to me, the line of her lips accentuated by her panties caught between them. I could see every part of her through the material, a map of her sex, the mound of her hood, the place I wanted to taste.

So I did.

Silky fabric against my tongue, the tang of her arresting my senses. Her body jerked from the pleasure of contact, a gasp filling her lungs and a sigh escaping them. Her thighs rested in the circle of my shoulders, my hands holding her hips, keeping her still when they wanted to move. But she didn't fight it.

Because she trusted me, I realized. I'd earned the trust of the girl who trusted no one. That rigid girl was supple under my touch, the cool stone turned to molten rock, hot and pliant and filling whatever space could hold her.

In that moment, that space consisted of my arms.

I hooked her panties, holding them out of the way before descending again, this time to taste her without restraint. The tip of my tongue traced the rippling flesh of her body, drew the edge of her sex into my mouth, teased it until it was swollen and slick. She writhed, color rising in blooms across her chest, her neck, brow furrowed and eyes clenched shut.

So I let her go.

She moaned her frustration, sitting up faster than her languor should have allowed. Her hands captured my face, lips crashing against mine. My hands roamed to her hair, wanting it loose, but I couldn't figure out how to let it down. Her fingers replaced mine, and so mine took the opportunity to relieve her of her panties completely.

When her hair was down and spilling across her naked shoulders, our hands exchanged places again—mine raking through the silky strands, hers unfastening my belt. We sat, twisted together, a mess of limbs and frantic hands.

She reached into my pants, closed her long fingers around my shaft, and stroked me.

A hiss escaped me as I curled around her, buried my face in her neck, my nose in the hollow behind her ear and lips closing over her fluttering pulse. With every stroke of her hand, I realized I was no longer the one teasing. Her free hand slipped my slacks over the curve of my ass, and when I shifted to press her into the bed, she stayed me, pushing back to keep me upright. Without discussion or influence, I knew what she was going to do, and though I wanted control, my body didn't. My body wanted what she wanted, and what she wanted was me propped on my knees with my pants out of her way.

Off came my shirt in three buttons and a fling of fabric of my own accord—Katherine was busy, and I wanted to see everything without obstruction. She had moved to her hands and knees before me, eyes on my cock and hand still closed around my shaft. I watched the parting of her red, red lips, the pink of her tongue extending, the hot shock of her wet mouth when it grazed my crown, then swept it, then swallowed it.

Dual moans—one deep in my chest, one rumbling around my cock in her mouth. My hand slipped into her dark hair and fisted, my senses on overload. Touch was consumed by the place where our bodies were joined. Sight was hijacked by flash points—her lips, her small nose, the crescents of dark lashes against her lily-white skin. The curves of her shoulders, the valley of her spine. The bend of her waist, the shape of her ass like a heart. I wanted in the split, wanted to touch it, invade it, taste it again.

But there was no denying her what she wanted, and I couldn't stop her if I tried—not only for her determination, but for my lack of will. She wanted me panting and didn't stop until I was. Not until I could feel the tight pull from deep in my body or the strained strands of her hair clenched in my fist. Not listening to the suck and pop of her mouth on my cock or the moan in her throat.

A throb, hot and deep, a wet slide of her tongue. And she let me go.

It was a smile there on her lips, held open by her own desire, and she turned around, the cleft of her body I'd wanted so badly a moment before presented to me like a fucking award.

She looked over her shoulder at me, on all fours, back arched, body open and ready. I wanted to grab my cock by the base and slam into her. But instead, I held her ass in both hands, spread her open, stroked the slick line of her body with my thumb.

"Roll over," I commanded.

She pouted. "But—"

I bent, planting my hand in the bed next to her, fitting her ass to my hips, cupping her breast with my free hand. I tasted her neck.

"In a few months," I whispered, "this is going to be one of the only ways. So right now, you're going to roll over, and I'm going to watch you come while I have the chance."

A labored sigh and a shift of her hips to cradle my cock in her ass were her only protests. She lay down and rolled over as I'd bidden while I kicked off my pants.

I climbed up her body, snagging one thigh on my way, fitting it to my ribs and spreading her open with the motion. The space between us closed, lips, chest, hips. My crown settled into her heat. Her hips rose. Mine flexed.

I slid into her, her body open and wet and waiting. Filled her, gave and took. Broke the kiss, watched her as her orgasm rose. Rolled my hips against the place she needed me, slipped into the place I needed her. Her eyes were closed, her brows coming together. Her swollen lips, red and parted. My name on her breath, but not the name she called me so often.

"*Theo.*"

She whispered the name I wanted to hear, the name that told me without saying that I was more. I was more than a night, more than a moment. I was more than a partner to raise a child with.

I was more than that. And that word, my name on her tongue and lips, told me she was starting to see it too.

She came with a series of gasps, a heaving of breasts, her chin pointed at the stars and her neck stretched in offering. She came with a pulse around my cock so hard, so tight, it throbbed with a deep ache of pleasure-pain. That breath froze for a moment, her lips locked open.

When her lungs kicked to life again, the sound of her drawing air sang, a gasp feminine and broken by desire and release.

And there was no holding back, no prolonging my own desire. I came with a deep, thundering groan, a galloping pulse, a pump of my hips. My hand clamped her hip, the other cupped her neck, my thumb forcing her jaw high, my eyes open but my vision dim. Flashes of imagery burned into my mind with every throb of my release.

Red lips stretched wide.

Black hair on white sheets.

Long white fingers hooked on my wrist.

The sound of my name again.

"*Theo,*" she whispered like it was a dream.

But it wasn't a dream. She was there, speaking my name, her body soft under mine, hot around mine, holding me tight in every placed we touched.

And my lips found hers, swallowed the word, wrapped myself around her so she couldn't leave.

I'd convince her to stay. I'd be patient until she realized she didn't want to be anywhere but right here with me.

I kissed her, a long, slow tangle of tongues and flex of lips, kissed her until she was sated and languid beneath me.

When I closed my lips, it was to look down at her, to smooth her hair.

To smugly smirk at her.

"Told you you'd pay for that."

Her musical laughter filled the room. Filled my heart.

And she tightened her arms around my neck and kissed me again.

DECISIONS, DECISIONS

KATHERINE

15 WEEKS, 5 DAYS

Theo frowned at the display of pacifiers, hands stuffed in the pockets of his slacks. "I still don't understand why we're at Target for this. I didn't even know there *was* a Target in Manhattan."

"Because," I reminded him as I scanned three different brands, hoping the baby would like at least one of them, "this way, our friends and family who don't live here can send something easily. Plus, there are five Targets, and this one is conveniently located enough that even our local friends will be able to come here and get things we actually *need*."

He sighed again. I hooked the scan gun under my arm.

"What's next on the list?" I asked.

He reached into his inside pocket of his suit coat, returning with a neatly tri-folded pack of papers. "Bottles," he said, glancing down the aisle and nodding in that direction when he spotted them.

We'd been wandering around for an hour, making fairly quick work of our registry. It was unconventional to register at fifteen weeks, but I'd insisted we do it now rather than wait. Primarily so I could sleep at night. Knowing we had to compile this one master list for the baby registry was a task that had been following me around for weeks. We'd done our research, and that list needed to be inputted into the database so I could be rid of the damn thing.

Theo had, of course, agreed without question, though he was irritated to be standing in the gleaming white aisles of the big-box store that so many New Yorkers despised despite the aforementioned convenience. He'd rather buy overpriced, off-brand toothpaste from a bodega than step foot in a corporate chain.

Until I'd asked. And then, like seemingly everything else, he'd complied for the sake of my peace of mind.

The last two weeks had been far smoother than I could have anticipated. Once I got past the initial strangeness of living in an unfamiliar place, that was. It had been a long, long time since I woke up in a place that wasn't my room in the old brownstone, and it'd been nearly ten years since I lived with strangers.

But Theo had been right about that, too. It didn't feel like we were strangers at all.

We'd found a routine—a simple one, but a routine nonetheless. He made breakfast every morning and packed me a lunch. Cooked us all dinner and spent evenings on the couch with me. Sometimes, we chatted about our days. Sometimes, we watched TV. Occasionally, we sat side by side with our laptops, researching strollers and cribs and the like.

Once, I'd walked in to find him sitting on the couch with music playing over the speakers, his face drawn in concentration and a book about ancient Mayans split open in his lap.

Never in my life had I seen something so gorgeous as that man in that tailored shirt and those slacks with his feet propped on the coffee table and a book on an ancient civilization resting where I would have liked to sit.

But rules were rules. I'd sat next to him where I belonged and just imagined I was that hardbound beast.

As we walked toward the bottles in companionable silence, I was reminded again of just how fortunate I was to have a partner like him. I pictured for a moment that he'd bowed out when I told him I was pregnant. Imagined walking these aisles on my own. And I was so thankful I wasn't.

I couldn't imagine being here with anyone but him. Not even my friends. Because with them, I was always the one who had it together. They'd be swooning and soft over the tiny clothes and miniature shoes, and I'd be shepherding us through the ordeal to keep us from having to permanently take up residence in the sippy cup aisle.

But with Theo, I didn't have to be the mother hen. I didn't have to have a schedule and itinerary.

I didn't have to be strong. And the feeling was both a relief and a curse. As blissful as it was to lean on him, the release from sole responsibility left me unsure of myself. I was too used to leading.

But he'd taught me to follow, starting with a dance in a swing club.

Living with Theo had unveiled two surprises—how easy it was and how badly I wanted him. We'd been busy with work, and I'd been exhausted from growing a person, I supposed, and so we really only saw each other at dinner and for a bit at night. He was terribly easy to get along with and terribly painful to look at. Because, heaven help me, I couldn't even glance in his direction without wanting to throw all the rules out the window in exchange for getting to kiss him whenever I wanted.

We stopped in front of shelf after shelf of bottles. Bottles with liners and bottles without. Fast and slow-flow bottle nipples. Four ounces, six, twelve. Bottles for babies with reflux and bottles with vents and bottles that were just bottles. Glass bottles, plastic bottles, boxes and boxes and boxes of bottles.

I frantically scanned them. I hadn't researched bottles. I didn't know how it had happened, but something in my brain had disconnected it from choice, deeming it too simple to require research. But as I stood there in front of an insurmountable choice, my throat squeezed shut, my feet stuck to the spot, and my eyes scrambled for recognition where I knew there was none.

Theo frowned at the boxes, shaking his head. "This is what I mean. No one needs this many choices. Have you been to the paper towel aisle? Who the hell needs twelve rolls of paper towels at once? Where do you even *put* that many paper towels in Manhattan? And don't even get me started on the toilet paper. The math on double rolls is enough to undo the fabric of space. I just can't understand why the fuck ..." He paused.

I thought he might have been looking at me, but I couldn't stop my mind.

"Kate, what's wrong?"

The question was so tender, so worried, that tears nipped the corners of my eyes. I looked down at two boxes, one in each hand, that I didn't remember picking up.

"This one says it's number one doctor approved, but this one says it's number one *mother* approved, and I don't know which one to choose, but I'm not sure what to do ... I don't know how to choose." The final word of the rambling run-on broke in my throat, and the vision of the boxes in my hands shimmered through a curtain of tears.

His hand, big and warm, cupped my cheek. He'd moved to stand in front of me, all that shiny white gone and replaced with the black of his suit.

With his free hand, he reached for the scanner. "Gimme the gun, Kate," he said gently.

I sniffled, relaxing my arm so he could take it.

He took the boxes, scanned them, and put them back on the shelf. "There. We'll get them both, and we'll let the baby decide which it likes."

When he turned back to me, I was still frozen, incapacitated. "It's too much, Theo. It's too much. Too many choices, too many things to get wrong. What if the baby has reflux? We won't have bottles for that."

Without argument, he swung his arm around and scanned the reflux bottles. "Now we will."

And then, he pulled me into his arms.

I buried my face in the expanse of his chest, breathed deep to try to calm myself. But instead, traitorous tears slid from my eyes and onto his beautiful suit.

I tried to back away, but he held me still, pressing a kiss to the top of my head. He rocked us, just the smallest shift, back and forth.

"It's not about the bottles, is it?" he asked, already knowing the answer.

He always did.

"No," I said miserably.

Another press of his lips into my hair, this time with a small chuckle through his nose. "I know it doesn't feel like it, but they're just bottles. If we need different ones, we'll get them. Flexibility in the moment, remember? It's how we plan for things we can't control."

"I know," I said, and I did. But I didn't feel it. "I...I don't know how to do this, and it scares me."

His arms wound tighter around me, the rocking coming to a stop. "I know." The levity in his voice was gone. "But that's why I'm here. We're deferring to me, remember?"

"Yes, I remember."

"So let me shoulder this stress. Trust me to take care of it."

"I do," I whispered. "I trust you."

Something in him stilled and came alive in the same moment. But he said nothing, just held me to him with strong, sure arms and a steady hand splayed across my back.

He didn't let me go, and I didn't let him go either. Instead, he held me in silence, and I knew without knowing that he'd hold me like that until I loosened my grip.

But I didn't want to. I didn't want him to go away, didn't want him to stop touching me. I didn't want a lot of things. Which led me to the realization there were a lot of things I *did* want.

I wanted him to stop the restraint, and I wanted to be unconstrained. For weeks, we'd been skirting around this, flirting with the possibilities of a relationship, toying with the boundaries set in place so firmly.

By me. Those boundaries were my construct. And if I wanted them gone, there was only one way to do it.

"I think I'm ready for the next phase in our experiment," I said with a small, shaky voice.

He leaned back, separating us by the smallest degree necessary to see my face. "Are you sure you want to decide this right now?"

"You mean, while I'm emotional?"

"No, while we're in the bottle aisle of Target."

When I laughed, he smiled, cupping my face, thumbing the cool track of my tears.

"Are you sure? Why don't we talk about it tonight," he said softly.

But I shook my head against his palm. "I'm sure. I'm tired of the restraints. I don't want the *once a week* rule anymore. The next steps are PDA, more frequent sex, and sleeping in the same bed."

He chuckled, his eyes dark and alive with possibility. Hope. "I thought we agreed to take things by increment."

I sighed. "We did."

That clever smile of his tugged up on one side. "How about we start with me holding your hand in Target while we look at breast pumps?"

"All right," I agreed with an amendment, "but first, kiss me. I've gone a week without your lips, and I don't want to miss them anymore."

When he drew a breath, everything smoldered—his eyes, his smile, the air between us crackling and hot. "Whatever you want, Kate."

The sweet softness of his lips surprised me, the week that had passed diluting the memory to swill compared to the pure potency of his kiss. It was arresting, robbing me of will and thought, of power and choice. It was a kiss that claimed me, a signature of his body and soul on mine that I couldn't erase.

I wondered if I'd be branded forever by him and knew with some degree of wariness that the answer was yes. But then he smiled at me and took my hand, ushering me to the breast pumps with a joke on his lips and a bounce in his step, and I forgot to care.

BIG SPOON

THEO

17 WEEKS, 2 DAYS

Zedd played over the speaker that night, the bass thumping as Katherine and I sat side by side on the couch. In her lap was a ball of pearly-white yarn, and in her hands was the beginning of a baby bootie. The TV played *Love Cabana* with closed-captioning.

It was a guilty pleasure we'd started watching as a joke but had turned into a nightly routine. We'd meant to make fun of it. Best-laid plans and all that. We were already on season three.

A week ago, she'd asked me for more in a Target aisle, tears in her eyes and a neat row of baby bottles in front of us. And, as promised, we held hands through Target for starters. The highlight of my week had been leaving that store with Katherine under my arm, her body against mine and her arm around my waist.

The door had been opened for PDA. And PDA had led to kissing.

naked in my bed.

And the world was suddenly full of possibility.

Subsequently, I couldn't keep my hands off her. And she didn't seem to mind.

Even now, her feet were in my lap, and my hand absently stroked her leg as Billy and Jeanine got into a screaming match over a spilled daiquiri. And by spilled, I meant Billy had dumped it down Jeanine's back and into the hot tub.

Katherine shook her head as she wound the yarn around her needle. "I'm not big on immature displays, but Jeanine deserved that."

"If they don't get kicked off the island this week, I'm gonna be convinced this show is rigged."

"It's scripted. They're all scripted. Reality TV is anything but real. Everyone knows that."

I chuckled, my hand shifting over the delicate bones on top of her foot. "It's so much more fun to imagine it's real."

"But it's not," she insisted, twisting the yarn again.

"So you've said." For a moment, I watched her fingers, the click of the needles and quick motion of her hands as she assembled the tiny sole of the shoe. "How long have you been knitting?"

She gave me a blank look. "You watched me start twenty minutes ago."

"No," I said on a laugh, "I mean, when did you learn?"

"Oh. A few months ago. We have a knitting circle at the library, and I was the only one who didn't know how. I'm glad I learned though. It's coming in handy." She held up her work in display.

I picked up the bootie she'd just finished, which sat on the coffee table. "This is the tiniest shoe I've ever seen."

Katherine smiled. "I know. There's a little sweater I want to make, too, and a hat and blanket to match. I decided on white since we don't know the sex of the baby yet."

"Just a few more weeks."

"I'll never understand people who want to be surprised by that information. There's already enough we don't know and can't control. Why wouldn't you want to know everything you could?"

I shrugged. "Some people like the anticipation, I guess. The mystery."

She made a face. "Lawless. I'm stressed just thinking about it. I would like to have a name chosen and color-coded clothes, all washed and folded and put away before the baby comes."

With a smirk, I said, "Funny, I would have figured you wouldn't label the baby with pink or blue."

"I'd rather not spend my free time correcting people who guess incorrectly."

"Fair enough," I said on a laugh.

The credits rolled on *Love Cabana*, and I picked up the remote. "Did you want to watch another?"

She sighed, bundling up her yarn and needles. "No, thank you. I'm—*oh!*" With a gasp, she folded forward, her hand flying to her stomach.

I was on my knees at her feet within a breath, searching her face for signs of distress, but there was only wonder. "What's the matter, Kate?"

She said nothing, just gasped again, her face lighting up with a wondrous smile. "The baby. I think … *oh!*" she said again, giggling.

Her hand shot out and grabbed mine, pressing it to the hard curve of her stomach.

"What am I—"

"Shh, wait…"

The silence was thick with anticipation, her hand on top of mine. The only sensation was the steady rise and fall of her bump as she breathed and the feel of her warm hand over mine.

I was about to give up when I felt it.

A thump against my hand, so fast, I wondered if I'd imagined it.

"Was that—"

"Uh-huh." She beamed, nodding.

Another thump, this one harder, and we both laughed.

"Oh my God," I breathed, laying both my hands on her stomach. "I can't…this is incredible."

But no more movement came, to our disappointment. I leaned in, angling for her lips, my hands still cupping her belly. And I kissed her, the magic of the moment filling every mingling breath, every flex of our lips, every sweep of our tongues.

She broke the kiss with a smile.

"Come to bed, Kate," I whispered, even though she didn't have on her lipstick tonight, her lips a dusty shade of rose, naked and natural.

Damn the rules.

"All right," she said. "But only if you'll stay all night."

My smile was boundless. "Your room or mine?" When I stood, I offered my hand.

She took it, answering, "Mine."

It was safer, I knew. One less variable for her to factor in or plan for.

"Anything you want, Kate."

She had just started to really show, opting for dresses with high waists and flowing skirts, and once home, she almost always stepped straight into leggings and T-shirts. Tonight she was wearing a *Team Tommy* shirt from a library fundraising publicity stunt we'd come up with after he and Marley Monroe broke up. He'd sold the T-shirts. She had written a breakup album about him that went platinum.

To be honest, I hated the sight of my brother's name stretched over the swell where *my* baby was.

I pulled her into me, smiling down at her, ready to get her out of that T-shirt. Not only so I could get to what was underneath it, but so I could throw it in the fireplace.

She smiled back, but something else was behind her eyes, words waiting at the corner of her mouth.

I kissed her to loosen them up.

I hadn't intended the kiss to deepen, but that was the nature of Katherine and me—we were in far less control than either of us would acknowledge. Her arms threaded around my neck, her lips open wide, tongue delving past mine, searching the depths. When I realized her ass was in my hand and my cock was rock hard, I broke the kiss.

"All right. I'm going to get ready for bed, and I'll meet you there."

"Okay," she said, smiling and flushed and breathless.

I kissed her again, this time slow and sweet. I couldn't understand how she fit so neatly against me, why her face seemed to fill my hand exactly, why her lips fitted to mine with the fit of a tailored suit. Strange. Beautiful. Utterly perfect.

We parted ways, hurrying in opposite directions so we could come back together.

As I changed and brushed my teeth, my mind zipped and zinged with possibility. Every step, every box checked, every marker passed had brought us closer to something bigger, something more. It'd brought us closer to *us*, to the place where we could be together fully.

And, if I played my cards right, maybe forever.

There was no logic behind the thought, only instinct I felt in my marrow. I understood her in ways I wasn't sure she understood herself. I understood what she needed and how to provide it, knew when to let her breathe and be and exist without constraint.

I could be her everything. She was already becoming mine.

Things were going exactly as planned.

I padded through the apartment, shutting off lights as I went, a little nervous and a little giddy at the prospect of spending the night with Katherine, something I'd waited for so long, it was almost as enticing as the prospect of sex.

Almost.

When the apartment was dark for the night, I stepped through the threshold of her room.

She had turned down the bed, the only light that of the small lamps on the nightstands. Her hair was long and loose, her nightgown delicate white cotton. The shadow of her body through the thin fabric was sensual without intention, curves I'd come to know quite well.

It was so strange to see a woman in a nightgown like that, almost formal or maybe old-fashioned. When she tucked her hair behind her ear and looked up, she froze but for her eyes, which dragged the length of my naked torso, not stopping until she'd noted every ridge and valley, skimming her eyes down my pajama pants and to my bare feet.

With a series of rapid blinks, she found herself. "I sleep on this side of the bed," she said matter-of-factly.

I walked around to the other side. "I sleep on this side, so it works for me."

She smiled down at her hands as she arranged the pillows. "We are a good match, Theodore."

"We are, Kate," I said as I slipped between the sheets.

She did the same, but before she could lie down or turn out the lights, I kissed her.

My hand cupped the back of her head as I laid her down, tasted the minty sweetness of her lips, felt the soft curves of her body through the thin barrier of her nightgown. Cupped the swell of her stomach that I loved so deeply. And her arms hung around my neck, holding me to her until the kiss slowed, then stopped.

"I should warn you," she started, her voice husky and hot, "I've never spent the whole night with a man in my bed—or a woman either. So please don't be offended if I accidentally push, kick, or hit you in the middle of the night. I don't typically like to be touched, and I can't speak to my reaction."

"You sound sure it will be violent."

"Like I said, I don't typically like to be touched. Except for when it's you. It's strange really," she mused. "I don't understand it."

"You don't have to understand it."

"But I'd like to."

I thumbed her jaw, looking over her face. "Maybe some things can't be explained."

"I don't believe in magic, Theo."

"I know you don't. But would you agree there's mystery and intrigue in things you don't understand?"

She frowned. "Everything can be explained in some way or another. Action and reaction. Science. Magic isn't real."

"You're uncomfortable leaving a stone unturned. You don't *want* to believe in magic."

"Because I take comfort in what's real."

"Because that doesn't require faith," I noted.

"I have faith. Faith in facts."

A smile brushed my lips. "Faith is believing *despite* the fact. And I'd argue that not all facts are black and white. You have faith in your friends, but there aren't a set of rules that you apply to your relationship with them."

"Our friendship is founded on respect and trust."

"Which were built with time, attachment, and evidence. But don't you think there's something beyond your experiences or chemicals that connects you to someone else? Something that motivates you to feel that's not strictly based in fact?"

Every corner of her face was touched with confusion.

"Okay, let me ask you this: is there something you can't explain that draws you to one of your friends?"

She frowned, thinking. "Val can make me laugh when it's the last thing I want to do. She always cheers me up. And Rin knows exactly what to say to make sense of things, which makes me want to tell her everything. That alone is singular. Amelia triggers a protection response from me, but I think that's because she's so small and innocent. I think Tommy has that instinct, too."

"Because you love her, and she seems vulnerable."

"Love is defined as a deep attachment. It's not unexplainable. It's survival. We need other people. We search for relationships and connections because without people, we'd go crazy. Even love for your child is a product of brain responses that form an attachment, so you'll be motivated to care for your baby. It's about progeny. About continuing the species. If you didn't love your baby and think it was cute, you wouldn't be so compelled to make sure it was safe and cared for. It's not magic. It's evolutionary science."

"Some would call that instinct."

"But instinct isn't strictly reactive. It's a response, not an initiative action."

I chuckled. "I dunno. Some instincts can be ignored, and some can't."

"I suppose that's true," she conceded. "But it's still a response."

"When I met you, there was something about you I had the *instinct* to know better. I knew the second we shook hands that we'd end up here, one way or another."

Her frown deepened. "With me pregnant?"

"No," I said on a laugh. "With you and me here, in bed, talking about the scientific merits of love."

She relaxed. "Well, that's just pheromones, oxytocin. I think our bodies knew we were a physiological match."

"I'd argue we were more well suited than just physically, wouldn't you?"

"Yes, I would agree," she said quietly. "The longer I know you, the more compatible I find us."

"Funny, I was thinking the same thing."

I brought my lips to hers, wondering how I'd found myself with a woman so resistant, so restrained, so averse to love and relationships. As I kissed her, I considered my motivation. Was it the challenge? The newness? The instinct to have and hold and protect her because she was carrying my child? Or was it more?

But I knew the answer, knew it with the certainty of a clairvoyant.

I was hers, and I'd do anything to make her mine.

And lucky for both of us, I never failed.

KATHERINE

My first thought when I woke was that of complete and total confusion.

I was hot—that was the first thing I noted—my hair stuck to my dewy face and nightgown tangled between my legs. And I was trapped, contained by heavy, thick restraints that should have sent me into a panic, especially when combined with the sweltering heat.

But I wasn't panicked at all. In fact, I drew a deep breath, curling into the hot confines of Theo's chest.

We were a knot of arms and legs, my face buried in his chest and his arms a vise around me. The thick rope of his bicep had become my pillow, threaded through the bend of my neck, his hand holding me to him by the shoulder. The only reason I could breathe was my nose had found the deep valley between his pecs, which doubled not only as a well of his scent—musk and soap and male—but a divot in which I could funnel air from the sweltering cage of his arms.

He woke with a drag of air through his nose and tightening of his muscles, somehow bringing me even closer to him. I hadn't even realized there'd been space. My lips brushed his skin with nowhere else to go.

"Morning." The word was rough, the sound sending a shivering desire through me.

It was as if the exact pitch and timbre of his voice had initiated the firing of a string of nerves in me. As if I were tuned specifically to him and no one else.

"I didn't hit you last night or anything, did I?" I asked, worried to hear the answer.

A laugh reverberated through him and into me by way of my rib cage. "No. I couldn't keep you off of me."

When I leaned back, he loosened his grip.

I looked up at him in disbelief. "I don't remember that."

"I wasn't actually sure if I could keep my hands to myself, so I stayed on my half of the bed with my back to you. You spooned me."

My brows drew together. "You're too tall to be the little spoon."

"Trust me, I know," he said, laughing. "I don't take threats of physical violence lightly, but no way am I anything but the big spoon. I half-expected to catch a bloody nose when I set the spoons in order." He watched me for a moment, amused. "You look confused."

"I'm surprised, is all. I slept so soundly, I don't remember a thing."

"At one point, I tried to put you back on your side of the bed, but the second I rolled over, you wiggled your way back."

Embarrassment set a hot blaze in my cheeks. "I'm sorry. You must not have slept at all."

But he slid his leg between my thighs, squeezing me tighter with that sideways smile on his lips. "Not until I ignored the warning and spooned *you* good and proper. Then I slept like a baby."

Ignoring the disconnect between my mind and body he'd so casually mentioned, I admitted, "Me too. You defy all the things I assumed to be true. It's … it's both a comfort and a point of contention. I both crave and am disarmed by you." She paused, her brilliant eyes searching mine, her thoughts shifting behind the irises. "Why do you want a girl like me?"

He frowned. "A beautiful, intelligent, driven woman?"

I shook my head. "I'm difficult. I'm inflexible. Calculating, cold."

"Oh, I dunno. I think you're *hot*." He was wearing The Look, his eyes smoldering and his lips lush and smirking.

With a roll of my eyes, I laughed. "You are so strange for wanting someone as strange as me."

He appraised my face, smoothing my hair. "You're different, and every difference you have, I admire. Everything you consider difficult and inflexible, I understand. We're very much alike, you and me."

"I know. But…Theo, you could have a girl who's beautiful and charming like you. You could have someone who would complement you, make you shine brighter."

"Well, that's the trick, Kate," he said, angling for a kiss. "I don't want anyone but you."

His lips connected with mine at the same moment something in my chest twisted, the feeling foreign, only instigated by him and him alone.

Never had I been so affected.

He was comprised of things I didn't understand, his presence alone enough to keep me both off-kilter and upright. But I couldn't imagine any other way. I couldn't imagine parting ways with him, going back to my old life. The woman I had been a few months ago was gone, an echo of who I had become. Everything had changed. And Theo had shepherded me through every step with patience and understanding, the incremental progress bringing us to this moment, this space.

He knew me. In an unreasonably short period of time, he understood me in ways I wasn't sure I even understood myself. It afforded him the ability to anticipate my needs, to guide me into a relationship in such minute degrees that I hadn't realized until that exact moment how deep we'd gone.

And the more shocking realization was that I wasn't scared. I couldn't be, not with Theo at the helm.

I wasn't scared because I trusted him.

If magic were real, Theo was Houdini.

He broke the kiss, though the press of his cock into my hips belied his lips when they said, "Come on, I'll feed you breakfast."

"Sausage and eggs?" I said with a smile and an arch of my back that ground my body against his.

A laugh. "Did you just make a dick joke, Kate?"

"What?" I said coyly. "Hot sausage sounds delicious."

"And I know how you like your eggs."

"How's that?"

"Fertilized."

Before I could laugh, he kissed me and gave me all the hot sausage I could handle.

MAKINGS OF A MAN

KATHERINE

19 WEEKS, 1 DAY

Two weeks had passed in a blur.

Phase Two of our relationship was in full swing. We were officially together and spent every spare second we had taking advantage of the newfound freedom.

That was how it felt—like freedom, not the shackles I'd thought it'd be. Beyond logic, it was a relief. There was nothing left between us, the rules checked off and retired, one by one. It was so strange to enjoy someone's company so much. I usually had a hard two-hour limit with other people before needing to retreat, requiring solitude to recharge.

It almost felt wrong to feel so right. It was a betrayal of everything I'd thought I knew.

And yet, here I was, enjoying every second of it.

I'd been busy at work after joining a committee against my will, but if I was going to land the promotion as a researcher, the committee would help since it was being run by a shark.

Library staff could be sorted into one of three categories: the young idealists, the old grumps, and the sharks.

The idealists were out to change the world through community outreach with projects ranging from inmates and new moms to—no lie—the wealthy. Rachel, one of our newest pages, had been trying to get a program together to reach out to the underserved wealthy in Manhattan, and on its fourth denial, she had a very public meltdown, complete with open sobbing and a brokenhearted monologue about the good we could do if we could only reach the rich with the power of books.

The grumps were their own breed, mostly working in circulation where things were the same every day. There was a stability of daily repetition they seemed to prefer. They typically stuck to the circulation room, sorting books that had been returned, or, as pages like me, shelving all the books that had been sorted. They abhorred the committees the idealists and sharks created in abundance. And though the grumps were generally well over fifty, I was easily categorized here.

And then there were the sharks. For some reason, the library system attracted a cache of ambitious individuals who should have been working as CEOs or lawyers but instead chose to make fifty thousand a year in the public library system. They advanced quickly, clustering around the top of the administration of each branch, and approached their jobs with the micromanaging and enterprising attitude of a politician. They were the suits of our industry, more interested in numbers and performance than anything, seeking high-profile programs and always looking for ways to get the library more government money.

In essence, they thrived on making things as difficult as possible for the rest of us, all in the name of efficiency. All it took was one jackass going to a convention, and for two months, they'd try to instill changes that would inevitably fail at everything beyond pissing off everyone in circulation.

I clocked in and put my things away, sighing with happy anticipation of the circulation room, where I'd find stacks of books all ready to find their way back to their home.

I grabbed a cart from the row of empties and wheeled over to fiction.

Mysteries were always fun first thing while I still had energy. I could clear a cart of mystery novels in fifteen minutes flat, even with the bottom shelf of the cart full. Notoriously, the lazy pages would leave the bottom shelf empty, as it was cumbersome to access. But despite my physical difficulty bending over lately, I always loaded the bottom shelf.

I was no louse, pregnant or not.

My cart was half-full when Eagan appeared at my elbow with Stephanie, a shark and long-time pain in my ass who had never truly worked in circulation.

She also happened to be the owner of the ass I'd have to kiss if I wanted that promotion.

I frowned at them. "Can I help you?"

Eagan's smile was shitty and cruel. "Efficiency check today."

Stephanie wore a suspicious smile of her own. She held up an RFID wand, which she could scan over every shelf I'd worked to ensure everything was in its correct place and order.

I stifled a groan.

"I'd like you to work in picture books today," she said, and the urge to throttle her almost overwhelmed me. "I don't know why you all avoid them so desperately."

"Because they take hours. You can't see the spines for the author names, and you could fit two hundred books on a single cart. Why *wouldn't* we avoid them?"

She laughed like I was joking. "Eagan took the liberty of loading a cart for you."

"I know how you like to use all four shelves, *Kate*."

My skin crawled. "Katherine," I corrected, glaring at him.

Ever since he'd heard Theo call me Kate, it was all he called me. After the first time, I'd hidden the extra carts so he'd have to make a hundred trips and carry them all by hand. And judging by his spaghetti arms, I was certain he hadn't even been able to pick up his precious stamp the next day.

"Whatever," he said, pushing the cart at me.

"I have three more where that came from, and I expect them all to be shelved by the end of the day. And shelved *correctly*."

"I always shelve them correctly," I snapped, not meaning to, my serenity and plans gone in a poof.

And then it was me who was gone in a poof.

Out of the circulation room I went, scowling and cursing them in my mind. I'd have to watch my back. All it would take was Eagan sneaking behind me to ruin my work, and I'd be in trouble.

If there was one thing I hated in life worse than being wrong, it was getting in trouble. I'd wring his skinny little neck if he messed things up for me.

I grabbed a wand of my own, just in case.

I pulled around a corner, heading for the children's library, nodding at my colleagues as I passed. And then I saw Rita and froze.

The library patron was hurrying toward me, her silver hair in disarray, her eyes rheumy and a little wild.

"Katherine!" she called, waving like a lunatic. Which I really had the inclination she was. She wore her shirt inside out as always—so the government couldn't track her T-shirt logos, she'd insisted—and her lime-green Crocs squeaked as she power-walked in my direction.

I glanced over my shoulder where, seconds before, at least three other librarians had been. Now, there was no one. They'd scattered like cockroaches the second they saw her.

Not that I could blame them. I'd have done the same, if given the chance.

It was an unspoken code, a constant game of Not It kicked into motion every time an undesirable approached for help. Like the ones who smelled like a dumpster. Or the ones who made a habit of urinating in chairs rather than getting up to use the restroom. Or the ones who came in weekly to try to sell us magazine subscriptions. Or the guys who masturbated in the stacks.

To be fair, there weren't *too* many of those, but there were enough to remember them when you saw them.

"Hi, Rita," I said wearily. "What can I help you with?"

I knew the answer before she said it.

"I wanted to know the significance of the number seven in the pyramids. You know they were built by aliens, right?"

In a feat of skill, I swallowed my argument and sighed my resignation. "Come with me," was all I said, turning for a terminal.

It was always an iteration of the same question. Rita came in weekly to delve deeper into the history of the number seven.

For the next hour, I endured an exhaustive overload of Rita filling the air with conspiracy theories while I researched our database and the print materials we had. Our results were a motley of flotsam and jetsam—like that one cubit of ancient Egyptian measure was seven palms—but she seemed satisfied enough by the time we were finished.

She paid me with a handful of warm gummy bears from her pocket, which I tried to refuse.

But Rita would not be denied, and rather than get stuck there any longer, I took the indignity with a, "You're welcome," and sent her on her way.

I then washed my hands for two full minutes under nearly scalding water.

Hours passed in blissful silence, and three carts later, I was nearly done and cheerfully smiling. Just a little bit longer, and this day would be done. And at the end of it was Theo.

"Heya, Kate."

My smile was gone just like that, replaced by a scowl and an irrational urge to throw a book at Eagan.

"Katherine," I corrected through my teeth.

"Steph's been behind you all day."

"Lucky for me, I don't trust you and caught every offense you tried to pin on me."

"Aw, come on. It's just a game. If you'd go out with me, I'd probably stop."

It was the third time he'd asked me out, and just like the other two, bile rose in my throat. "I'm pregnant with another man's child."

He shrugged. "Far as I'm concerned, that just means you put out."

I gaped at him, and he laughed, rolling his eyes.

"I'm kidding, Kate."

"Katherine, you plebeian." I turned back to my shelf.

"Seriously, what's that guy got that I don't?"

"Besides respect for others?"

"Sure."

I huffed. "For starters, a foot on your height and a foot that'd be in your ass if he saw you talking to me."

"Jeez, so touchy."

"I wouldn't go out with you if you were the last man on Earth. I'd rather barbecue you and become a cannibal than save the species."

"You say that now, but wait until Mr. Suit leaves you high and dry."

"Mr. Suit? That's the best you've got? Seriously, do you even read books, or do you just look at the pretty pictures? No wonder you put me in children's. Must feel like home. Here, you can start with this one."

I handed him a picture book, and he looked down at the title, frowning.

"*Thomas and the Pee-Pee Problem.*"

"Happy reading," I said, grabbing the handle of my cart and steering myself away from him. "Try not to hurt yourself."

I wheeled my cart away with my nose in the air and my mind full of expletives, noting the time as I passed one of the government clocks on the wall. One hour, and I'd be in Theo's arms.

And that was just the motivation I needed to set a smile on my face as Eagan gaped at my stiff back from the children's section, right where he belonged.

THEO

I sat in an ocean of crib pieces, Creedence Clearwater Revival bouncing out of my speaker. John Fogerty sang all about the bad moon rising, and flipping through eighteen pages of instructions, I had to agree.

The furniture had come while Katherine was at work, so I'd put it where we'd discussed, making a few executive decisions when things didn't fit exactly as we'd thought they would. I went with my gut.

Hadn't failed me yet.

I'd hoped to have the crib finished before Katherine got home, but judging by the number of screws and washers I had to get through, that wasn't happening.

Two screws in, the doorbell rang.

I hopped up and trotted down the stairs. Ma and I had a deal that she wasn't to answer the door when I was home. Problem was, Ma didn't listen and hated losing her independence, so if I didn't hurry, I'd find *her* hurrying, a sight that never ceased to leave me imagining her falling. Her reflexes were too slow now for her to hurry anywhere.

But when I entered the living room, she was nowhere to be found.

And thank fucking God. Because what I found on my stoop would have put her in an early grave.

"Heya, Teddy."

John Banowski's voice was deep, weathered by years and roughed by cigarettes, one of which hung from the smirking seam of his lips.

Rage, deep and unbridled, tore loose under every square inch of my skin. "What the fuck are you doing here?" I asked with fake, flattened distance, stepping out to close the door behind me.

Six years hadn't aged him much, though his hair was shot with silver, the creases around his eyes deeper. He was a beast, imposing in stature, aggressive in stance, handsome in spite of it all.

"Is your ma home?"

"None of your fucking business. Now tell me what you want or get the fuck off my stoop."

"Came to ask you about this." He shifted, reaching behind him to pull something from his back pocket. His hand reappeared with a folded, slightly dirty pack of papers. "Fuck is this, Ted? I thought we had a deal, and here I get divorce papers." He waved them in case I hadn't picked up on what they were.

"We do have a deal. That doesn't mean Ma can't have what she wants. What the hell do you care anyway?"

"You're tryin' to squeeze me out. I read the story in the paper Tommy's little creampuff wifey wrote, tellin' the world about his poor old ma. You think you can get ridda me by telling the papers all the goods you've been paying me to keep quiet? You think your ma can send me these papers, and you'll be through with me? You think I don't still have leverage? 'Cause there's no need for Tommy's secrets anymore. I've got one better—*you.*"

"Nobody's trying to squeeze you out," I said with a tight jaw. "Nothing's changed. But if you're stupid enough to tell Ma and Tommy about our deal, it *will* be over."

He took a drag of his cigarette, exhaling smoke in my face. "The second you quit with the checks, this's the first place I'll come. Can't imagine what Tommy'll think about you payin' me hush money all these years."

"Oh, I'd be more worried about what he'd do to your sack-of-shit face. Never mind if you hurt Ma. 'Cause in that case, you'll have to watch out for both of us." I stepped into him, eye to eye, glare into burning glare. "And I might be the nice one, but I'm the one who will fuck you up beyond repair." I straightened up when he pushed off the doorframe. "Next time you need to harass me, you fucking call me to do it, or the deal's off. I don't wanna have to put you in traction, old man."

A laugh, a cold, haughty laugh. "You just keep that cash coming, Teddy."

"Sign those papers. Let her go."

But he was already turning to leave. "Yeah, sure. I'll get right on that," he said, and I watched him walk away.

For a long moment, I couldn't move, grappling with the sight of my father for only the second time in twenty years. But then I found a way to carry myself inside with mannequin legs, walking stiffly to the kitchen where I poured myself a drink.

Thank God Ma was out with Tommy and Amelia. Thank God John and I were on the same page.

And thank God things were fine.

For now.

I downed a glass of scotch and poured another just as the door opened.

Katherine appeared in the entryway, looking exhausted and utterly radiant despite the fact. And all I wanted, all I needed, was her in my arms.

I strode across the room, scooping her up with a laugh and a question that I swallowed when I kissed her. I kissed her long and hard, kissed her until she was soft and pliant in the circle of my arms. Kissed her until I wasn't mad or scared or hurt anymore.

When I broke away, her lids were heavy and lips were smiling. "Well, hello."

"Hello," I said and kissed her again.

I kissed her with abandon, with wildness. I kissed her with singular purpose.

To erase John Banowski from my mind.

MATHMAGICIAN

THEO

20 WEEKS, 2 DAYS

"Kassandra," Katherine said, smiling down at her pasta, fork spinning in her linguini.

"Kassie. I like it."

The joke earned me a stern look. "No nicknames. Maybe we should name her something like Jane so you won't give her a pet name."

"Like Janie?"

She rolled her eyes, but she was smiling. "What about Sarah, after your mother?"

"Too confusing to have two Sarahs in one house. What's your mom's name?"

Her humor was gone. "Susan, but she changed it to Sparrow when she turned eighteen."

I watched her for a second, waiting for the punch line. One

"Well, I can't think of a nickname for Sparrow other than Birdie or Cuckoo."

A ghost of a smile flickered on her face. "A cuckoo isn't even in the same family as sparrows, but my mother *is* crazy. So, there's that."

I kept on, not wanting her to unpack anything she wasn't ready for, regardless of my curiosity. "What about Natasha? Gabrielle? Yvonne? Genevieve?"

"Those are names of hot spies, not babies."

"Well, babies grow up," I reminded her.

One of her brows rose. "You want your *daughter* to be a hot spy?"

"Good point." I forked some penne. "What about something like … Hope? That way, there's no nickname."

She nodded, her smile spreading. "I'll add it to the list."

I took a bite, my eyes finding the sonogram picture on the table while we ate for a moment in companionable silence. We had come to Del Posto to celebrate three momentous occasions. Our first official date, Katherine hitting the midpoint of her pregnancy, and the cherry on the sundae—this afternoon, we'd learned the sex of our baby.

The fuzzy black-and-white sonogram lay on the table, a series of photographs of our daughter. Her small arms, hands fisted in some and open in another, her tiny feet kicking. She had moved around the whole time, the ultrasound tech chasing her measurements.

But what had struck me beyond seeing her kick and move and suck her thumb was even more simple and strange. It was her profile, white against black, the button nose and curves of her lips. Her cheeks and little chin, the shape of her head. One day soon, that little head would rest in my palm. Those little lips would smile at me. That tiny hand would hold my finger.

That little girl would one day call me Daddy.

That morning, I'd sat in the chair next to Katherine in the dark sonogram room, her face turned to the screen, most of the time spent in silence while the tech measured the baby's forehead and amniotic fluid and spine and a dozen other things she never explained the significance of. And I held Katherine's swampy hand and documented the moment, etching it in stone so I could remember it always. The look on her face, the joy, the discovery when we saw our daughter for the first time.

I loved Katherine with a fierceness I'd never known.

There had been no moment to pinpoint, no lightning bolt of realization. It had grown like ivy—in slow tendrils and unfurling leaves, day by day, hour by hour. It had been happening since the first time I laid eyes on her, in every minute spent with her, in every breath and heartbeat between us.

I loved her.

And God, how I wanted to keep her.

"Hope," Katherine said again. "I like that one."

"Me too. It's sweet for a little girl, but she could have a professional adult job and it's classic enough to work." I loaded my fork. "What do you think she'll do?"

Katherine made a face at me. "That's an impossible question. We don't even know what kind of disposition she'll have."

"Well, we could assume she'll be like us in some sense."

"That isn't a safe assumption. I'm nothing like my parents."

It was the second mention in a handful of minutes, which led me to believe it was safe to ask, "What are they like?"

Another look, this one flat. "My mother changed her name to Sparrow. I'm sure you can imagine what kind of mom she was."

I chuckled. "So, she's an accountant?"

She frowned. "No, I'm not even sure she can do math without a calculator. She's a yoga instructor."

"It was a joke, Kate. What brand of hippie is she? Weed and conspiracy theories or vegan and reiki?"

"Vegan and reiki. She actually thinks dream catchers catch dreams."

A laugh shot out of me.

"I mean it," she said. "She psychically cleans them on Saturdays."

"That's…"

"I love her, but she drives me crazy. We are exact opposites."

"How so?"

She set down her fork and folded her arms on the table in front of her. Her face was touched with both amusement and annoyance. "For my thirteenth birthday, all I wanted was a gift card to a bookstore. That was it. I explicitly requested that, a vanilla cake with strawberry icing, and *no party*. But she didn't listen—she never does. Instead, she deemed the occasion too momentous to let pass without a hoorah. So, she showed up at school during lunch, floated into the cafeteria with balloons and chocolate cupcakes, and sang 'Happy Birthday' in front of all my peers. I thought I was going to melt into the floor and die."

I laughed, only because it was so outrageous. "It's like she didn't know you at all."

"Doesn't. Doesn't know me and doesn't listen when I tell her who I am or what I want. That night, she threw me a surprise party with a bunch of kids from school I didn't even know. I think all their mothers made them come, maybe with bribery. I can't imagine why else they would have shown up." She sighed and picked up her fork again. "It's classic Sparrow—I ask her for something, and she not only ignores my request, but goes in the complete opposite direction. I think it's her own method of control, an effort to fix me, prove to me that there's a better, happier way to live, if only I'd give it a whirl. That rationalization helps me endure, coupled with the knowledge that she means well. But I'm glad there are several thousand miles of distance between us. She has boundary issues but square miles help."

"I'm guessing she wasn't bent to find out you're pregnant when you didn't have a boyfriend."

She shrugged, her attention on her food. "I haven't told her yet."

I stilled. "You haven't told your mom you're pregnant?"

"She's been on a spirit journey in Washington for the last two months, and I didn't want to tell her until we were out of the first trimester."

I hadn't moved. "A spirit journey."

"A spirit journey." She didn't elaborate. She had more important things to attend to, like her pasta.

"Where did you say you grew up?"

"Sedona—land of a thousand psychics. My kindergarten teacher read tarot cards for us during recess and didn't believe in the word *no*."

Ten pieces of the Katherine puzzle snapped into place at the admission.

My straight, serious Katherine had grown up in fucking Sedona to hippie New Age parents who believed in magic. It was no wonder she craved bounds and rules and order. I wondered how in the hell Sparrow Lawson had handled having a daughter like Katherine.

"How about your dad?"

"His name is Dave, and he's the lead singer of an Eagles cover band."

"Please tell me he has a ponytail."

"Of course he does. How could he not? It's the color of graphite, and he doesn't use a ponytail holder—he keeps it in a leather cuff."

A laugh burst out of me.

"You're surprised. Everyone is surprised."

"I expected them to be scientists or mathematicians or professors. Intellectuals."

"I wonder sometimes if they had been, if I'd have ended up *their* opposite. Whatever genetics they passed on to me were not applicable to them, and their attempts to nurture me into a spiritual being didn't stick. For a long time, I thought I was adopted. If there'd been such thing as Photoshop and if my parents knew how to use computers,

I'd have convinced myself they fabricated the photos of my mom in the hospital with me. I even had a fantasy about being switched with another baby in the hospital."

"You wanted to find reason where there was none. Sounds nothing like you," I joked.

"I couldn't ever understand how it was possible. I had no rules. None. And it was so dire, I ended up making rules of my own, not only for myself, but for them. We had a chore chart hanging on the fridge, but it wasn't to motivate me. It was to motivate them, with little gold stars and extra allowance for their favorite mystic shop. Nothing motivated my mother to do the dishes like the prospect of buying more crystals."

"I can only imagine little Katherine in the kitchen with sheets of foil stars in primary colors."

"I won't lie, it was fun to coordinate rules and systems, but it was emotionally exhausting. I felt constantly depleted. In fact, I didn't know it was possible to be in any kind of relationship and it not exhaust me of all my emotional resources. At least, not until you."

A smile brushed my lips with a tightening of my heart. "I'm glad I could make things easy for you."

With a laugh, she said, "If only I made them easy for you."

"Oh, trust me, it's easier than you think, Kate." I leaned back in my seat, eyes on my fork as it pushed pasta around without intent. "When my dad left us, Ma had to work three jobs to keep us out of the rain and put clothes on our backs. Tommy acted out, started getting in fights, especially when it came to kids getting bullied or picked on. So that left me to keep things together at home."

Her smile fell gently into a compassionate expression.

I continued, "I did the laundry. Picked up groceries for dinner. Made sure Tommy and I stayed after school if we weren't doing well in class to get tutoring. I wrestled Tommy into bed on time and made sure we weren't late to school. Because I was the man of the house, and part of that responsibility was to support Ma. I got a hardship license and work permit when I was fifteen. Got a job stocking groceries and convinced Tommy to do the same."

"I'm sorry, Theo," she said quietly.

"Don't be. Growing up fast wasn't a bad thing—it taught me how to be responsible, and it showed me early on what's important to life. Family. We care for the ones we love, and we show that love however we can. We protect them, no matter what. We do whatever we have to to keep them safe from harm. For you, that came in creating order where there was none."

"But you did it out of love. I only feel resentment. It's...it's so hard for me to be flexible, to share myself with anyone. Because my fear is that I will be completely depleted, and what is taken from me won't ever replenish."

"Well, that's why we're taking it slow, Kate. It's why I took my lemons and made lemonade."

"I took my lemons and made lemon juice."

"Once diluted, and with the help of a little sugar, lemon juice *is* lemonade. I like to think we're making lemonade right now."

She smiled down at her hands as she smoothed her napkin in her lap. "Where is he now? Your father?"

My mouth dried up, my tongue covered in sand. "We didn't know what happened to him. He just...disappeared. Ma couldn't afford to hunt him down for child support or even a divorce. Tommy figured him for dead, but we woulda heard. They're technically still married."

"Really?" she breathed.

"Really. It wasn't until a few years ago that I knew what'd become of him." I took a breath and spoke words I'd never uttered, not to a single living soul. "When Tommy's career broke out, our father showed up asking for money."

Everything about her was still. She said nothing.

"You know how Tommy hid our past, Ma, everything from the public? Well, John Banowski was prepared to blow that cover with a well-placed phone call. So I paid him to keep quiet. *Pay* him," I amended. "Every month, I write that son of a bitch a check. And I sleep like a baby knowing Ma and Tommy are safe from him."

"They don't know?" She was frowning, her brows drawn.

"They can't know. He's a monster, Kate. They're better off assuming he's dead or living in Costa Rica or on Mars. Subjecting them to him would only hurt them all over again. I know it did me."

She reached for my hand, wrapped her slender fingers around my square ones. "You protect everyone you love so well, Theo."

"I try. I don't always succeed. Even now, I might have gotten myself in too deep. Ma filed for divorce, and John showed up to shake me down about it. He thinks I'm trying to cut him out, threatened to tell Ma and Tommy I've been lying to them for all these years."

Her jaw flexed, her eyes hardening. "After giving him monthly checks for six years?"

"It's my own fault. I knew what I was getting myself into. I'm just not sure how to get *out* of it."

"You could stop paying him for starters."

"And then he'll tell Ma and Tommy."

"You could head him off and tell them first."

I sighed, the sound heavy. "I will, if it comes to that. If he keeps giving me hell, I will anyway. But I'll have my own hell to pay when I do."

"They'll understand, Theo. You'd never hurt anyone on purpose. All you do, you do for others. It's so much more than we could ever repay you for."

"Kate, all you have to do is exist. That's payment enough for me."

She flushed, smiling.

"Anyway, I hope the baby won't inherit the Banowski knack for getting into trouble."

That earned me a smile. "It's probably safer to assume she'll be nothing like either of us. In fact, she'll probably take after my mother and be reading our tea leaves before preschool."

"Good. We can put her to work."

She made a face.

"What? Kids are expensive."

At that, she laughed, the sound musical and vibrant. "I just imagined a toddler version of our baby sitting at a crystal ball."

I felt my smile all the way into my bloodstream. "Did she look like you or me?"

Color bloomed in her cheeks. "She had your eyes."

"Boring brown?"

"They're not boring. They're hypnotic, a place without depth, a place to get lost. I'm fairly certain that was how you got me to sleep with you."

"I thought it was my smell," I countered.

"That too. You smell incredible."

"I thought you were going to climb me like a ladder right there in the middle of the club."

"You made me feel…" She paused, correcting herself. "You *make* me feel like I've been starving my whole life, and I thought my depravation was just the way life was. That living in a constant cycle of exhaustion and retreat was just how relationships worked. That's the best way I can explain it—I was starving, and you are a feast. You even engage my salivary glands."

"I've never felt so desired as making your mouth wet."

"That among other things." She was smirking, smug and wry and absolutely gorgeous.

"Kate, are you coming on to me?"

"Maybe," she said, making a show of taking a bite of her dinner, which—thankfully—was almost gone.

"You know something, Kate?"

"What?"

"I sure am glad I knocked you up so I could woo you."

She laughed, that musical sound I loved so well. She was Kate through and through, soft and smiling. Katherine was long gone.

Served her right. It just wasn't fair to be the only one.

In my life, there was one thing I knew I would have—a family. It was a construct I only understood in theory, pictures painted from television and movies and Norman Rockwell paintings. I'd never known what it was like for the mother and father to be in love, to be a team. To raise their children in a safe, secure place, not the kind that had come from crime or depravity but security born in love. I wanted family vacations in the Hamptons. I wanted road trips and a family dinner every night. I wanted matching Christmas pajamas and soccer practice.

And I wanted it with her.

Everything I'd ever wanted was sitting across from me, smiling only for me.

"What do you say we get out of here?" I asked, echoing the phrase from the first night, *that* night.

Recognition lit her smile. "I'd say, lead the way."

.

KATHERINE

As I watched Theo's broad fingers slip the knot out of his tie, a thought crossed my mind that I couldn't shake and didn't want to.

Maybe magic is real.

In his way, Theo *was* magic. It was in everything he did, every touch, every word, every action. And the real magic was in how I'd been affected. Because the way I felt and the depth I felt it was beyond my understanding, a foreign flicker in my chest, my attachment to him a hook in my heart. The thought of being parted from him gave me physical pain, an ache and longing so deep, I couldn't fathom its meaning.

Not unless magic was real.

Which meant I'd been wrong all along.

He turned, pulling his shirt out of his waistband, hands moving for the buttons, but when he saw me standing there, in the middle of the room, staring at him while I tried my best not to cry, he stepped into me and framed my face with his hands.

"What's the matter, Kate? Is something wrong?"

I shook my head, overcome. "No, everything's right. I…" I swallowed the stone in my throat, forcing admissions and truths down. I'd deal with them later. Right now, I only wanted one thing. "Kiss me, Theo."

But for a breath, he watched me. His own admissions hummed through him, but he didn't speak.

And then he gave me what I wanted.

His lips.

The surge of emotions in my chest didn't ebb like I'd hoped. It wasn't a distraction. It was an amplifier. I felt the change in me, felt the stir of it against my skin, felt the thrum of it in my pulse.

I was not myself. But I was more myself than I'd ever been.

I didn't understand it, but I didn't want to fight it. I'd been fighting myself for far too long, and I could feel the release of my grip on who I'd thought I was, what I'd thought I wanted.

And it was all because of him.

He held my face like I was a precious thing, kissed me as if he'd never kiss another woman, touched me like I was a treasure he'd searched for his whole life.

With deft hands, he undressed me, never breaking the kiss. My dress slid to the floor, our languid lips slow and deliberate as he slipped his hands into my panties and pushed them over the curve of my ass. My bra, unfastened with a neat snap of his fingers, joined the pile, and when his hand was free, he palmed my heavy breast, testing the weight with tender reverence.

My fingers weren't still either. They made quick work of his shirt buttons, his belt, his zipper. He kicked out of his shoes, stepped out of his pants, pulled my hips toward his when I slid my hand down his back and into his underwear. My intent was to remove them, but my hungry fingertips wanted to taste his skin, the soft curve of his hard ass a wonder of musculature.

I turned us around in a slow sway like we were dancing, putting his back to the bed, stepping him into it, pressing him to sit. His arms curled around my waist, bringing me close, my body between his thighs and his face buried in my burgeoning breasts. And I watched him, tracing the smooth plane of his forehead with my eyes, marveling at the thick crescents of his lashes, the lush swell of his lips as they closed over my nipple. The pink of his tongue. The angular bridge of his Roman nose. The silky black strands of his hair against the white of my fingers.

He was beautiful, devoted in ways that were unfathomable in depth and beyond my understanding. I'd once thought it was perhaps only the baby that had triggered this in him. But if I combed back through the months, analyzed every touch, if I went back to the beginning, nothing had changed. From the first time he'd touched me, I had known. I had known he was different, that what we shared was *other*. It was why I'd run from him.

I'd known he would change me. And I would never willingly step into change.

It was a fault of mine, born from a desire to protect myself. But there was a level of protection I could never fully provide, discovered in him. In the way he gave and gave, in every moment of patience, in every word he spoke. He would do anything for me, my partner, lover, friend.

This was the pinnacle, the height of my understanding, the closest to love I could imagine.

I shifted, sliding one knee outside his thigh and into the bed, climbing into his lap. The other knee mirrored its twin, my hand cupping his neck and my lips finding his. Broad hands squeezed my ass, our height difference erased as I brought my hips to his, sought the hard length of his cock. The smooth crown brushed the aching center of me, drawing a deep moan from him, a moan I swallowed. His hands flexed, spreading my ass, shifting my hips until he breached me.

The kiss finally broke, our eyes locked and lust-drunk, lips parted and breaths mingling, the tip of my nose brushing the bridge of his as I lowered my hips, filling myself with him.

A fluttering of his black lashes, a deep, heavy sigh, the click of our bodies as we fit together, unmoving but for a pulse of his cock inside of me and an echoing flex of my core.

Words sat weighted on my tongue, foreign but for the feeling they evoked. Words that paled next to the fathomless, nebulous emotions I felt, but they were the best I had.

I couldn't say them. But I could show him. So I did.

First with my fingertips on the smooth line of his jaw, with my eyes that searched the depths of his, eyes that could see the tether between us as clearly as if it were a tangible thing. Then, with the rock of my hips, I took my pleasure and gave it back in a wave. It was an exchange, a dance we knew every step to, one that had become second nature, a latent instinct.

He drew a breath that drew me into him and captured my mouth with a press of his lips, a sweep of his tongue. And with every motion, every breath, every heartbeat, I heard the words of my heart echoed back to me through him.

Every wave of our bodies brought us closer, my body opening up, my hips settling deeper, the grind of my clit against him spurring me, the pressure hot and building, seeking a vent, an escape, a release. Slow we moved, achingly slow, painfully slow, the intent to hold out, hold off, but the effect was the opposite—the throb of his cock, the pulse of his desire brought me closer, close enough to forsake my plan strictly for want of my pleasure.

Deeper was the grind of my hips, harder was the flex of his. Faster came the wave, tighter his fingers squeezed.

A throaty moan, rumbling and low. He took control of my hips, buried his face in my neck, buried himself in me to the sting of my thighs against his, the swell of his cock inside me. My orgasm was stayed, my attention wholly on him. The thick, ropy cords of muscle tight under my hands. The noisy rush of his breath. The pinch of his brows and the painful grab of his hands. With a hard thrust, he stopped us both for a single protracted moment of complete abandon. And he came with a deep throb and a silent cry before he raised me up and slammed into me to the beat of his heart.

And still, in the mindless stretch of his release, as he took what he needed, he gave me what I did, his body meeting mine without intent to press that delicate flesh between my thighs in the rhythm I desired, the angle and pressure I sought. But he did, that attunement of our bodies and the sight of his pleasure triggering a chain reaction that shuddered down my spine.

The orgasm first commandeered me. I was a creature of feeling and nothing more, my body its own and my mind lost. I was aware only on the very fringes, only in the places we touched. My sight was gone with a flash and a burst, my will dissolved.

I rode the feeling, drifting back to the ground like a cottonwood bloom, spinning and floating in the eddies of my desire. But before I made landfall, he kissed me.

Possession. It was a kiss of possession, bruising and deep, volumes and volumes of words spoken without sound. It was transcribed, transferred in the most elemental of ways, impressing upon my heart all the ways in which I was his and he was mine.

A warm, salty tear slid over the curve of my cheek and into the seam of our lips. His hand cupped my jaw, his thumb brushing the track.

The kiss broke. My eyes closed, my face turning into his palm so I could press a kiss to its soft center. I didn't want him to see me cry, didn't want to speak. I hoped he wouldn't ask, because if he asked if I was all right, I wouldn't be able to hold myself together.

But he didn't. He knew without knowing. He saw without seeing. It was his way, the simple understanding, the intuitive grace with which he handled me.

He tucked me under his chin and wrapped me in his arms. Twisted to lay us down. I burrowed into his chest, my tears coming steady, my breath coming deep, filling my lungs with the clean scent of him.

I was a stranger to myself. But I didn't want to go back to who I had been.

I couldn't if I tried.

His fingertips grazed the curve of my shoulder, sparking fire.

And magic, for a moment, was real.

A WING AND A PRAYER

THEO

20 WEEKS, 3 DAYS

Without a word, everything changed.

She told me in the way she kissed me, the truth of her heart alive in every teardrop, riding her shallow breath. And I basked in the knowledge that I'd found what I'd wanted for so long.

For her to lean in to us. For her to choose me.

For her to love me.

It was her trust in me, finally deep enough to unclench the fist around what she'd once believed was true.

I kissed her then, kissed her until her tears were dry and her body wound around mine, eager for more. So down I moved, taking her with my lips until I tasted another orgasm on my tongue. I sheathed myself in her, loved her like I loved her—with deliberate care, with calculated patience. With all of me, I loved her.

And we fell asleep wrapped in each other's arms, heartbeats synced and breaths measured and evenly matched.

Just like us.

Morning came too soon, the day promising to be hectic. But in that quiet moment, before the clock began to tick, it was just her and me and the creeping sunlight.

A sigh dragged in and out of her lungs, one of her arms slung around my middle, her head resting on the curve of my shoulder and her hair spilling onto the bed. Her belly pressed into my side, lamentably keeping her hips from me.

"Good morning," she said, her voice husky from disuse.

"Morning," I echoed. My arm snaked around her waist, and my hand splayed across the curve of her stomach.

Her leg slipped between mine. "I've never called in sick, but I'm tempted to this morning."

I chuckled. "I know. Tommy and Amelia are at a fundraiser for children's literacy this morning, and afterward, we have a meeting with the USA Times. I'm not going to be back until after dinner."

I couldn't see her face, but I swore I heard her frown.

"Don't worry. I'll have dinner in a Crock downstairs for you and Ma."

"Oh, I wasn't worried about that. I've been successfully feeding myself for twenty-six years. I just dislike being apart from you."

"I dislike it, too." I kissed the top of her head.

Another sigh, this one forlorn. "I wish we could at least meet for lunch."

"Why? Is Eagan not behaving himself?"

She made a derisive noise. "Yesterday, he checked a bunch of books in and changed the return dates so they wouldn't have fees. Under *my* login. Stephanie was furious with me. And he had the nerve to tell me he'd done it. Stephanie didn't believe me, and he lied to her and said he hadn't. Stupid cretin."

"I'll kill him," I said flatly.

"Not if I kill him first," she countered.

"Well, tonight we'll stay in. The finale of *Love Cabana* is on."

"And I think I'll finish Hope's sweater."

I leaned back, smirking as I looked down at her. "Hope, huh?"

She shrugged, but a smile curled the very corners of her lips. "I was trying it on to see if I liked it."

"And what do you think?"

"I wish it had more syllables, but I think I like it very much. Plus, you love it, which makes me love it more."

The word *love* from her lips set a hot stir in my chest. Love. Such a fanciful word with so many meanings. I loved the way she said our baby's name. I loved the way she loved me. I loved the child we'd made, and I'd never even seen her.

I felt the word on my tongue, the shape of it round and open. I kissed her so I wouldn't speak it.

Mindful of the time, I let her go. "Come on. Let's get this over with."

She smiled, and I slipped away from her, getting out of bed. When I turned, she hadn't moved.

Her body was comprised of rolling curves—cheek and chin, shoulder and elbow. Waist and hip, breasts and belly. Her eyes were swimming shades of blues just then, picked up and reflected by the white sheets, her cheeks pink and lips rosy.

She was the most beautiful thing I'd ever seen, swollen with my child, radiant and fresh and smiling up at me.

So I climbed back in bed and told her so.

An hour later, we were nearly late, the two of us rushing around each other in a dance of compatibility. We'd gotten Ma set for the day, and as I took a sip of my coffee, Katherine adjusted the knot of my tie. I fiddled with the shoulder of her cardigan where it was caught under her shirt collar while she took the last bite of her toast. And just when I kissed her nose, the doorbell rang.

I frowned, checking my watch. We had to go. In fact, I was surprised Tommy hadn't already busted in with Amelia in tow. It crossed my mind that it was him, but the thought held no logic. He'd have just walked in.

I strode to the door, and what I found nearly knocked me over.

A woman the exact duplicate of Katherine—plus twenty-five years, a healthy dose of patchouli, and maybe an alternate universe— stood on the stoop with a smile on her face and a carpetbag on her shoulder.

"Hi there," she said, her voice musical. "Val said Katie is staying here. Is she here now?"

"Mom?" Katherine said from my elbow.

Sparrow's eyes shifted, widened, and softened, all in a heartbeat. She moved for her daughter, and I shifted out of the way to let her by. I'd been completely forgotten.

She opened her arms, reaching for Katherine, who stood stock-still and ramrod straight, arms at her sides as her mom wrapped her up in a hug. Katherine's eyes shot to me with the panic of an SOS.

"Oh, Katie-Bug," she said into her daughter's hair, rocking her where they stood. "I missed you, honey." When she leaned back, her face was warm and admiring, emotional and a little intense.

"What are you doing here, Mom?" Katherine asked robotically.

"Well, when my journey was over in Washington, I decided to come this direction to see you."

"You didn't call."

"I know, honey. But last night in Chicago, I had a dream and knew I had to get here fast." She looked off with a wistful expression on her face, using her hands to help her explain. "I was in a meadow at night, the Milky Way splitting the sky in two. And as I looked up in wonder, a leaf fell from the stars and floated down to my hand. When I looked down, there were tiny eggs stuck to the veins, and they began to tremble and shake and split. And from their casings came sweet little ladybugs. I knew it was a sign. So here I am, and look! My little ladybug is having a baby!"

She wrapped Katherine up in her arms again as I stared, gaping. Katherine was made of stone.

"Ladybug eggs hatch larvae, not beetles," she said flatly.

Sparrow laughed, that tinkling musical sound. It was unnerving how alike they looked and how openly different they were. "Oh, Katie. It's been too long."

"What are you doing here, Mom?" Katherine asked again.

"Well," she started, finally releasing Katherine, who immediately relaxed with distance, "your father and I released each other again, and I thought, where better to go than to see Katie? I can't believe you're pregnant! Spirit wanted me to come here." Without warning, she reached for Katherine's belly, smoothing her hand over the curve. "Ooh, we should do a reading for the baby later. I'll let you choose which tarot deck you want."

I thought Katherine might actually be trying to crawl out of her skin like the pupal stage ladybug of her mother's dreams. I resisted the urge to put myself between them.

Katie-Bug. No wonder Katherine hated nicknames.

I'd known Sparrow was out of touch with Katherine's needs, but it seemed she was as deeply set in herself as Katherine was. I had to admit, I didn't dislike Sparrow. I found her charming in her way, the small woman with dark hair in a kimono that smelled of sandalwood and patchouli. But I definitely wanted her to get her hands off

Katherine and take three steps back.

For a second, Katherine blinked at her mother, who had turned and was inspecting me openly but without judgment, like one would look at a piece of art or a steak in a butcher's window.

Katherine cleared her throat. "Mom, I'd like you to meet Theodore Bane."

"I hope it's okay that I call you Theo. I'm a sucker for nicknames. Now come here, I'm a hugger." She reached out with slender arms and wrapped me up in a warm, pleasant hug.

I glanced at Katherine, who watched us like we were covered in Ebola.

"It's nice to meet you, too, Mrs. Lawson."

At that, she laughed. "Please, call me Sparrow." She turned to Katherine. "Is this your boyfriend, Katie?"

Katherine's eyes widened, then blinked. Her lips parted, but she didn't seem to have an answer.

My face was smooth, but a flash of surprise and concern jerked in my ribs. She couldn't call me her boyfriend, and a few hours ago, I had been sure she loved me. But Kate—my Kate—had disappeared the second her mom walked in. And in her place was Katherine.

She was clearly uncomfortable, clearly caught off guard, so I forgave her instantly and spoke for her. "Katherine and I are cohabitating. Getting used to each other before the baby comes."

Sparrow frowned. "You're not together?"

"I didn't expect judgment from you on relationship status," Katherine said matter-of-factly.

But Sparrow shook her head with a laugh. "Oh, no—I didn't mean it like that. Only that I can't seem to imagine you having sex with anyone but a boyfriend."

Katherine paled, probably at the word *sex* coming so casually coming from her mother's mouth. "Theodore and I experienced a condom malfunction."

Sparrow's face opened up with laughter, the backs of her knuckles brushing her lips. "Well, that'll do it."

"So, why are you here, Mom?" she asked for a third time.

"Like I said, your father and I released each other, and I wanted to get away. So here I am!"

"Did you have a plan?" Katherine asked, her exasperation contained.

"Well, I wanted it to be a surprise, and look how nice that was."

"I hate surprises," Katherine said.

"I know. I was teasing," Sparrow said, hooking her arm in her daughter's. "But you're always so busy. So I thought maybe if I didn't make a big production out of it, you'd see me when it was convenient. I don't need much in the way of attention, Katie. You know that."

Katherine made a derisive noise.

"I really did need to get away," Sparrow said a little quieter, a little calmer.

Katherine's lips flattened. "Where will you stay while you're here? Theodore and I have to leave for work."

"Oh, I'll figure something out."

"Do you have a hotel booked? How long will you be here? Does Dad know where you are?"

"No, I don't know, and yes. You worry too much, Katie-Bug."

"Well, what are you going to do today?"

"Oh, I don't know. Maybe I'll wander around Central Park. Or there's a mystic shop in the East Village I haven't been to in years. I need to pick up some more sage. I ran out in Milwaukee. I swear, that hotel was a murder stop."

Katherine's eyes met mine in a plea.

I cleared my throat. "Sparrow, come meet my mother. Maybe you can stay with us for a bit."

Katherine's face tightened, and I swore in my mind for having read her wrong.

Sparrow's face lit up like a firecracker. "Oh, Theo, that would be *wonderful*. You'll have to let me read your tea leaves. Or I could clear your aura, though yours is solid," she said, her eyes tracing the air around me. "Very masculine, very steady. You picked a good one, Katie." She bumped Katherine's hip with hers.

Katherine barely moved from the impact, like a cliffside against a hurricane.

I ushered Sparrow into the living room with Katherine following us like a wooden doll. Once I introduced Sparrow to my mom, they struck up a conversation, affording Katherine and me a split second of privacy. I reached for her hand.

"You okay?" I asked quietly, my mind tracing the crack that had, out of nowhere, split between us.

"No," she answered definitively.

"Hey," I whispered, stepping into her. The motion caught her attention, and her eyes locked on mine like a lifeline. "I've got you. Okay? We'll figure it out."

She nodded once, but her brows were drawn.

I wanted to pull her into my arms, to kiss her, to remind her she was safe. We were safe. But the display in front of our mothers would only make it worse, I knew.

I suddenly loathed the fact that I couldn't see her at work today. Because even though her hand was in mine and she'd agreed with the words I'd spoken, I could feel the slip, a backward step that I hoped was temporary.

Because I wouldn't lose the ground I'd gained.

KATHERINE

I watched my mother unroll her satchel of reiki crystals, chatting her face off to Sarah as she arranged them on the windowsill to recharge.

I was unable to get a handle on the situation. I had a checklist for today. One for the week. One for my pregnancy. One for me and Theo. And my mother was not on any one of them. I'd had no time to plan for her, no time to mentally prepare for her presence. And now, she was not only in New York, but she would be staying with us.

My mother, who was more unpredictable than an infant.

My mother, who was splitting up with my father. Again.

Last night, I'd let go, found myself glamoured into thinking that magic was real. That Theo and I were different, that he could be the exception to the rules I'd lived my life by. But as I tracked my mother as she fiddled with her crystals, I was reminded of those truths, the cold, sterile facts.

Magic was no more real than her crystals and tarot cards. Love was no more real than soggy tea leaves and sage smudging, and my off-again, on-again parents were proof positive. And if I'd been caught up enough to have forgotten that, I was in far too deep.

Theo was wound almost as tight as I was, though he was watching *me*. He checked his watch in a twitchy movement that was very much unlike him.

"We need to go," he said quietly, cupping my elbow in his massive hand before addressing our mothers. "We'll see you two tonight."

"Have a good day, honey," Sparrow called, hurrying over to invade my space once again with a crushing hug.

Theo stiffened next to me. I got the distinct impression he was both charmed by my mother and fighting an impulse to pry her off of me.

The second she let me go, he steered me toward the door like my bodyguard. I wanted to be mad at him for inviting my mom to stay with us, but I couldn't find it in me. I'd have invited her myself, because if I knew my mother, she'd have ended up in a hostel or some seedy motel where she was sure to get held up or worse. She had no sense of danger—she trusted the universe to take care of her, and by her estimation, the universe typically provided.

In this case, it was certainly not the universe. It was Theo who'd provided.

I sucked in a breath through my nose as we stepped out of the house and onto the sidewalk where Tommy and Amelia waited. On seeing us, their faces bent in concern.

"What happened?" Tommy asked.

"My mother showed up unannounced."

Amelia's face opened up with compassion and concern. "Oh no."

"Oh, yes. Sparrow is currently unrolling her yoga mat in the guest bedroom downstairs," I said pointedly, though the words were tight with my tamped-down hysteria.

Tommy didn't seem to understand, but he and Theo had one of their silent conversations, which ended up with his brows drawn. "I hate to rush, but we're late. Car will be here any—oh, there it is."

A black Mercedes pulled up to the curb.

Amelia reached for my hand, and thank God she didn't hug me. I'd been surprise-hugged too many times this morning for my comfort.

"Are you okay?"

"Not even a little."

Her little face pinched. "It's gonna be all right. We'll talk tonight and sort it out, okay?"

"Okay," I said without believing in the possibility that *anything* would be fine.

She gave my hand a squeeze and turned for the car where Tommy held the door for her.

Theo stepped around me, shielding me from the street, our friends, the world. His face was a cool mask, but his eyes belied his worry.

"Kate, listen to me." He caught my chin in his thumb and forefinger to angle my face to his.

He was the sum of my awareness the second our eyes met.

"We will make rules, boundaries for her. She'll stay downstairs. I'll have the door installed at the top of the stairs, and I'll put a lock on the inside. Hell, I'll make enforceable visiting hours if I have to."

God, how he knew me.

The ache in my chest twisted. "It won't stop her. She *has* no boundaries, and rules mean nothing to her. My life is an arrangement of neat, tidy blocks, always in their exact place. And my mother is a toddler, come to knock it all down. She can't follow rules, Theo. She doesn't understand how."

"I'll make her," he promised, not understanding that the task was impossible.

But I didn't have it in me to argue.

So I sighed and said, "Okay."

His arm slipped around my waist, bringing me into him. I was surrounded by him, the comfort immediate and bone-deep. "I've got you, Kate. Nothing's gonna get through me."

With another sigh, I relaxed into him. And when he kissed me, I almost forgot that my life had just gone nuclear. I felt as if yesterday hadn't happened.

As uncomfortable as I was, there was at least comfort in the familiarity of my old self, the one with the rules that had kept me safe all my years. Theo and I were compatible on all levels, and that was enough for me. It was the best I could offer, the most I could give.

I just hoped it was enough for him.

OH NO CHI DIDN'T

KATHERINE

22 WEEKS, 5 DAYS

Amelia, Rin, and Val's faces were pinched in disgust around the bar table.

"Did you just say mucus plug?" Val asked with a wrinkle of her nose.

"Yes," I answered. "It's what keeps amniotic fluid from leaking out of your cervix."

The three of them groaned collectively.

A shudder racked down Amelia's back. "I heard most people poop a little when they push."

"It's very common," I confirmed. "You use the same muscles to push as you do to defecate."

Val made a face. "As long as Sam stays on my side of the curtain

"You know, the curtain. So you can't see what's happening down there."

"There's no curtain, Val. Only if you have a cesarean, in which case someone's hands are buried in your insides."

She paled. "What do you mean, there's no curtain? Like, you have to…you have to see the…all the *stuff* and the…oh my God, *what do you mean, there's no curtain*?"

I shrugged. "There's no curtain. I've been watching YouTube videos to prepare myself. Childbirth is disgusting. There are so many *fluids*. Not to mention the placenta, which is an incredible organ. Once you have the baby, you then have to birth the placenta. And don't even get me started on vaginal tearing."

Another groan.

"New topic," Val declared. "If I have to think about my vagina getting blown inside out anymore, I'm gonna throw myself off the roof." She picked up her drink. "How's it going with Sparrow?"

I sighed. "In the week that she's been here, she's cleansed the house, worked on everyone's aura, and burned enough sage to make my eyes water when I walk in the house. Poor Theo can't figure out how to feed a vegan. Mom's been eating kale salad and pasta for every meal."

Rin laughed. "I can't believe she just showed up like that." When I gave her a look, she amended, "I mean, I can believe it. I'm just surprised that it actually happened."

"And she and your dad are getting divorced again?" Amelia asked.

"Apparently," I answered. "When I asked her what happened this time, she said their spirits were out of alignment. What the hell does that even mean?"

Val's brows drew together in thought. "Like, I know if your root chakra is out of alignment, it's supposed to knock all the others out, too. Maybe it's like that."

I groaned. "Not you, too."

"Listen, I'm not gonna lie, I want your mom to read my cards real bad," Val said.

"Reading tarot is more about cues from the person you're reading for and finding connections where there are none. There's nothing mystical about it," I countered.

"Couldn't you say that it's about reflection?" Rin asked. "You read the cards and see what you want to see, and that helps you frame up your current state rather than thinking about them actually telling the future."

I frowned. "I dislike that implication. It's not therapy. It's a deck of cards."

Val shrugged. "It's fun is what it is. The older we get, the less magic there is in the world. Like, remember how Christmas used to be so full of magic?"

"We celebrated the solstice," I said.

"Ugh, you are such a killjoy." Val's gaze swept the ceiling.

"So you're telling me it's better to be lied to as a child and find out that Santa was just a cruel story to make you behave and that your parents were the gift-bringers the whole time? That they fooled you all those years? You'd rather believe a lie than know the truth?" I pressed.

"If it's for a good cause, I don't see why not," Val said.

"And that's the difference between us," I said. "I don't want to be emotionally manipulated by a lie. I want the truth, no matter what. I don't want to believe in something that isn't founded in fact. *When the truth comes around, all the lies have to run and hide.*"

Amelia's eyes narrowed in thought. "Deepak?"

"Ice Cube."

A laugh burst out of Val. "*Reality is wrong. Dreams are for real.*"

"Tupac," I said.

"*Life without knowledge is death in disguise,*" Val challenged.

That one I really had to think about. "Talib Kweli."

"*I drop science like girls be dropping babies,*" Rin rapped.

"Ol' Dirty Bastard," I said on a laugh.

"Aren't there some things that can't be backed up in fact?" Amelia asked. "Like a gut reaction to something, something unexplained?"

My insides flinched. "Like love?" The question was pointed, almost accusatory.

"Sure."

"You know I don't believe in that."

"But you love us," Amelia argued.

"That feeling is built on years of you showing up and proving your loyalty. It's built on trust and mutual respect. Yes, I love you. But that word doesn't imply something that can't be explained. I could make you a graph if it would help."

"And how about Theo? Think you could love him?" It was as sly as Amelia ever got to ask me a question with a segue like that.

My lips flattened. "I care for Theodore very much."

"That isn't what I asked."

"Well, it's the best answer I have. Love isn't any more mystical than my mother's tarot cards."

"Fair enough," Val said. "But who's to say you won't love Theo like you love us? A relationship based on trust and respect?"

"Because I can't use that word in relation to a man. The implication is too much to stomach."

"What implication?" Val asked.

"That it will equate to marriage, which is a construct I refuse to subscribe to."

Amelia pouted.

"Don't look at me like that. You've met my parents."

"I think they're sweet," she said.

"Sweet? They've been married and divorced more times than Elizabeth Taylor. Except *to each other*. They even lived together when they were divorced. Anarchists."

"They're nonconformists, which means they're not without rules. They just have their *own* set of rules," Val said.

"Well, their rules make no sense, and I need my rules to make sense. Why get married if you don't think you're going to stay together? What's the point?" I asked.

"I don't know," Rin said. "But they're happy, aren't they? Isn't *that* the point?"

I sighed. "I don't know. It's nonsensical. I thought for a second that things might be different with Theo and me. That maybe I'd found what you guys have."

"Love?" Amelia asked hopefully.

"God, no. But that partnership, the meeting of my match. And really, I have, just not in the fairy tale way. In the practical way. That's the one good thing about my mom showing up. She reminded me of my rules and set me straight. Really, I should thank her."

Now, Amelia was pouting.

"I care for Theo, and I think he will continue to be the perfect partner. But love? Love is no more real than mood rings, and marriage is a trap that ends in divorce."

Amelia frowned, thumbing her wedding band. "I don't think that at all."

I softened, reaching for her hand. "You and Tommy…you're different. You love each other so much, you're getting married again in a few weeks, just because once wasn't enough."

"And the first time, it was fake," she added pointedly.

But I continued, "You two believe in the same kind of magic, so it works. For me…well, it's like an atheist trying to date a Lutheran. Doomed from the start. But Theodore and I are on the same page.

We're partners. We believe in logic and reason, not fairy tales. That's why we work so well together. It's all relative to who you're with and your belief systems. If all the things line up, your relationship will thrive and grow."

"And you and Theo are thriving and growing?" Rin asked.

I smiled. "We are. He just makes everything easier. And as uncomfortable as this pregnancy has made me, he's made the whole thing less scary. It doesn't seem so intimidating."

"God, I never even thought what it would be like if you were alone," Rin said.

"It would have been much, *much* harder," I answered. "I need a steady hand, and Theodore always has his extended, just waiting for me to need it."

The three of them smiled wistfully.

"He's perfect for you," Val said. "I knew someday, someone would come along and snag you, someone who just *got* you. Although, I'll admit, I didn't think he'd be that tall."

Laughter bubbled out of me. "Or that handsome. I was sure I'd end up with someone like Eagan."

"An asshole?" Val asked.

"An intellectual. I think it might actually be a genetic disposition to be smaller if you're smarter. Easier to route more blood to the brain," I joked.

"I mean, Theo's no plebeian," Amelia added.

"It's true," I said. "He's highly intelligent. I wonder sometimes what he would have become if he'd gone to college. But the truth is, he's resourceful, and no matter how he got there, he'd have been successful. He and Tommy owe it to street smarts. The school of hard knocks and all that."

"There's plenty to be said for that. Some people are just destined to be successful," Amelia said.

"I wouldn't call it destiny. I'd attribute it to experience and circumstance, amplified by the Banes' high testosterone output."

Val snorted a laugh.

"What? It makes them far more determined and aggressive in their goals and thrill-seeking."

"And in the bedroom," she added with an eyebrow waggle.

I smirked. "Yes. And that."

Amelia leaned in. "Is it weird to have sex when you're pregnant? I mean...a baby in the room is bad enough, but a baby in the *womb*?" Her little nose creased.

"She doesn't know what's happening, so I don't really think about it. Although, once she woke up, which was distracting. It's hard to concentrate when your fetus turns a complete circle in utero while you're getting nailed."

They grimaced, laughing off their discomfort.

Val's smile widened. "I want to know if it's weird sleeping with twins. Like, do you ever look at the other one and get turned on?"

Amelia and I simultaneously winced.

"They look nothing alike," I said flatly.

Rin and Val shared a look, but Amelia was nodding.

"Seriously," she said. "I don't even put them in the same stratosphere. Theo's so...well, he's so serious. And his smile is backward. And his hair is too short."

"Tommy looks like a savage. I really wish he'd shave his face," I said. "He'd never be on time if it weren't for you and Theodore. He couldn't even order his own groceries without Theo."

Amelia laughed. "That's true. He'd drive you crazy."

Rin and Val just shook their heads.

"You guys are so weird," Val said. "They are exact copies."

"Except they're not at all," I insisted. "Tommy is the king of the smash and grab, and Theodore is the voice of reason."

"Which is why Theo is perfect for you," Amelia noted again. "Maybe someday, you'll find yourself believing in magic."

"I don't need magic to be happy," I said. "I think I just need him."

"I'll drink to that." Val raised her glass. "To the men we need, even though we'd be damn fine without them."

And with a laugh and a clink of our glasses, we drank to that.

IT WAS AFTER EIGHT BY the time Amelia and I made it home, parting ways on the sidewalk.

I was ready for bed.

I didn't care that it was too early to sleep—I'd wake up at four in the morning, ready to party. All I wanted were pajamas and my bed and Theo. And not to be standing.

My feet were swollen and smooth, the bones in the top buried somewhere under my skin. I wanted my flats off. Maybe Theo would massage them. I liked when he massaged them very much.

Smiling, I entered the house. Sarah had already retired to her room, and I scanned the room, walking lightly so as not to draw the attention of my mother. She'd follow me around talking for an hour, and after spending the last two hours extroverting with my friends, I was done.

I snuck up the stairs, ears perked for signs of her but found none. Theo wasn't in the living room or kitchen like he usually was, and I frowned my disappointment.

I'd find him just as soon as I had on loungewear and my feet were free.

On my way to my bedroom, I paused, hearing the scoot of furniture in the baby's room.

My frown deepened.

I pushed the cracked door open.

My mother was hinged at the waist, dragging the changing table across the hardwood floor. The rug had been rolled up and propped in the corner, the crib pushed against the wrong wall, and the armchair was facing the wrong direction, just out of the way of whatever path she had the changing table on.

"What are you doing?" I shot.

She jumped, giggling as she fell back on her ass in surprise. "Katie, you scared the life out of me."

I scanned the bedlam. "*What are you doing?*" I asked again, trying to quiet the surge of irrational rage and violation.

"The energy in this room was all wrong, Katie-Bug. The chi was hitting walls and flying out the window, so I'm just putting everything where it belongs."

I unceremoniously dropped my bag in the hall, rushing into the room. "It belongs where I put it," I said, grabbing the changing table and throwing my weight behind it.

"But you don't want to put the crib that close to the window, or her energy will get sucked right out." She flung her hand from the top of her head toward said vortex window.

I pushed blindly at the stupid changing table, which was heavier than I remembered. Probably because Theo had moved it before.

His name climbed up my throat and stuck there. I swallowed it down with my inexplicable tears.

"Feng shui is not science, Mom."

"Maybe not to you, but it is to me," she said quietly as she stood. "I'm sorry, baby. I was just trying to help. Here, let me move it back."

I shrugged her off. "I've got it."

"Come on, Katie. Let me help," she said with aching kindness that did nothing but fan the frantic flame in my heart.

My control was lost, gone in a bang and a flash.

"No!" I cried, hot tears stinging my eyes as I let the changing table go and turned on her. "You're not helping, don't you see? But of course you don't see," I reminded myself. "You can see the future in a deck of cards, but you can't see how this would upset me. Do you know me at all? Do you understand me in any context? I want things the way *I* want them. Theo and I put these things where *we* wanted them, and you didn't even ask. You didn't ask a single question, just came in here and did. You *had* to know this would upset me, which makes you cruel. And if you didn't, you're just blind."

Angry tears rolled down my cheeks, not only for my frustration, but with guilt. She looked so small, her face bent in sadness and regret, as her shoulders curled in on themselves. She was cowed and cowering, and the apology written all over her only made the whole thing worse.

I felt him before I saw him, his presence behind me drawing the attention of every nerve in my body. When I turned to him, his face was tight with concern, his eyes scanning the room, my mother, and then me.

"I…I'm so sorry," Mom said, sniffling. "I wanted to surprise you, but I…you're right. I should have known. I'll put it all back just like it was," she promised.

I couldn't speak. All my energy was tied up in trying not to cry.

Theo's hand was on my arm, pulling me into his side.

"It's all right," he said even though it wasn't. Nothing was. "Just leave it where it is. I'll put it all back."

"No, it's my mess. I'll sort it out," she insisted, stepping toward us to shoo us out. "Go on. I'll make it right."

He nodded, guiding me out of the room. I was trembling, my knees unsteady, my lungs locked, my thoughts spinning. I couldn't understand why I was so upset, why I was hysterical over something so stupid as furniture. I felt unheard, misunderstood by the one person who was supposed to know me better than anyone.

But she never had heard me. She never did understand.

When we stepped into Theo's room, I forgot my mother instantly—what waited there shot my lungs open in a gasp.

The room was lit by glowing, golden light, filtered through the white sheets of a blanket fort. It was held in place by tethers stuck to the walls, the sheets draped in a feat of engineering, the interior strung with fairy lights. When I peered through the parted entrance, I found floor pillows and throw pillows and blankets laid out like a nest.

He kicked the bedroom door closed but didn't stop walking, steering me around the bed, toward the tent.

"How... what ... what is this?" I asked stupidly as he bent, ducking into the tent.

His hand reappeared from the entrance, seeking mine. "A blanket fort."

I slipped my fingers into his palm. "Well, I can see that, but... why the hell did you make a blanket fort?"

When I climbed in, my eyes widened. It was dreamy and cozy, more like a room than a temporary play tent. The lights were so soft, the textures and feathery lightness of the pillows swallowing me up. He was sitting with his long legs stretched out, his torso propped on one elbow. The other hand pulled me down to him.

"Well," he said, wrapping me in his arms, pulling me into his chest, "I ordered a pillow fort kit for the baby and was testing it out. I wanted to make sure I knew how to do it and that all the pieces were included. And that it was as epic as I imagined."

I looked up at the little lights, noticing a string of dangling pom-poms in a rainbow of colors wound through the lights. "You did this for the baby?"

"Mmhmm."

"But why? It'll be a year before she can enjoy it."

"Because I've decided I'm going to be the best dad ever, and who could earn that title without making a five-star blanket fort?"

I laughed, the sound muted through my stuffy nose. My tears hadn't ceased, they just weren't angry anymore. My throat closed up.

"It's perfect," I said quietly.

He held me to him, his hand shifting up and down my back through a silent moment.

"I'm sorry."

"Why are you apologizing? There's nothing to be sorry for."

"I'm irrational and emotional, and I was just cruel to my mother."

I could hear him smiling when he said, "You're pregnant, and your mom just overstepped. I can't imagine anyone would be rational and devoid of emotion. Especially with you and your mom."

"But that's the thing. She hasn't done anything wrong. She was only trying to help, and I was s-so mean to her. I don't want to be mean. I don't want to feel any of this," I blubbered, the words dissolving.

"Shh," he soothed. "Don't do that, Kate." The words were so tender, so gentle, that they only made me cry harder. "I mean it. I have never seen two people so different with the same genetic code."

"You and Tommy are nothing alike," I countered.

"Other than our looks, no we aren't, and you know it," he said on a laugh. "But we've got nothing on you and Sparrow."

I groaned, burrowing into his chest.

"Know what I think?" he asked.

"What?"

"She makes you feel out of control, and right now? Well, you're already there. She just cranks up the pressure cooker, and you blew. It was bound to happen. Honestly, I'm surprised it took this long. Last night, when she pulled out her crystals at dinner and started telling my mom how they could help cure her Parkinson's, I thought that was it. I was ready to grab you by the waist and haul you out of the room if you climbed over the dinner table to throttle her."

Another laugh against the ache in my chest.

"She doesn't mean to hurt you. Not that she couldn't try a little harder or maybe pull her head out of her ass long enough to realize how you feel. But she doesn't mean to upset you. You know that, right?"

I sighed. "I do know." I moved to push myself up. "I need to go say I'm sorry."

But he squeezed me tighter, holding me to him. "Shh, just stay here for a minute." When I was settled back into his chest, he said, "Don't beat yourself up. The construct of her universe is founded in things you don't believe in. And your world view is based in the exact opposite—fact, not faith."

The ache warmed. "We were talking about that tonight," I said into his chest, closing my eyes, sinking into him.

"About what?"

"Compatibility. About finding someone who subscribes to the same dreams and constructs as you do. It's why Tommy and I would never work, but you and I are in perfect sync."

"While we're on the topic, I'd like to note for the record that I'd like to take a pair of scissors to your *Team Tommy* shirt and throw it in the garbage."

I leaned back, smirking at him. "You aren't jealous, are you?"

He slipped his thigh between mine, his hand finding my belly. "This is mine. *You* are mine. The last thing I want is another man's name on your body. Especially not my fucking brother's."

I chuckled, cupping his jaw, marveling over the flickering desire and possession in his voice, in his words. I should have been offended—I was no one's but my own. But I wasn't offended at all. I wanted to be his. I wanted him to own me with the respect and care he'd always shown me.

I wanted to be his, and I wanted him to be mine.

There under the fairy lights, in the blanket fort he'd made for our unborn child, I felt peace and safety I'd never known before. I hadn't even known it was possible.

And I didn't want it to end. Not ever. I wanted to live in that moment forever and ever, safe and secure there in his arms where no one could touch me.

"I wish it could be like this forever," I said softly, breathing the words, giving them life. Forever was what I wanted, and I wanted it with him. Just like this.

"It can," he said. "It will, Kate. I promise you that."

And he sealed the promise with a kiss.

FOREVER AND EVER, AMEN

THEO

22 WEEKS, 6 DAYS

F orever.

  She'd said the word last night in the tent. And I'd promised her I'd make it so.

I stood with my palms on the glass top of the case, surrounded by twinkling diamonds. I'd worried when I walked into the jeweler's that I wouldn't be able to find one she'd like. That somehow, as well as I thought I knew her, I wouldn't be able to find a ring that would suit her. It had to be exactly right—not too big, not too flashy. Nothing that would be heavy or catch on things, but nothing too simple either. It had to embody *her*, the mix of direct simplicity and beautiful complexity of Kate herself.

I'd circled the room, hands in my pockets, peering into the cases,

And then I saw it.

Delicate, simple, the band of gold set with a marquise diamond that was small enough to be dainty but large enough to shine with all the brilliance I found in her. The wedding band was actually two pieces, pointed in the centers to frame the diamond, the bands lined with tiny diamonds of their own.

Three pieces. Three of us. Me, Katherine, and our baby.

For weeks, I'd considered this, weighed out this next step, the big step. I'd played it out in five steps, calculated the outcomes with precision. I'd give her the ring. Ask her the question.

If she said yes, well, that one was easy.

If she said no? Things would get complicated.

We'd never even discussed marriage, not really, and we hadn't said the word love aloud. But I knew her, even by her own admission. I knew she loved me. And that would be enough for me.

But it didn't hurt to ask.

As long as she loved me, I could take no for an answer. I just hoped I wouldn't have to.

She'd noted once that I knew what she needed before she needed it, and this was just another case in point. We were a match, and I didn't believe there was a single thing life threw at us that we couldn't handle. If we'd survived all we'd been handed so far, we could survive anything. I'd happily spend the rest of my days making sure *she* was happy. Because my reward was her. It was my family. It was my child and our future.

Katherine had asked me for forever, and that was something I could provide.

Something I'd do anything to provide.

And all I had to do was ask.

KATHERINE

I trotted down the stairs with a smile on my face, looking for my mother.

Theo had left me that morning, sated and calm and more peaceful than I'd been in what felt like forever. Honestly, it might have been *ever*.

We were on the same page, exactly and perfectly. Forever was here. We had arrived.

And the peace and comfort that knowledge gave me was beyond measure.

By the time I'd come out of Theo's room last night, looking for my mom, she had retreated to her room, the baby's room put back exactly as it had been, exactly as promised. My guilt had plagued me to nearly knocking on her door—a boundary I was typically hard-pressed to breach—but I'd caught myself, heading back to my bedroom where Theo waited for me, shirtless and reading a book about the Roman conquest of Egypt.

This morning, I was glad for the time, thankful for the reset of sleep. For the first time in a long time, I felt like everything was going to be okay. Better than okay.

It was hope, alive and thrumming in my heart.

"Mom?" I called, rounding the corner into the living room.

But she was nowhere in the common space. Around another corner and to her room I went, pausing outside her door. Fleetwood Mac played softly in the room, the scent of incense drifting under the door and into the hallway.

I took a breath and knocked.

"Come in," she called through the door, and after smoothing my skirt, I reached for the doorknob and did just that.

She sat on her bed, looking forlorn, her Mucha tarot deck in hand and cards laid out on her comforter. She offered a small smile.

"Hey, Katie," she said softly.

"Hi, Mom," I answered, closing the door behind me. I moved to the bed, sitting on the very edge so as not to disturb her cards.

"How'd you sleep, honey?"

I hated that she'd asked about me when I'd been so awful to her. "Fine, thank you. I looked for you last night, but you'd already gone to bed."

"I just felt so awful, Katie. Once I set the room right, I took a long bath and thought about what you said."

"I shouldn't have said so much. You were only trying to help, and I was ungrateful and hurtful. I'm sorry, Mom."

But she shook her head, setting her cards down. "No, it's me who's sorry. You were right—I had no right to move things around, and I can't seem to foresee when I'm going to do the wrong thing. It's just that I convince myself time and time again that I know what's best for you, and that if I can just show you, you'll see. I try to bend you, but I wind up breaking you instead." She sighed, straightening the deck with her eyes on her hands. "If I'd really thought about it, I'd have known. But I was so sure of myself that I didn't."

"Mom…"

"Forgive me, honey. I…I'm going to try harder. I promise."

"Of course I forgive you," I said. "Will you forgive me?"

"For what? You didn't do anything but put me in my place, which I think I needed."

"I was irrational and cruel. I know you were trying to help."

"Well, best-laid plans of mice and men. No matter what we plan for, there's always a chance it'll go wrong. A good chance, I'd say."

I chuckled. "A good perspective to keep in mind. My interview for the research position is today."

At that, she lit up. "Well, that explains the cards. The deck says you've got good things coming. The Empress is abundance, the nine of cups is a wish coming true, the ace of pentacles says an opportunity is coming. I think today is going to be lucky for you."

I sighed, but I found myself still smiling, if for nothing more than she believed in me. "We'll see how it rounds out. Have you heard from Dad?"

Her smile faltered, something about her shifting incrementally into sadness. "Yes, he's called a few times. But I haven't answered."

"What happened? You never told me."

"Well, Katie...for a long time, I felt like a ghost. He didn't see me even though we were together all the time. It was like we were nothing more than roommates, without passion, without fire or spark. Just...complacent. It wasn't one thing or another, just a drifting. I couldn't seem to find him anymore. I was invisible. So I made myself disappear."

I watched her as she tried to smile, then as she picked up her cards and placed them on top of the deck.

"I'm sorry," I said, meaning it.

"Oh, it's all right. Sometimes, when we're together a long while, you take the one you love for granted. Learn from my mistakes and make sure Theo knows you care."

I nodded. "That's excellent advice. I struggle with how to show him. He's a minimalist—there's nothing he wants that isn't functional, and if he needs a thing, he buys it. But he does so much for me, every day, always. I don't want him to feel neglected, not when I appreciate him so much."

"Well, I think everyone feels appreciated in different ways. Him anticipating your needs speaks to you, though I don't think he's overly conscious of it. It seems latent. Maybe it's the same for you. Maybe you're already doing what he needs without realizing it."

"Maybe, but I'd still like to show it."

Mom smiled. "I think if Theo needs something from you, he'll ask you for it. Then all you'll have to do is say yes."

I tried to imagine what he could possibly ask of me. To wear negligee he'd bought me perhaps. To wear my red lipstick. To sit with him while he read or to maybe take a weekend trip together. I'd say yes to any of that and more.

I couldn't imagine saying no to anything he asked. He'd gotten me agree to move in with him, which was something I never thought I'd do. He'd gotten me to slip into a relationship, one I didn't want to end. I hoped it wouldn't.

He'd promised me last night that it would be just like this forever.

And I believed him without question.

COMING UP ROSES

KATHERINE

24 WEEKS, 2 DAYS

I sat in the chair in Stephanie's office, wondering if I'd actually heard her right.

"I was very impressed by your work on the inmate outreach committee, and despite Eagan's concerns, I found you to be our best candidate for the research position. Congratulations."

"Thank you," I said, unable to say anything more.

I'd been waiting for nearly two weeks for the announcement, and I'd been sure I wouldn't get it. Eagan's campaign had been a massive pain in my ass. He'd tried to set me up no less than half a dozen times, sabotaging me at every opportunity.

Fortunately, I was much smarter than him. He had no stealth, so conspicuous, I'd have had to be an idiot not to catch him. I carried a RFID wand with me as a rule, checking and double-checking my shelves to make sure they were in alignment. I made quick work of every cart I filled, sidestepping his hurdles, addressing every patron he'd sent to find me—even the tedious ones—with expedience. He'd been hoping to slow me down. What he should have known was that I was always a step ahead of him.

I stayed a little late, showed up a little early. Made my presence known in the committee, which I found I enjoyed far more than I'd thought I would.

And it had paid off.

I smiled, realizing fully that I'd done it. I'd gotten the promotion. And if anything happened with me and Theo, I'd be all right. I could survive on my own.

It seemed almost unnecessary now that we were together, a precaution I'd hopefully never need to invoke. But I was proud of my efforts, proud that I'd overcome the challenges placed before me.

More than anything, though—I was damn near giddy to have beaten Eagan.

"You should have plenty of time to get through training before you take your maternity leave. The timing will be perfect. We'll have a new page trained in your place, and you'll shadow Francine until you're gone. We'll start you full-time when you get back."

My smile widened. Francine was one of my favorite researchers. I didn't think I'd ever heard her make a joke.

"Thank you so much, Stephanie. I won't let you down."

"I know," she said with a smile of her own as she stood, extending her hand. "It's why I hired you."

I gave it a shake, and when we parted ways, I floated down the hall toward circulation like a balloon, looking like I'd swallowed one.

Phone in hand, I texted Theo.

I got the job!

Little dots bounced as he typed back. *I knew you would. Congrats, Kate. Can I bring you lunch and a kiss to celebrate?*

That would be the best celebration I could imagine.

Good. Rub it in Egghead's face yet?

I smiled down at my phone. *Not yet. Looking for him now.*

Tell him I said hi before you ruin his life.

Deal. See you in a bit.

You sure will. Never had a doubt in you, Kate.

My chest was hot and tingly and full of joy. *Thank you. You're my favorite, you know that?*

Ditto. Kissing you in two hours.

Hurry up.

I slipped my phone back into my bag, rounding the corner into the circulation room. I'd miss it in here, the solitude, the order of it all. But it was an advancement, one that would be good for my career and one that would get me far away from Eagan.

I found him scowling at a cart, loading it with more force than was necessary. The books hit the metal with a thump and a clang.

"What's the matter?" I asked innocently. "Arms sore from all that wallowing?"

He shot me a glare. "I can't believe you got the job."

"I don't know why you're surprised. I mean, aside from that I made it through your harassment."

Eagan huffed, grabbing another stack off the shelf. "Now you're going to be gone. You'll be in the research department every day."

I made a face. "You did all this so I'd stay in circulation?"

When he turned to me, it was with an exasperated expression on his face. "Honestly, Katherine, are you such a robot that you can't see that I like you? I've asked you out. Multiple times."

I frowned. "You're a creepy perv. I didn't think you actually meant it beyond trying to sleep with me. Even though I'm pregnant. Hence the creepy pervness."

"Of course I want to sleep with you. You're hot, even pregnant."

"Thanks," I said flatly.

"Whatever," he scoffed, plunking another stack on his cart. "I thought we'd be a good match."

"I live with my boyfriend."

"I know."

"Who impregnated me."

"I know!"

I paused, watching him rage-load the cart. "You are an odd little man."

"I've had a thing for you for years, Katherine. You're just too weird to even see it. So have fun with Francine in research. And good luck with your *boyfriend*."

"He said to tell you hi, by the way."

Eagan groaned.

"You should have just asked me out. You know, before this." I gestured to my stomach.

He slowed, glancing at me hopefully. "Would you have said yes?"

"No, but at least then it wouldn't have turned you into a megalomaniac."

Another groan. "Bye, Katherine," he said, pushing his cart away in a rush.

"You didn't load the bottom shelf," I called after him.

He flipped me off over his shoulder.

I sighed, though I found myself smiling. Things were working out, looking up, coming up roses. My life seemed to be aligning in the most wonderful and hopeful of ways.

And there was nothing that could get me down.

THE SAME PAGE

THEO

26 WEEKS, 6 DAYS

Everything about the night was perfect.

Tommy and Amelia's wedding—their *real* wedding—was short and sweet and beautiful. I stood at my brother's side for the second time as he promised her forever, this time fully intending to do it. Truth be told, I thought he'd meant it the first time without realizing, that night a marker, a beginning none of us had fully comprehended. But we'd felt it then.

This time was even better. This time, we all knew the truth.

Their love was beyond us all.

My throat closed up when Tommy's voice broke during his vows, as he spoke of all the ways she saved him, all the ways he loved her. And my eyes found Katherine's where she stood behind Amelia, clutching a bouquet over the swell of her stomach. Her eyes shone. *She* shone, lit from the inside, her skin luminous, pale against her dark hair but for the flush of her cheeks and the red of her lips.

God, how I loved her. Tonight I would tell her.

And I'd make her mine, permanently and legally.

The ring box in my pocket whispered to me like it had been for the weeks I'd been carrying it around, waiting for the right time, the right moment. I'd told no one, the secret mine, guarded with the tenacity of the Queen's guard over the crown jewels. No one would know until she knew.

And tonight was the night.

The hyperawareness of her aversion to surprises had been niggling at me since I walked into the jeweler. But she'd wished aloud for us to be like this forever, and I'd promised her it would.

The ring in my pocket would just make it official.

I wanted to share my future with her. I wanted to give her my name. I wanted to say I do, and I wanted to hear the words from her lips. I wanted her to know I'd never love anyone else.

And I hoped beyond hope that she felt the same.

Dinner had just finished, the plates cleared and the music started. The first dances came and went, and we watched as Tommy spun Amelia all over the dance floor like a pro, the light on their faces contagious, shining on everyone in the room and filling them up with light, too. And then the dance floor opened up, calling us all to join them.

So we did.

Katherine's hair was up, twisted and curled and pinned elegantly to reveal her long neck. The bridesmaid dresses were muted neutrals, dove grays and soft shades of champagne in varying styles, all of them Grecian. And Katherine looked like a goddess. Layers of chiffon draped artfully over her shoulders, hung over her stomach, sweeping the parquet with levity that made her look as if she were hovering a few inches over the ground.

Never in my life had I seen anything so lovely.

I spun her around, reveling in her laughter as I pulled her back into my arms. I held her as close as I could, wishing I could bring her flush to me. I wanted to feel the press of her body against mine, but the baby was in the way.

So I took what I could get, any way I could get it.

Her smile was open, wide and free. Here in my arms was my Kate. My forever.

The transformation in her went far beyond her growing belly. She had become Kate, fully and completely, relaxing into us. Leaning in. Smiles came easier, her laughter won sometimes with little more than a glance. Everything about her had softened with her trust in me and her faith in us.

She'd finally committed to me. And it was time I officially committed to her.

Katherine smiled up at me. "What?"

"What, what?"

A chuckle. "You have a look on your face like you want to say something."

My heart flipped. "Oh, I have things to say, Kate. So many things."

But instead of speaking them, I kissed her smiling lips.

She sighed. "Tonight has been absolutely perfect."

"I was just thinking that."

"Everything. This venue. The food. The ceremony and the party. This suit on you."

"This dress on you," I added, thumbing the creamy chiffon tie of her dress.

"It just feels right," she said. "Such a strange thing to feel, that there's a deep and unexplainable *rightness* to things. I wonder what that is," she mused. "The shared experience—collective effervescence, it's called—of so many people in one place? I read a study once that compared the feeling of exaltation when you go to church to the same way you feel at Comic-Con or a concert. It's the collective experience, but it affects us all differently, personally, so we feel that we're singularly experiencing the sensation."

"Or maybe it's just *right*."

She smiled. "Well, that would imply a fatalist quality to things."

"You don't think there could be other forces at work? Scientific forces?"

"I've never seen math on fate," she joked.

"What if—follow me here for a minute, Kate—what if the universe is a big machine, one that's been rolling and turning its cogs for billions of years? And we're this tiny, little piece of this big machine, and each piece inside has its own trajectory. And what if there *was* an order to things, and if our little brains could fathom it, if we could actually grasp the math, we could see the path for each piece? What if certain pieces were drawn together using chemical reactions, like the connection of hydrogen and oxygen to make water? Fate doesn't have to mean there's a conscious being guiding those pieces. It could just be our best explanation for physics we can't possibly understand."

Her pretty face was touched with amusement and connection. "That is a theory I'd like to read more about."

Amelia materialized beside us, looking sheepish. "I'm sorry to interrupt, but I need a hand in the ladies'. I love this dress, but needing three people to help me pee is the worst."

"I'll be right back," Katherine promised, hitching up on her tiptoes as she stretched for a kiss, which I provided.

I sighed happily, slipping my hands in my pockets as I watched them go. My fingers closed over the ring box and turned it around, testing the corners.

Tommy stepped up next to me, my duplicate in almost all ways, including his pose. Our eyes were still following them.

"I'm the luckiest guy in the world," he said with a lovesick smile on his face. "How I ever convinced her to love me, I'll never know."

"Well, when you're not being a pain in the ass, you're pretty lovable."

"Flatterer," he said with a smirk.

"You've met your match."

"I have," he said quietly.

"And I think I've met mine, too."

He stilled but for his face, which turned to me.

"I know it's crazy, but I love her. I've never…I just didn't even know it was possible to feel like I do. I'd take a fucking bullet for her. I'd wither away and turn to dust without her. She's it. This is it."

He watched me for a protracted moment. "I don't think it's crazy at all."

It was my turn to lay a look on him. "What, no quip? No warning?"

"If it were me before Amelia, I'd have told you you should get your head checked. But now that I know? Theo, if she's it, then go get her. Look at me. Have you ever seen me this happy?"

"Never," I admitted.

"And it's because of her. I didn't know how miserable I was until she got caught up in my life. Until she saved me from myself. I want that for you. I want you to be this happy. I want you to have what I have. I knew from the second I saw you and Katherine together that this was it. You found her, Theo. Do whatever you have to do to keep her."

I nodded, swallowing hard. "Tonight. I've been waiting for weeks, and I don't want to wait a minute longer."

He clapped me on the shoulder, his face alight as he pulled me into a hug.

"Then don't. Go get your girl."

KATHERINE

Val giggled, losing her balance in the bathroom stall as Amelia peed.

Rin, Val, and I held armfuls of tulle and chiffon with Amelia's face in the middle, so much fabric that we couldn't see around it.

"This dress is ridiculous," Amelia said shortly as she finished up.

"It's gorgeous," Rin amended.

"Gorgeous and ridiculous." The toilet flushed somewhere beyond the layers of white fabric.

She sighed and stood, and we shimmied out of the stall, Val scanning the room to make sure it was empty before an unprepared guest accidentally saw her ass.

Once in the safety of the space in front of the sinks, we helped set her to rights.

"God, Amelia, everything has just been perfect," Rin said with a wistful smile.

Amelia smiled. "You're next."

Rin laughed. "I'm not in any hurry. In fact, I bet Val will be before me. I told Court two years, and I meant it."

Val snorted a laugh. "If Sam and I get married before you and Court, you and me are going to have a sit-down. Court's waiting on you, you know."

"I do know, and he'll keep waiting until I'm sure he's not going to club me over the head and drag me back to his cave."

Amelia gasped. "Oh my gosh—you should have a double wedding like in a Jane Austen novel."

One of Val's eyebrows rose. "Would you have wanted to share your wedding day with one of us?"

She laughed. "Fair point."

"Anyway," Val started, "who knows? Maybe it'll be Katherine and Theo next."

It was my turn to laugh. "Theo and I are perfectly happy exactly as we are. He knows I don't believe in marriage. We're partners. We're committed. We don't need the party and the ring and the name change."

"You have to admit, the party and the ring and the name change are appealing," Val said.

I shrugged. "It makes me more uncomfortable than anything."

"Okay, what about the tax break?" Rin asked.

"Now, *that* I can understand," I answered.

"You two look so happy." Amelia beamed. "Wedding or no wedding, I'm glad you found him. I'm glad you found each other."

"Me too." I beamed back.

She straightened herself up in the mirror, and we talked and laughed as we walked out of the bathroom together.

Effervescent. It was the perfect word to describe how I felt, like fizzy, floating bubbles and sparkling joy. It was an effect of the psyche, I knew. But I didn't care.

It felt too good to question.

Theo and Tommy stood side by side at the edge of the dance floor like they'd been waiting for us, twin sentinels in midnight suits, hands hooked in their pockets and matching expressions of joy when they saw us. And without forethought, I found myself in his arms.

He kissed me tenderly, and before I knew it, my hand was in his. I thought we would head for the dance floor, but instead, he towed me toward the garden.

I didn't ask why, didn't wonder what we were doing, just blissfully followed him.

I'd follow him anywhere.

It was quiet outside the tent, the music and laughter far away. The night was warm and cloudless, the garden lush and green, dotted with low lights. Past a fountain we went and into an alcove of vines and wisteria.

And there we stopped. We said nothing. He turned to face me, the adoration and reverence on his face filling me with a surge of that feeling. The rightness. It was everywhere—skating across our skin, zipping in the air between us, filling our lungs and transferred in our breaths. He kissed me, kissed me with a deep longing, a hundred promises, a thousand wishes.

He kissed me until I was breathless and boneless, my self quiet and my body alive.

"When I met you, I never thought we'd end up here," I mused, my hands skimming the lapels of his suit.

"Making out in a garden?" he asked with a sideways smile. The Look was on his face, but something about it was deeper. Different.

"Oh, I might have guessed that, but not that I was pregnant. And not that you would become my partner." I searched his eyes. "I'm so happy I found you. I'm so thankful for you, for the way you understand me. I just … I'm so happy, Theo. And it's all because of you."

"Really? Because I think it's because of you."

"Why?" I asked with a laugh. "For incubating our baby?"

He pulled me closer, his smile shining on me like the sun, warming me all over. "Among other things."

"Kiss me," I whispered with a smile I only granted to him.

So he did. He kissed me softly, a tender exchange, touched with veiled intention that sparked my curiosity.

Theo broke the kiss to gaze into my face with adoration. "Remember when you wished it could be like this forever?"

"I do," I said with a smile.

"Is that still what you want?"

"More than ever."

"Good. Then I have something to ask you."

My smile slid off my face as he dropped to one knee. His hand disappeared into his pocket, returning with a little velvet box, which he opened with a creak. And on a bed of white satin sat a band of gold adorned with a sparkling diamond, shining with moonlight.

His face, his beautiful face was turned up to mine under the soft light of the moon.

"Theo, what are you doing?" I breathed, panicked.

"Asking you to marry me. Because all I'll ever want is you."

The ring blinked at me. I blinked at it.

Shock, cold and sharp, ripped through me. Everything I'd thought I knew, everything I'd thought we were, came to a halt, the brakes slamming with all their force. But the contents of the car kept moving, flying into the windshield, testing the limits of the seatbelts, leaving bruises and broken bones that I had the horrible realization would never heal.

The construct of my life and my future came crumbling and tumbling and rumbling to the ground of my heart.

I dug through my thoughts with frantic hands, trying to find something, anything to make sense of what he was asking. For months, he had challenged my beliefs until the boundaries were confused and the fences weak. But on the proposition on his lips, I realized with shattering certainty that I hadn't abandoned them.

I'd built my life inside of them, and they wouldn't be breached so easily, so quickly.

Of all the people in all the world, I'd thought he was the only one who understood me. All this time, I'd thought we were on the same page. But the ring in his hand and the look on his face told me we weren't. I had been grossly misunderstood.

I had never considered marriage. I had never spoken the word *love*. I wanted him, wanted to be with him forever if he'd have me. But not like this.

Anything but this.

I couldn't make snap decisions. I wasn't capable. Especially when it came to something of this magnitude.

In that moment, without the comfort of warning, without the time to consider what he was asking, there was only one thing I could do.

Default to the relationship construct I'd stood upon my entire life.

"But…Theo, I…I don't believe in marriage. I told you in the beginning."

The flicker of fear on his face gutted me. "You were serious?"

"You've met my mother, and you know me better than I know myself. Whenever am I not serious? I…I don't know how…I can't…"

Panic, caustic and bitter, buckled my knees.

Before I knew I was falling, I was in his arms. He helped me to a concrete bench where I sat with tingling hands.

"Breathe, Kate."

I drew a loud, deliberate breath through my nose and held it.

"Let it out," he commanded.

So I did. "I…I'm sorry. I was unprepared for that question."

A loud sigh of his own, the hurt in his voice clear as he said, "I should have known better than to surprise you. You hate surprises. I justified this to myself so far that I was convinced this was what you wanted. I love you, Kate."

Love. The word knocked the wind out of me, tilted the horizon. I leaned into him so I wouldn't fall.

"I thought we were on the same page," I said half to myself, the words quiet and mournful. "I thought you understood."

He shifted, moving to kneel before me again, taking my hands in his. "I'm sorry. I'm sorry to have caught you unaware. But from the second I met you, I have loved you. I didn't understand how or why… at the time, I didn't realize what it even was. And once I figured it out, there was only one thing to do. This." He looked down at my hands, thumbing my left hand, third finger. "I've only ever wanted two things in this life—to be the father I never had and to be a husband to a woman I love. Then I met you. And now my dreams are all right here in front of me." He shook his head, raised his gaze, met my eyes. "I can let go of marriage if you love me. I can do anything if you love me."

A succession of words, letters strung together to make sounds. A paragraph. A question.

And everything changed.

He'd impressed his boundaries on me, and now that I knew, I had to respect them—I had no choice. He had always respected mine. Had I known his, I would have done the same.

With the truth, I would break his heart.

I would break my own heart.

"Theo…" I whispered his name, and he knew. I saw the tear of his soul in two syllables.

A pause, thick with a truth neither of us wanted to acknowledge. "You don't love me." Cold. Distant. Broken.

My throat closed, stinging and hot. "I've never felt like this about anyone."

"But you don't love me." His face was stone. The words were miles away.

"I don't believe in love," I said, begging him to understand. "And I can't promise you something I don't believe in."

He let go of my hands and stood, blocking the moon, casting me in his shadow. The moonlight threw a halo around him like an angel.

"If you don't love me, there's nothing left to say. If there's no hope that we can be anything beyond a set of rules and a baby, then we've reached an impasse. If there's nowhere to go but here, I won't be satisfied. I love you, Kate. I've done all I can to prove that love. I've given you everything, and gladly, because I thought we were moving in the same direction. But you stopped, and I kept going."

My hands found each other, twisting together like the twist in my chest. "I thought you knew. I'm sorry. I'm so sorry." The word choked off, my tears rolling down my cheeks, my chest split and burning. "I don't want to be without you."

"I don't either," he said, his voice low and trembling. "I haven't asked you for a single thing but this—to love me. And this, I can't let go."

This was what he wanted—to break up. I couldn't say the words he needed to hear, but I could respect this. I could give him this even if it killed me.

Val ran up, smiling and panting and completely unaware. "God, there you are! Come on, they're leaving! We need to go light sparklers!"

She snagged my hand and ran, pulling me behind her. And when I looked back, there he stood in the moonlight, watching me leave.

And I knew then that our forever wasn't the one I'd envisioned.

It was one I'd never imagined.

One without him.

THIRD
TRIMESTER

THE END OF THAT

THEO

27 WEEKS, 1 DAY, 12:01

The cab was silent as a tomb.

Katherine sat close enough to touch, her face turned to the window and her hands clasped in her lap.

She should have been in my arms. She should have been smiling instead of crying. She should have had my ring on her finger.

But none of those things were true. And our reality had shifted into a place I didn't understand and had no patience for.

A matter of inches separated us. But it was a chasm, a yawning, empty space with nothing but wind and broken dreams.

I'd never been one for frivolous dreams. Tommy was the one with the wild imagination. I was the one who relied on the tangible, the fact. I'd thought Katherine and I were a fact, a solid truth. I'd thought we were on the same page. But what I'd thought was a step, she'd thought was the pinnacle. We'd reached the top for her, and as

I looked up that staircase to the future I wanted, I found I couldn't let it go.

So I had to let her go.

I tried to reject the thought, the impossibility of it staggering. But facts were facts.

I needed her love, and she didn't love me.

And that was the end of that.

The taxi pulled up to the house, and silently, we exited. Through the front door, into the dark house. Up the stairs and into our living room. My living room.

She stopped, turned to face me, stood in the middle of the room in that beautiful dress, swollen with my child, my heart in her palm and tears in her eyes. "Theo, I'm sorry. I wish I'd known what you needed."

My chest, my shoulders, rose and fell with a weighted, definitive breath. "I thought it was clear, Katherine. This was never casual for me."

"It wasn't for me either," she said quietly, shining tears on her cheeks. "This was why I didn't want to see you this way. Because I knew either I would hurt you or you would hurt me. I knew it would fall apart. I knew we would end up here, and now, it's happened." She shook her head, her eyes cast down. "I should have stayed away."

"I'd argue that this was probably inevitable. And I'm not sorry we tried. I'm only sorry I failed."

"You didn't fail."

"Are you sure about that? This was what I wanted. It was what I've always wanted from you, from the first second I kissed you."

"But I can't give that to you. I-I told you," she said through a sob.

"I should have listened," I said, my voice rough. "But I thought I knew better. That'll teach me." I turned for my room, more exhausted than I'd ever been.

"What do we do now?"

I glanced back at her over my shoulder. "You don't have to do anything. It's me who has to figure out how to stop loving you."

And I walked away with no hope that I actually could.

IMPASSABLE

KATHERINE

28 WEEKS, 1 DAY

Pity was written all over Amelia's face, and misery was written all over mine.

It had been a week since the wedding. Since the end.

Theo and I had barely spoken beyond the bare minimum required to share living space. Meals had been prepared in advance of dinner, but he hadn't graced the dinner table, citing work. He'd stayed gone, stayed away.

I was miserable. And when he was home, it was unbearable.

Neither of us had brought up *us*. We hadn't been in the room together long enough to even try.

Amelia had come up almost the second that she and Tommy came home from their honeymoon, and she'd listened with wide eyes as I recounted the whole horrible happening to her.

"I... I can't believe he just asked you like that," she said. "Had you guys ever even talked about marriage?"

"Only on the day I told him I was pregnant. And we joked about it then. Seems neither of us knew the other was serious."

"What are you going to do?" she asked gently.

"I don't know," I answered, casting my gaze to my hands in my lap. "I don't know that there's anything we can do. We want different things. For the first time, we're out of alignment. Or maybe we were out of alignment the whole time and just didn't know."

"I can't believe this. I can't believe you found each other and want each other and aren't together."

"We're fundamentally different in the one place it matters the most. His idea of relationships is founded in love and marriage. Mine is founded in partnership, not passion. I can't say things I don't mean or step into a construct I don't believe in just because I want to be with him. And he can't abandon the idea of love and marriage for me. He needs a promise I can't give him. He's given me this boundary, and I have to respect it. There's nothing I can do."

She pressed her palm to her chest, her eyes wide and shining. "That breaks my heart."

I nodded, swallowing tears of my own. "It breaks mine, too." With a deep breath, I said, "But that doesn't change the fact that we're having a baby. We have to find a way to be partners again, to put our feelings away so we can do what needs to be done. So, I have to talk to him. This is all my fault. I knew this would happen. I knew I'd hurt him. I knew I'd get hurt. This was everything I was afraid of."

"Do you really think you could have stopped it? Do you think you could have stayed away?"

Another sigh, my ribs tight and aching. "No."

"Well," Amelia started, "I know you'll figure it out. And I know you doubt the possibility, but I hope you find a middle ground. You found each other, and losing each other like this is just so unfair."

I tried to smile, the gesture thin. "Thank you," I answered without hope. "How was Tahiti?"

She brightened up. "Oh, it was beautiful and relaxing and perfect. All we did was lie around in the sun, eat, and nap for a week."

"And bone."

She laughed. "Yes, and bone."

I found myself truly smiling for the first time in a week. "The wedding was beautiful. I'm so happy for you and Tommy."

"Thank you. And … well, I have other news, too," she said, her cheeks pink and eyes bright. "I'm pregnant."

My lungs shot open in a gasp, my hand flying to my mouth. "Oh my God!" I flung myself at her, wrapping her in my arms in an uncharacteristically emotive gesture fueled by my ache for touch, my relief in not being alone in my pregnancy, my happiness for her and Tommy, my inability to contain my emotions.

She laughed, catching me. "We'll have baby Banes just a few months apart."

I leaned back, beaming. "I didn't even know you were trying."

"I just got off birth control last month."

"Those Banes and their high testosterone," I said with a shake of my head. "So virile."

"So very virile. Apparently, they can get a girl pregnant with a well-placed glance."

"Well, I assume Tommy has The Look, same as Theo. I don't know that anyone could escape a look like that."

"Oh, he has it. We were doomed from the start," she said on a laugh that died in her throat. She reached for my hand. "I hate this."

"So do I. But we'll figure it out. Theo and I work well together and are pragmatic enough to sort this out. I think … I think, once we do, we'll be very good friends."

"What if you can't be friends?"

A flash of pain shot through my chest. "Then we'll have to separate." The tickle in my nose stung. "I hope it doesn't come to that."

"Me too," she said with the saddest look on her face.

"I'm going to talk to him tonight. He's been avoiding me all week. I might have to camp out in front of his bedroom door to pin him down, but I've got a book and a floor pillow and all the time in the world."

"Can we meet for lunch tomorrow? Or, if you want, call me tonight and come up. I'm here for you."

"I know. Thank you. I'll be all right, but lunch tomorrow would be nice. I'll text you tonight anyway. I know how you worry."

"I do," she agreed. "I just…I want you to be happy, and I hate that you're not. I was sure you and Theo were *it*. You're so well suited."

"I thought so, too. The hardest part is, as much as I hate it, I understand. His father leaving made him wish for a nuclear family. I can't argue with that."

"And your parents being flaky made you want to avoid love and marriage completely. I don't think he can argue with that either."

"Oh, he can. He was right. He hasn't asked me for one thing, except this. And this is the one thing I don't know how to give him. I *can't* give. I don't understand love. All I know is that I want to be with him."

"Couldn't that be considered love?"

"Not in the way he means it. I just…I wish we could have taken it one day at a time, one week at a time, a month, then a year. I wish I'd known how he felt. When you were little, you dreamed about your wedding day, your babies, of finding a man who would love you. But when I was little, I dreamed about being alone. About being self-reliant because my parents were not. They needed me, and they took without replenishing what they'd stolen. They were codependent when they were together and even when they were apart. Even the idea of marriage is tainted by their constant state of flux. When they split up, we all still lived together. Do you know how many 'aunts' and 'uncles' I saw shame-walking out of the house in the morning? That's not commitment." I shook my head. "I know it's not like that for everyone. I know you and Tommy are happy being married. But I just can't imagine being beholden to someone else for the rest of my life. That commitment sounds like it would require so much energy that I would deplete to the point of emptiness. I don't know how I would withstand having someone need so very much from me."

"But won't a baby do the same?" she asked gently.

"Yes, and that will be hard enough on its own." My voice broke. I swallowed hard. "He is the perfect mate, the perfect man. And someday, he'll meet someone who will love him like he loves. I'm just not capable. I'm not equipped for love." My breakdown was complete, the words gone, choking and catching in my throat.

"Come here," she said gently, pulling me into a hug to rock me. "It's all going to be okay. I know it doesn't feel like it right now, but I promise it will."

I bit down on my bottom lip, bit back my tears, felt the stretch of our baby in my body, felt the raw edges of my heart.

And I hoped against hope that she was right.

THEO

It had been the longest eight days of my life.

I'd made it my mission to stay away, stay out of the house. The charity function I was planning had ended up being a boon—it'd afforded me an excuse to avoid home. Eight dinners I'd eaten alone. Eight breakfasts wolfed down in a cab. Seven long, cold nights alone in my bed, unable to sleep, unable to think of anything other than the girl down the hall. The girl I loved.

The girl I couldn't have.

The frustrating and maddening girl who was carrying my baby. The girl I'd given my heart to, the girl who didn't want it.

All my dreams had been washed away with the tide, leaving me empty of anything but longing and regret. I should have talked to her before proposing. I should have listened to her when she warned me. I should have known the second I met her mother. But I'd been blinded by what I wanted. I'd justified my actions, made my choice strictly based on my dreams without considering hers.

If I had, I would have known the answer.

I should have known better.

I should have left well enough alone.

I should have given her a warning, more time.

But time wouldn't have changed anything. She didn't want to get married, and she didn't believe in love.

Which didn't change the fact that I did. It didn't matter how much I loved her. I couldn't love her enough for both of us. I couldn't bend her to what I wanted. It was one of the reasons I loved her. She was unflappable, sure-footed, and confident. And that was exactly why I'd lost her.

I'd finished work hours ago, but I knew she'd be home, waiting for me. So I walked. I walked from Midtown, passing Bryant Park and the library, pausing to admire the light posts she'd told me about months ago, when hope still existed and possibilities lit a fire in me. I walked the long city blocks to Washington Square Park, sat at the fountain, admired the arch as the sun went down and the marble lit up. And hours later, I'd dragged myself home, hoping everyone was asleep.

With a sigh, I unlocked my front door. The house was dark and silent—a good omen. I crept through the house, up the stairs. But when I reached the landing and glanced into the living room, that longing I'd thought I kept tamped down let loose in a rush that brought me to a dead stop.

The lights were off but for a lamp next to the couch, and in the low light, she looked posed in her perfection, too beautiful to be real. Her face was soft and slack in sleep, her dark lashes and rosy lips a contrast to the pale of her skin. Her head rested on her arm, which lay hooked behind her head on the arm of the chair. Her hand cupped the curve of her belly in a protective gesture, almost as if to reassure herself the baby was there and safe. The white muslin of her nightgown stretched and draped around her breasts and belly, her hips and legs, the light brushing the curves of her in gentle strokes.

There were so few things in this world I truly wanted, and she was almost all of them. The sense of loss was blinding, the desire to pick her up and carry her to bed overwhelming, the wish that she were still mine and the knowledge that she wasn't nearly bringing me to my knees.

The ache in my heart twisted and burned as I walked to her with wooden legs, snagging a blanket from the basket next to the couch, unfurling it as I approached. I slipped it over her with gentle care, not wanting to wake her, not wanting to touch her for fear it would sting.

But a lock of hair was strewn across her face, and before I could stop myself, I brushed it away.

She stirred, inhaling deeply, stretching languidly. Her eyes fluttered open. "Theo?"

"Shh. Go back to sleep."

The corners of her lips tugged into a frown. She pushed herself up to sit. "I was waiting for you," she said, swinging her feet around to the ground.

"I'm home. Come on, let's get you to bed."

"No," she said with a shake of her head. "Please, will you sit with me for a minute?"

I swallowed, locking my face, shuttering my heart. I took a seat in an armchair without speaking.

She took a breath and met my eyes. "You've been avoiding me."

"I've had a lot of work to do."

"Work never keeps you out past ten, Theo."

A week ago, I'd ached to hear her call me by my nickname that she was so averse to. Now it only reminded me of all I'd lost.

"What did you want to say, Katherine?" I asked, unwilling to give her anything she hadn't explicitly asked for.

Her brows flicked together. "This is unbearable."

My jaw flexed. I didn't speak.

"I know this is my fault. I should have been more clear from the start."

"And I should have listened."

Pain shifted behind her eyes. "I have another proposition. I...I know we can't go back. But what's happened doesn't change the fact that we're having a baby. So we need to find a way to move forward. My first question is, do you want me to leave?"

That split in my heart widened. "No," I answered with firm certainty. "I don't want you to be alone. And I want to be here when the baby comes. I don't want to be apart from her any more than I want to be apart from you."

The click of her throat as she swallowed. "All right," she said with a small, shaking voice. "Then we need to figure out how we can be partners again. How we can be friends. I...I miss you."

"I miss you, too," I admitted, hating that she was right. I just didn't know what to do about it.

"What if we make new rules? Rules to help us?"

"What do you suggest?" Hope was my curse. It rose like the sunrise.

"For starters, we need to stop avoiding one another. We need to know we can be around each other without it hurting."

"But it does hurt, Kate."

"It does. Won't that lessen with time?"

"Theoretically."

"It's a theory I think we should test. Because even though we're not together, we're bound. I don't want to feel this way, but knowing I've lost you as my friend is too much to endure. And I don't want to go back to being strangers. Do you?"

"No."

A pause. "Will you start coming home for dinner again?"

My sigh tested the limits of my ribs. "Yes."

"We can start there. I'll stay out of your way. It hurts me, too."

I watched her for a protracted moment. "I hate this. I hate this so fucking much, I can barely stand to share air with you. Because every breath hurts. Every single one, Kate."

Tears shone in her eyes, clinging to the corners. "I know," she whispered. "But nothing about us has been conventional, Theo. There is no option to run away. So we have to decide not to. We have to face what we are even if it's not what we want." She shook her head, glancing down. "I'm sorry."

"So am I."

I couldn't stand to see her cry, couldn't stop myself from moving to her side. From holding her, from closing my eyes and burying my face in her hair. From feeling her body against mine and memorizing the sensation, the warmth radiating from her and into me. I couldn't help myself.

And this would be my greatest challenge.

I swallowed my emotion, swallowed the things I wanted to say. Swallowed my wishes and dreams and kissed them goodbye with a kiss to her forehead. And then I stood.

I had to, or I wouldn't be able to stop myself.

"Amelia said it would all be all right," she said, swiping tears from her cheeks. "But it's hard to believe there will come a time when this doesn't hurt."

"It will."

I said it for her sake. And I said it with the hope that it would come true but without the faith to believe it.

SEMANTICS

THEO

31 WEEKS, 4 DAYS

hree weeks crawled by, and little by precious little, we found a new normal.

It wasn't any normal I wanted, but it was better than the alternative—life without her.

The progress was slow, peppered with stilted conversations and strained silences. Conversations that systematically avoided painful truths. And somehow, we found a way to be roommates.

Friends seemed almost out of the question.

It wasn't made easier by the chemistry that still had us under its thumb. Even that morning, as I rinsed my dishes, I could feel her watching me, her gaze heavy with things unsaid. Desire warmed her face. And I still hadn't figured out how to override the urge to kiss her or the hope that a kiss would wash our pain away.

But it would be a lie, a temporary stay of execution. There was no way to bridge the gap between what we wanted—what we *needed*.

"The house is voting in *The Eye* tonight," she said, dusting crumbs off her hands. "Can we watch after dinner?"

"Sure. If Todd gets off the hook, Barry might lay him out on live television."

She laughed. "I don't know why no one is blaming Janet. She's the one who kissed both of them."

"As hard as Barry's been campaigning, I'm pretty sure Todd's a goner."

"I think Janet planned it. Todd's her biggest competition. I don't trust her."

I smirked. "You don't trust anyone."

"Not true," she said, picking up her toast. "I trust you."

That dull ache that had taken up residence in my chest flared. "Well, I'm exceptionally trustworthy," I joked, drying off my hands. "I'll see you tonight, Katherine," I said, fisting my hand as I walked to stop myself from reaching out to touch her.

"Have a good day, Theo."

I smiled my best fake smile, turning the corner to trot down the stairs, then down again into the basement.

Tommy was already there, his long hair pulled into a knot at his nape. A Tribe Called Quest was blaring, Q-Tip telling us to wipe our feet really good on the rhythm rug as Tommy curled the hand weights in reps.

I knew exactly where he was in today's workout cycle, and while he finished up, I stretched a little, cracking my neck and flexing my shoulders as I scanned the rack for a heavier load.

He racked the weights and stepped back as I stepped up, squaring up in front of the mirror.

"Punishing yourself?" he joked.

"No," I lied.

The strain on my biceps agreed with him.

"You're miserable," he said.

"I'm fine."

He folded his arms. "Sure. You look fine."

I hissed, unable to answer. The sum of my focus was in my trembling muscles.

"There's got to be another way."

My eyes darted to his in warning.

"What? This clearly isn't working for you."

Nineteen, twenty. I racked the weights, huffing. "Doesn't matter what I want, does it?"

"The way I see it, it's a matter of semantics. You both want the same thing, but you're calling it different names."

I hung my hands on my hips, glaring at him. "You're telling me, if Amelia said she didn't love you and refused to marry you, you'd be content begging for scraps?"

His brows drew together. "No."

"Exactly."

"But that's not who Amelia is. If she refused me, it would be for different reasons than Katherine—it would be because she didn't want me. Katherine wants you. She just holds issues with the words and constructs."

I shook my head. "I don't know how to get past that."

"That's because you have an inflexible view of right and wrong. Black and white."

I snorted. "Please. Have you met yourself?"

"Takes one to know one, Teddy."

My eyes flicked to the ceiling.

Tommy picked up his weights, shifting to get his feet just right. "Maybe you need to redefine your idea of a relationship."

"If she doesn't love me, what possibly could we be doing

together?"

"Maybe she loves you but only at her best capacity. Maybe this *is* the most she can give. Does it matter whether or not she says it if you know how she feels?"

"How can I know how she feels if she doesn't tell me?"

He gave me a look and curled one weight. "Oh, you know. Don't lie and say you don't."

A noncommittal noise slipped out of me.

"Maybe it's *you* who's being inflexible, not her." A hiss and a curl. "Can you let it go? Can you let her be with you and care for you however she needs?"

"That's all I've done, Tommy—let her be whatever she needs. This is the one thing *I* need. How can I live without the thing I want so much?"

His hands lowered, and he turned to pin me still with two words. "For her."

Anger and longing surged. I shook my head. "It hurts too bad."

"Worse than not having her at all?"

"Goddammit, Tommy, it's not that simple."

He shrugged, unaffected. "Doesn't seem all that complicated. If you want to be together, it seems like you're the only thing in your way."

"I don't know how to do that. I don't know how to just pretend like it's fine that this is all we'll ever be. It's like we're business partners who've entered into a merger. So that's how I've gotta treat it. I can't keep loving her. I can't stand the pain."

Sadness shifted behind his eyes. "You're a stubborn son of a bitch."

"Takes one to know one."

That earned me a ghost of a smile. "Just think about it, Theo. Because if you can figure out how to put your fucking ego away, you could have her for good."

"You don't know that. She won't promise me that, so how

could you?"

"Call it a hunch," he said, turning back to the mirror to start up his reps again.

And I waited for him to finish, staring through a spot on the foam floor, trying to find truth in his words. The thought of rolling over, of slipping back into her arms, was almost too much to resist.

I could be whatever she needed. But I didn't know how much more I could sacrifice when she'd sacrificed so little.

I felt like I was being punished for my feelings, for what I wanted. That if I didn't hold on to this, I would lose my everything I'd always wanted. I thought through it, considered giving it up. Saw my life without a wife, and although it hurt, it was better than not having her at all.

But a life without love? Without those four letters, that one word that promised me her heart? That was one thing I couldn't do.

Maybe Tommy was right. Maybe this was the best she could give.

I just didn't know if it was enough.

QUEEN OF SHEBA

KATHERINE

34 WEEKS, 3 DAYS

The room was a sauna.

Outside wasn't particularly warm anymore—fall had broken the sweltering heat of summer—and even if it were, the brownstone had been fitted with central air when they renovated.

The reason I was sweating like an ice cube in a fireplace was a combination of the additional thirty pounds, the hormones required to regulate my body temperature, and the thirty-some-odd faces staring at me.

I kept my eyes on my hands and the task before them—pulling wads of tissue paper out of a pink bag with an elephant on the front.

If it hadn't been for my friends' insistence, I wouldn't have agreed to a baby shower. If I'd fully realized how uncomfortable I'd be as the center of attention, I would have refused.

How bad could it be? Theo had asked me.

Answer: sweaty, itchy, *get-me-the-hell-out-of-here* bad.

The men who had accompanied their women looked as disenchanted as I felt. At least they had booze. All I had was a stupid lemonade.

Under what felt like obscene mounds of tissue paper was a plethora of breastfeeding supplies. Breast pads. Lanolin—otherwise known as nipple grease. Boob-shaped ice packs. Silicon nipple shields.

Seriously, the word *nipple* was on every package.

"Thank you, Val," I said after I'd listed each item aloud for Amelia, who was compiling a list for thank-you notes. "My nipples will be thankful for your thoughtfulness."

She winked, shooting a finger gun at me. "I'm here for you and your nipples."

The crowd chuckled.

Rin cleared the paper, taking the gifts from me to repack in the bag as Theo handed me another gift.

"Ooh, that one's from me!" my mother called, waving at me.

I was immediately terrified.

In the bottom of the bag were little baggies—tea, I realized on inspection. Spearmint, rose hips, red raspberry leaves. I shot her a look when I saw blue cohosh. She was beaming.

"Blue cohosh is dangerous, Mom."

She waved a hand. "Oh, psh. We'll use it once you go into labor, not to induce."

Theo and I shared a look, agreeing silently to put it directly in the trash.

"And that red raspberry leaf tea will help soften your cervix, get you all ready for the baby! I'm just gonna throw it out there that sex will help that, too. You two don't have to be involved to do her a solid, Theo. Small mercies!"

"This is not the place to discuss my cervix, Mother!"

"Moving on!" Amelia chimed too cheerfully and far too loud, her face the color of a rutabaga as someone handed me another present, defusing the bomb with legs that was my mother.

I felt like the Queen of Sheba with attendees waiting and my king at my side.

Theo was close enough that our thighs touched, our chairs set up like thrones in front of our friends and family. He was probably another reason for the sweat list. We hadn't been this close in what felt like forever. The contact had me hot all over and fighting the urge to climb into his lap and kiss him.

The weeks that had passed did nothing to quell my feelings for him. We'd at least found a routine, a new normal, a way to be friends.

And I hated it.

I hated being in the room with him without being able to touch him. The tension was almost unbearable, the unspoken words screaming between us. Even when we felt almost normal, the shadow of what we once had been hung over us like a thunderhead.

But we'd settled into it as best we could. Theo seemed to be faring better than me. The last few weeks, he'd softened, smiling more, avoiding me less.

To be honest, that made it all so much worse.

Worse and so much better. Because it was a taste of what I'd had once, and that taste reminded me that I was starving to death.

He smiled at me, and I wondered how he wasn't sweating at all. He had a full goddamn suit on. I wore a black sundress with a light cardigan the color of an apple, and I felt like I was about to combust. The bottom layer of my bangs stuck to my forehead, and my breasts, which had doubled in size, sat heavy on the shelf of my belly. I brushed the back of my hand on my forehead, and it came away damp.

"Is there more?" I asked pitifully.

"Nope. You did it," he said.

"Oh, thank God," I breathed.

Rin busied herself combining things into bags and moving things out of the way while my mom helped her clean up remnants of paper and tape and ribbon. Amelia stood, hooking her pen in her notebook with a blissful smile on her face. She'd just started to show, and she looked beautiful—small and glowing and all belly. I, on the other hand, looked like a hippopotamus—shiny, fat, and grumpy.

"All right, it's time for games!" she cheered.

The men in the room collectively sighed. I buckled, my eyes widening and back straightening.

I reached for Theo's hand without realizing, and he spoke just when I noticed. "Hey, let's take five first. Everybody grab a refill before Amelia forces you all to make toilet paper diapers on your boyfriends."

I sighed, relieved. "Thank you," I breathed.

"Come with me," he said, helping me to stand and steering me toward the stairs. He snagged a fresh lemonade off the table on the way, and once we were upstairs, he headed us to the patio.

The second we were outside, I felt ten pounds lighter. The breeze was light, touched with a chill that felt like heaven on my overheated skin. I sighed, twisting my hair to expose my neck.

He handed me the paper cup, which I took, drinking greedily. Another sigh when it was gone, and his big hands took the rope of hair and lifted it up, fanning my bare neck with a baby bingo card he'd pulled from his pocket.

I closed my eyes and sighed again.

"I don't think I've ever heard you sigh so much in a five-minute span."

I could hear him smiling, and my lips smiled in answer.

"This was a terrible idea."

"It's one of those things we do for everyone else more than

ourselves. They want to be here. They want to celebrate."

I snorted a laugh. "There's not a single man downstairs who *wants* to be here."

A chuckle. "Fair enough. But did you see your mom's face? Your friends? I think Amelia's waited her whole life to throw a baby shower."

"Honestly, I'd do it just for her, if she asked me. Which she didn't, by the way. She *told* me."

"She can be really bossy when she sets her mind to it."

"You're telling me."

"Feel any better?" he asked, still fanning my neck.

"Much," I answered, wishing I'd said no when he smoothed my hair and took his hand back.

For a moment, we were silent, looking into the empty courtyard as the breeze stirred around us.

"Thank you," I said, reaching for the rail, my eyes on the greenery below.

"For what?"

"Everything. For taking care of me. For knowing what I need, always. For saving me."

"You don't need saving, Katherine."

I hated when he called me that.

"Just because I don't need saving doesn't mean it doesn't feel good to be saved."

"Well, good, because I happen to like saving you. It makes me feel useful."

"You're one of the most useful people I know. And the closest thing to perfect I've ever seen."

He stilled. I swallowed hard, regretting saying so much.

"There's no such thing as perfect," he said after a moment.

"I know. But for me, you are." I stared through the brownstone behind ours, the bricks and windows blurring. "I wish it were different, Theo."

"So do I."

"How is it possible that we could care for each other so much and not be together?"

"I wonder that every day. Living with you through it all is torture and bliss. Because I want to spend every second with you, but you're not mine."

"Every day is hard," I agreed, the door open and the words coming without thought or will to stop them. "Every day, I wonder if something will change. If we'll wake up and be back where we were. Or if something in us will reconfigure, and we'll suddenly be on the same page again."

"Me too," he said quietly. "I miss you."

I turned to face him, searching the depths of his eyes. The pretense was gone, the falsity of our friendship exposed. "I miss you, too."

He drew a heavy breath and opened his arms, stepping into me. "Come here," he said.

So I did.

I wound my arms around his narrow waist, buried my face in his chest, breathed in the familiar scent of him, lost myself in the comfort of his arms and the feel of his lips pressing to my crown.

I wanted so desperately for things to be different, wanted so much to give him what he needed. I wanted to understand how I could change my perspective. I wanted a new definition of love.

But maybe this *was* love. And it was neither the brain chemicals I'd so proudly waved around, nor was it unexplainable magic. Maybe it was this, the feeling I had right now. The sense of belonging, the sense of purpose.

He was home. And I'd boarded up the windows and locked the door behind me.

If it was love, would it mean a way back in? Would it mean I could have him again? Was it possible I was wrong about everything?

Could I give him what he needed?

Could what he needed be everything I wanted?

His hand slipped into my hair, cupping the back of my head, holding me to him for just a moment longer.

"We'd better get back inside," he said, his voice rough with emotion.

I wondered if it was the same emotion locked in my throat and decided it was.

And so, I followed him inside, questioning the things I thought I knew.

If anyone could ever change my mind, it was him. But if I was wrong, we'd only be in for more pain. I'd only hurt him worse.

And that was something I just couldn't bear.

RECKONING

THEO

22 WEEKS, 5 DAYS

Every man in the room wore a toilet paper diaper but me.

I laughed, the neck of my beer hooked in my fingers. I brought it to my lips for a pull.

Even Katherine laughed openly, pointing at Rin's boyfriend, Court. I didn't think I'd ever seen a man so deeply disturbed as he was in that moment, donning a loincloth of two-ply over an expensive cobalt suit with a scowl to rival a Roman general.

The doorbell rang over the ruckus. Katherine and I exchanged a glance that transmitted an unspoken thought. Almost everyone we knew was in this room.

"Maybe it's a package," I said.

"It's Sunday," she studiously pointed out.

I stood, striding to the door, unprepared for the man on the

John Banowski, tall and proud, in clothes I'd paid for and a cigarette I'd bought in his fingers. "Son," he said in lieu of a greeting.

I tried to step out, hoping to close the door before anyone saw him, but he caught it with his palm, keeping it open.

"Havin' a little party?"

"Yeah, and you're not invited. What the fuck are you doing here? I told you to call me if you—"

"Just wanted to bring these to you." He reached behind him, his hand returning with the same pack of papers he'd had before.

"Are they signed?"

I reached for them, but he jerked them away. "They are. So, how much are they worth to you?"

Fury rose in my chest, my jaw clamping shut. "You sorry piece of shit. You took everything from her, and you can't give her this one fucking thing?"

"Hey now, don't get all worked up. I got no problem signing them—that's done. It's handing them over I thought could use a little…incentive."

The pop of my jaw. The clench of my fist. My shoulders square and back straight as a fucking razor. "How much do you want?"

"That all depends."

"On what?"

He leaned in, sneering. "On how much you're willing to give."

"I don't owe you one fucking thing. You've taken enough from us. Now give me the fucking papers before I go in there and end all this once and for all."

His eyes narrowed. "You wouldn't. They'd never forgive you." He scanned my face as a slow smile crept onto his. "Nah, you're too smart for that, aren't you?"

I leaned in. "Try me."

"Theo?" Katherine's voice came from behind me, kicking me

back into reality. She pulled the door open and went dead still.

"Well, well, well. Who's this?" John asked.

"None of your fucking business, like I said. Get out of here. Call me like I told you."

He tsked. "You've got terrible manners, son. Look at that. My grandkid in there?" He jerked his chin in Katherine's direction.

Katherine's hand slipped into mine. "Come back to the party, please," she said, the words quiet and touched with fear.

"Yeah, Teddy," he said with mock cheer. "Come on, let's get to the party."

He pushed past me before I could stop him—Katherine had my hand, and she was too close for me to put my hands on him for fear she'd get hurt in the scuffle. Helplessly, I watched him enter. I saw the din and activity in the room still and then stop. And in the center of it all were Tommy and my mother, staring at him with pale shock and absolute disbelief.

"Johnny?" Ma breathed, her brows knit together in confusion.

"Hey, babe. Long time." He was smirking, looking casual as the day was long, scooping a handful of nuts off the table of food. He tossed one in his mouth. "Look at you, Tommy. Last time I saw you, you was practically in a diaper just like that."

"What the hell are you doing here?" Tommy shot, his body drawn tight as a bowstring. "Theo, what the hell is he doing here?"

"What, your dear old dad can't come to the party? Don't act so happy to see me. I'd say I was surprised Teddy didn't tell you all about me comin' around. How come you been hidin' me, Teddy?" His eyes glinted, sharp as switchblades.

Ma stood with Amelia's reluctant help. "Teddy, what's he talkin' about?" She looked scared, small and wounded, like a bird with a broken wing.

"Nothin', Ma. He's just makin' trouble."

She cast a look in his direction.

Tommy stormed through the crowd, ripping the toilet paper off as he walked. "Tell me what the fuck you're doin' here, old man," he said through his teeth, stepping into John's space, not stopping until they were nose to nose.

"Ask your fucking brother. He's the one who's been tryin' to keep me away for six years."

Slowly, Tommy's face turned to mine. "What?" he asked, the calm in his voice dangerously deceiving.

I met John's eyes. "You stupid son of a bitch," I said, my body shaking. "Trying to keep you away? Like you give a fuck about anybody but yourself." I faced my brother. "Six years ago, he came here to blackmail you. So I paid him to stay away. And he's been doing just that until he got the divorce papers. They're in his pocket. He came to sell them to me."

There was zero time to react. Tommy's fist cocked and sprang like a cobra, connecting with John's nose with a smack and a crunch and a spray of blood. Someone screamed. I moved for Tommy, who had John by the lapels of his leather jacket, just as Court and Sam reached him. They pulled Tommy off and held him back as I shoved John toward the door.

"Get out," I yelled, shoving him again. He stumbled toward the door from the force. "It's over. Give me the papers."

"Or what?" he shot, swiping his ruined nose.

I grabbed him by the shirtfront, bringing him close. "Or else we'll take you to court and ruin what's left of your fucking life."

His eyes narrowed. "Big words, Teddy."

"Give. Me. The papers."

He shifted for his back pocket, providing the papers.

I let him go and snatched them with a snap.

John ran the back of his hand across his mouth, inspecting the gore that had come off on it. "Good riddance," he said, spitting a gob of blood on the hardwood. "Never were worth my time, anyway. Even at ten grand a month."

Rage, red and hot. I dived for him without thinking, swinging without stopping. The crunch of bone against bone. The slick heat of his blood. Over and over again—for how long, I didn't know.

Gravity ceased as I was pulled off him, picked up, carried away, snarling. Through the haze, I saw Ma standing stronger and harder than I'd seen her in years.

"Get out," I heard her say. "You've done enough."

And with a sneer and a limp, he did just that.

I was set on my feet, my eyes still on the door he'd walked out of. Tommy stepped into my line of sight, his face drawn and eyes dark as midnight.

His jaw clenched as he stretched to his full height. And I knew what was coming before he did it.

I took the hook in the jaw without trying to stop it, my body twisting from the force of it, the sting radiating down my neck, tightening my stomach.

With a shake of my head and a hard series of blinks, I could at least see again. I straightened up and smoothed my clothes, which were dotted with my father's blood.

But Tommy had already turned, stalking toward the door. Amelia ran after him, her face wide with fear, calling his name. And with a hard slam of the door, he was gone, too.

The party was silent, our friends standing wide-eyed in the living room, surrounded by pink balloons and streamers. It was Rin who broke the tension by shifting to pick up a few paper plates and cups from the coffee table. Val followed suit, and then everyone was moving, hastily cleaning up.

Ma was crying.

I stepped toward her, but she took a step back.

"Six years," she whispered. "Six years, you've been lying to us."

My hand moved to touch her arm but paused, falling to my side again. "I only wanted to protect you."

"Not like this, Teddy. Not like this."

She turned her back on me.

"Ma, please—"

"Not now," she pleaded. "Not right now. Please, excuse me," she said, shuffling toward her room.

Katherine intercepted her, offered her arm, met my eyes with a nod before turning her full attention to my mother.

I looked over the worried faces of our friends, who had all paused in some effect, their expressions touched with pity and fear.

"I'm sorry," I croaked. And I turned for the stairs to escape.

But there was nowhere to run.

I rushed into my bathroom, leaning on the counter with my hands splayed, knuckles split. My hair was a riot, my suit rumpled and speckled with blood.

I'd made a mess of everything. Every single thing I touched.

It didn't matter what I did, didn't matter how I tried. Didn't matter what I wanted or what I gave in the hopes that I'd get it back.

I'd ruined it all.

"Theo?"

Her voice from behind me. Her worried face in the mirror. She moved to my side, laid her hand on my arm, shifted to move in front of me. I let the counter go and stood, looking down at her with my brows drawn in pain and regret.

Her hand on my jaw, a brush of her fingertips. "Let me help you."

But no one could help me.

She turned for the sink, reaching for a washcloth from a stack. The sound of water running, the splat and drip as she wrung the cloth out. And then she turned to face me again.

I was too tall for her to reach easily, so in a feat of grace and physics, she hopped herself up to sit on the counter. "Come here," she said gently.

So I did.

She reached for my waist, pulling me closer. I fit myself between her legs, my hands on her thighs, her face so close to mine. I lost myself in her eyes, but she didn't meet mine.

Instead, she scanned my face, followed her cloth as she cleaned me off, pressing the cool compress to my aching jaw.

"You did the right thing," she said, "even though it feels like you didn't."

I closed my eyes.

"They'll see. I promise."

"You can't know that."

"They'd have to be blind not to, Theo. You did the right thing," she insisted. "You were right to try to protect them from him."

I swallowed hard, shaking my head. "I should have been honest, Kate. I should have let them decide for themselves."

"But you protected them for all these years. You shielded them from him. He could have ruined Tommy. I can't imagine Tommy would have let that slide or would have paid to keep him quiet. John would have blown everything for Tommy. And, yes, Tommy and Sarah are angry and hurt. But give them time. They'll come around. I know it."

I bowed my head. "How do you know?"

She tilted my chin so I'd meet her eyes. "Because they love you, Theo."

"I thought love wasn't real."

"Well, maybe I was wrong."

Before I could speak, she shifted, slipping off the counter. "Leave your clothes in the kitchen, and I'll make sure they get cleaned."

"All right," I answered softly. "Kate?"

She turned, her hand on the doorframe. "Yes?"

"Thank you."

A smile, small and devastatingly earnest. "You're welcome, Theo."

THEO

It was dark out by the time I showered and changed, our living room upstairs abandoned, leaving me wondering where Katherine was. Not in her room, the doorway open and dark.

The sound of crinkling paper drifted up the stairwell, and I followed it.

I had apologies to make, though I didn't know if I deserved forgiveness.

Katherine, Amelia, and Tommy worked silently to clean up the mess of the party, and a flash of guilt tore through the already sickening remorse I harbored. I should have been here helping, too.

I should have done a lot of things.

Amelia and Katherine offered smiles, but Tommy ignored me. The only indication that he'd seen me was a renewed fervor in depositing cups into the trash bag in his hand.

"I'm sorry," I said, staring at him, willing him to look at me.

"Fuck your sorry," he spat, chucking a paper plate into the bag.

"What was I supposed to do, Tommy? I know I shoulda told you, but he was gonna expose you and Ma both. Call the media, do interviews. Rip everything you'd so carefully hidden down to the ground. So really, what would you have done?"

"Sent him to the hospital."

"Which woulda done what? Made him keep his mouth shut?" I scoffed. "All he wanted was money. And if he didn't get it, he was gonna hurt you and Ma. I couldn't stand for that. But I shoulda told you, Tommy. And I'm sorry."

He threw the trash bag on the coffee table and laid the full weight of his gaze on me. "Yeah, you shoulda told me."

I watched my brother, reading his thoughts. Because what Tommy really wanted was to reconcile with that bag of shit who'd lent us his genetics.

"He was never gonna be what you wanted."

"How do you know? You paid him to stay away."

"Because he's an opportunist. He doesn't give a fuck about anybody but himself. And he would have used anything to get what he wanted. You, me, Ma. Jesus, Tommy—you act like I stole some precious thing from you. We weren't off playin' catch."

"God, you're so high and mighty, Theo," he shot, stepping into me. "You handled it all on your own, just like everything else. Can't let anybody in and can't share the burden. Can't be weak. Can't be vulnerable. It's why you're so messed up that you got shot down by Katherine. If you hadn't been vulnerable, you wouldn'a gotten hurt. That about right?"

"Fuck you," I spat. "Fuck you, Tommy."

"I'm just sayin'. This is how you roll. Things woulda been different with him if we'd all sat down and talked about it."

"What part of *he wanted your money* don't you fucking get?" I fumed, close enough to feel the heat waving off of him. "I swear to God, you're so hardheaded. I couldn't crack your skull if I took a fucking pickax to it."

"That's enough!"

We froze, turning to the sound of our mother.

Her face was bent, her dark eyes shining and lips tight. "Sit down," she said, her mom voice firm and hard.

"But—" Tommy started.

She pointed to the couch, her jaw flexed and eyes hard. "Sit."

Tommy and I shared a look before doing as we'd been told.

Katherine and Amelia hurried to help Ma around the couches, depositing her into an armchair before slipping silently upstairs.

Ma watched us with disappointment all over her face. "Stop fighting, both of you."

"But he—" Tommy spat before Ma cut him off.

Never did know when to keep his mouth shut.

"I said, enough! Zip it, Thomas Banowski, right this second."

He shot me another look and sat back, scowling.

"Ma," I said gently. "Ma, I'm so sorry."

But she shook her head. "He wanted money all those years ago and held us ransom. I hate that you didn't tell me, Teddy. But I woulda done the same."

My throat clamped shut. "Ma…"

"Never in your life have you ever done anything out of spite or anger. You live your days serving everyone but yourself. If you'd thought there was another way, you woulda taken it. I…I'm sorry I was so mad. But seein' his face just…" The word trailed off, and she lost herself for a moment. Her lips pursed. "It's over now anyway. Don't you give him one more penny, Teddy."

"I won't, Ma."

Tommy was furious. "I can't believe you're just gonna let it go, Ma. Six years, he kept this from both of us. He saw that man and didn't tell us the son of a bitch was even alive."

Ma gave him a look. "You feel better now you know he is? Did seeing him answer all your questions? Are you satisfied now you popped him in the nose? Tell me, Tommy—do you feel better or worse?"

An angry flush smudged his cheeks, his eyes shining, nostrils flaring. "Worse," he admitted.

"Your brother was trying to spare you this, can't you see that?"

His Adam's apple bobbed.

"You don't wanna admit it, fine," she said. "But you know it's true just as well as I do. All he's ever done is take care of you."

"Ma—" I started.

"Don't interrupt," she snapped. "Tommy, you find forgiveness in your heart for your brother who tried to protect you."

He met my eyes, dark and endless as my own. He swallowed.

I waited.

He knew, and he kept me waiting longer before finally speaking, "I know you were trying to protect me, but I'm still fucking mad about it."

I sighed through my nose, my brows still drawn, but my heart eased. "Wanna hit me again?"

That earned me a flicker of a smirk. "Kinda."

I rubbed my jaw. "Man, you haven't taken a swing at me in five years."

"Six."

My brows rose with my smile, and we said at the same time, "Clarissa Merryton."

"You deserved that, too," he said.

"I did," I admitted.

Ma smiled, but the expression was tight with exhaustion. "I love you boys more than life itself, and to think your father has come between you at all cuts me to the quick. He has hurt us all enough. I don't want to give him any more, not one minute of time, not one iota of energy. Deal?"

"Deal," we said in unison.

"Good. Now, come here and hug your ma."

We helped her up and wrapped her in a hug. Took turns kissing her cheek. And Tommy and I clasped arms. He pulled me in for a hug, clapping my shoulder with his free hand, squeezing tight enough to sting so I'd know how sorry he was, that I was forgiven, and how bad it'd hurt him—the whole encounter. It was too much, too thick with emotion to even peel back.

But that was what we did. We protected, and we forgave.

Because that was what love was.

IN TOO DEEP

KATHERINE

37 WEEKS, 1 DAY

"**A**re you sure you don't want a water birth, Katie?" my mother asked in all seriousness.

"I am unflinchingly sure," I answered flatly. "I've already written my birth plan."

She waved a hand. "Oh, that's flexible."

"No. It's not."

Sarah chuckled. "I can't believe in three weeks, I'll have a baby to hold."

"And then another one a few months later," Mom added.

Sarah beamed. "It's an embarrassment of riches. A year ago, I was more prepared for Tommy to end up in jail than a wedding chapel, and I figured Teddy for a perpetual bachelor. And look at us all now. Babies and weddings galore."

I tried to smile, knowing she didn't intend to dig at me for not marrying Theo.

We'd been living in a constant state of *almost*. Almost touching. Almost speaking. Almost friends.

Forever seemed like such precious little to promise him to end the almost. But with a glance at my mother, I was reminded exactly *why* the marriage level of forever was impossible. She didn't understand words like *forever* and *commitment*.

She shook her head, doe-eyed and sighing. "I wish Katie and Theo were having a wedding."

"Mom," I warned.

She wore a magnificent pout. "I know, I know. You two just seemed so happy together."

"We're happy now."

She gave me a look.

"What?"

"You are *not* happy. I have witnessed firsthand your moping around and hangdog looks at each other across the room for weeks. It's clear you love each other, and I just can't fathom not being with someone you love."

"You can't fathom staying with someone you love either."

The pout turned to a frown. "What do you mean?"

"I mean you've been divorced from Dad *four times*. Can't you just call a fight a fight and work through it?"

"Your father and I don't fight," she said matter-of-factly.

It was my turn to give her a look.

"Have you ever seen us fight?" she asked, folding her arms across her chest.

"No," I admitted with a pout of my own.

"Exactly. We're happy together, and we're happy apart. Why is that so hard to understand?"

"Because it's too fluid," I blustered, shifting on the couch. "It's lawless, boundless."

"But honey, that's love," she said. "It's not a straight line, and neither is life. *Life* is fluid. Why shouldn't love be?"

I shook my head. "Love isn't real."

Sparrow gaped like I'd just burned a stack of tarot cards in front of her. "Of course it is."

"It isn't! It's not some magical patch you can fix your relationships with. Say I love you, and all your sins are forgiven. You throw the word around like *hello* and *goodbye*."

"That's because the whole world is made up of love. It's what motivates almost every person on the planet. It's the energy that binds us together."

"Energy doesn't bind people together, Mom." Impatience, thick in my words.

Her face screwed up. "That's the silliest thing you've ever said, Katie. I can *see* it binding you and Theo. Your auras are so connected, they practically explode like fireworks whenever you're in the same room."

"Auras aren't real."

"Okay, fine. Then tell me this. Tell me you don't feel the bond with your baby."

"That's different," I huffed. "That's chemical. That's familiarity. I'm carrying her around all day, every day, anticipating the day she's born. That bond is instinctive."

"That bond is *love*. You're about to meet that baby, and your whole world will revolve around her. Survival of the species has little to do with it."

"Couldn't it be both?" Sarah asked.

We turned our faces to her.

"Why does it have to be one or the other? And the better question is, why does it matter? Katherine, you're going to love that baby in ways you can't even comprehend. You've already got an inkling…I can see it on your face even now. That love you have for your child is transcendent. The moment she's born is the moment your life stops being yours. It'll be hers, and you won't think twice about the sacrifice. You won't even notice the shift. *That*, honey, is love. It's automatic. You won't know you're in it until you're too deep to get out."

Tears, burning and hot, stinging my nose and the back of my throat. My vision tunneled.

The moment she'd said it, I knew it was true, against logic, against all I'd thought I knew.

This was love. Love for my child, uncultivated, unlearned. I hadn't even seen her, and I loved her. I loved every little finger and every little toe, counted every minute until she arrived so I could kiss every one. She hadn't done a single thing to earn that love but exist.

Love was automatic.

And if my love for my child was automatic and true, then there was another truth. A truth that had been right there, right in front of me all along.

His name was on my lips, written on my heart, etched on my soul. I'd never believed in fate, never subscribed to soul mates. But if ever there was a man who was my exact match, my most perfect equal, it was Theo.

And if that wasn't love, I didn't know what it was.

That word was defined by his existence.

I had fallen without knowing what was happening, without understanding the shift between us, in me. There was nothing I had to do, nothing for him to explain. There was no course to take, no box to check.

My love for him was a fact. It existed whether I believed in it or not.

"Katie, honey, are you okay?" Mom said, moving to my side,

taking my free hand.

The other was pressed to my belly. Hope shifted against my palm.

I nodded, unable to speak.

"Love is a gift," she said, her eyes shining with tears of her own. "And you are so loved. There has to be a way for you and Theo. Because that boy loves you."

"He does," Sarah added. "I didn't think I'd ever see the day he met his match, but Katherine, you are it."

"He…he asked me to love him, and I told him I couldn't. I didn't realize I already did." The words were thick in my throat, broken.

"Then it's easy, Katie," Mom said, smiling. "All you have to do is tell him."

And that was all I wanted to do. I wanted to run out of the house and through the streets of New York, calling his name. I wanted to find him and tell him I loved him.

Sarah shifted to pick herself up with shaky hands, smiling and crying and hauling herself to her feet before I could help. She stepped toward us around the coffee table, shuffling her feet, her mobility limited. My eyes widened—I moved to stand, to meet her halfway. But before I could reach her, she took a step, her foot hooking in the coffee table's leg.

She went down with a thud and a crack, her hands too slow to catch her, her foot still hung in the table. Her leg twisted at an unnatural angle, the cry from her lips raising every hair on my body, setting every nerve on end.

I rushed to her, pushing the coffee table out of the way around her leg. She groaned as I knelt beside her, turning her onto her back with gentle care and alarm screaming in my ears.

"Mom, call 911," I commanded, my voice calm and my hands brushing Sarah's hair from her wrenched face. "Then get my phone and call Theo. Tommy and Amelia are with him. Hurry!" I snapped when she didn't move, jolting her into action.

"Sarah," I said with an eerie calm I didn't feel, "you're okay. I think you might have broken your leg."

"Hip," she gritted through her teeth, her eyes pinched shut. Cool sweat bloomed on her cheeks, which had paled to an alarming shade of gray.

I glanced down her body as my mind whirred through emergency procedures I'd learned in Girl Scouts. "Mom, come sit with Sarah," I said, trading places with her, placing her free hand on Sarah's.

Her eyes were wild, her voice trembling as she gave details to the dispatcher.

I shot to my feet, running for the linen closet. With my arms full of sheets and towels, I ran back into the living room, snagging a pair of scissors from the kitchen on my way. The sheet I cut into strips in record time, fueled by the sounds of Sarah's pain. One strip was for her ankles, which I tied together. I passed a hand towel to my mom.

"Go wet this with cold water, please."

She nodded, her face pale as she took it and hurried to the kitchen.

"The ambulance is on its way, Sarah," I said, hoping to distract her. "I'm going to make a brace out of towels and tie them to you. The more stable it is, the better it will feel."

Sparrow handed me the wrung-out, folded towel, but my hands were busy rolling up towels.

"Cool her forehead."

She did.

I kept talking, catching her gaze and holding it. "When I was in Girl Scouts, a girl in my troop named Farrah Silver used to terrorize me at camp. Ants in my bed, stole my soap, threw my sheets in the mudbank of the river. The works." The tear of the sheet, the flash of my hands. "Once, she replaced one of the other girl's shampoo with Nair, and after that, she was everyone's best friend. It was that or baldness, and no twelve-year-old girl would pick anything but asskissing under those odds."

A flicker of a smile, tight with pain, touched Sarah's lips.

"So, we were at camp, heading out to trail ride. We headed to the stable, and Farrah walked straight up to the biggest horse they had—Diablo. Why they had a stallion evil enough to be named after Satan at Girl Scout camp is beyond me." I positioned the rolled-up towels from hip to knee on either side. "Our leader had ridden up ahead of us to check the trail was all right after a rainstorm. Farrah, of course, started showing off and spurred Diablo, but he barely moved other than to buck her off. I swear, she flew ten feet and hit the ground in a puff of dust."

"That little girl was a menace," Mom said with a shake of her head.

"I'm sure she's either in prison or is a CEO. Anyway, everyone just stared at her while she wiggled around on the ground, yelling. Not crying. *Yelling* obscenities at us. And no one helped—they just laughed. Laughed! Especially Rachel, the bald one. So, I got off my horse and made a brace out of sticks and a T-shirt."

"You gave her your shirt?" Mom asked.

"Nope. I used hers. She put ants in my bed? Well, I saved her ankle by exposing her stuffed training bra to the troop."

She laughed.

Sirens wailed in the distance just as I took Sarah's hand. "It's going to be all right. I know it hurts, but it will be better soon. They're going to have all kinds of good stuff for you, like morphine and ice packs."

The doorbell rang.

"I'll get it," Mom said, rushing to the door.

I expected to hear strange voices of paramedics, not my mother gasping.

"Dave! What are you doing here?"

My head snapped around so fast, I nearly got whiplash. My father sagged miserably on the stoop.

"Honey, I've missed you. I've been going crazy without you all this time. I know I haven't loved you like I should, but I came to prove I'd cross the world for another chance. Let me make it up to you, babe. Let me love you like you deserve."

"Oh, Dave," she sighed, falling into his arms. "I've missed you, t—oh!"

The noise of the sirens rose to ear-splitting decibels just as a fire truck squealed to a stop beyond the door.

And then the commotion really began in the way of half a dozen first responders, my crazy parents, the gravely injured grandmother of my child, and a contraction so intense, I thought I might split in two from the extraordinary blinding heat of it.

And all I could do was hang on to Sarah's hand and hope.

THEO

Chaos.

The cab screeched to a stop just down the street, which was blocked by an ambulance and a fire truck.

I threw the door open and ran, leaving Tommy and Amelia behind me.

Chaos, red and frenetic, sirens and lights, strangers in uniforms with no familiar faces.

I wound through paramedics and firefighters, bolting through the open door of my house, my gaze darting across faces, looking for one I knew.

Then I found one, a pale face wrenched in pain and drenched in sweat.

"Ma," I called, beelining for her.

Two EMTs were moving my mother onto a body board, her body so small. She reached for me.

"Teddy," she croaked, her voice trembling and tight.

I clasped her hands. "What happened?"

"I fell, tripped on the coffee table like a clumsy old fool. Katherine took care of me."

"Kate," I whispered.

Her brows tightened even more. "Honey, check on her. I think she's having contractions, but she's too proud to admit it."

I froze, my heart stopping for the fourth time since I'd rolled out of bed that morning.

"Go. I'm okay," she insisted. "There's nothing anyone can do for me that hasn't already been done. Go make sure she's all right."

I kissed her forehead, trading places with Tommy before wheeling around to look for Katherine.

I caught sight of her in the kitchen, face hard as stone, pacing a rut in the floor with her mom in her wake. The closer I got, the worse my dread.

"Theo," she breathed when she saw me, the hard facade she'd put in place cracking and crumbling. She launched herself into my arms.

"Kate." I cupped her head, holding her to me. "Are you okay?"

"I'm fine. God, Theo—it happened so fast. She stood and took a step, and I couldn't catch her. I tried to get to her, but she fell and—" A noisy hiss, and her body locked, curling in on itself.

I let her go to inspect her. "What's the matter?"

"Nothing." She ground the word out like grain against stone.

Sparrow's face was pinched with worry. "I think she's in labor."

Katherine shot her a look. "I am not in labor. I am not supposed to go into labor for three weeks. Three full weeks."

"These things happen," her mom assured her, placing a small hand on her back.

"Not to me they don't—*ah*!" She doubled over, hanging on to my arm.

"We're going to the hospital," I commanded.

Katherine's expression was petulant. "No, we are not. I am not having this baby yet. I am not in labor. It's just stress. I need a glass of water and to lie down. That's all." She dragged in a breath deep enough that her nostrils almost stuck together.

"Kate—"

"I am not in labor!" she shrieked, edging hysteria without warning. "I haven't even lost my mucus plug! I have a list, Theo. I have a list and it's not checked off and I'm supposed to have *three whole weeks*. It's not happening now. It's not!"

I pulled her into my arms, deciding the first thing I needed to do was calm her down. "Okay. It's not happening now."

"Thank you," she said miserably against my chest.

A man I'd never seen before appeared next to Sparrow with a glass of water in his hand and a ponytail that would have made Tommy Chong green with envy.

"For Katie," he said with a lazy smile. His glasses were tinted, but I was eighty-nine percent certain he was high. "I'm Dave. Niceta meetcha."

I took his hand with numb detachment and pumped it once.

The bedlam swirled around us—people and sirens and my injured mother, Katherine's mother, and her father, who'd come without warning. And in my arms was my Kate, crying and groaning and most likely about to have our baby.

There was nothing to do but get shit done.

I scooped Katherine up and carried her to the couch. Gave her a glass of water. Pulled a paramedic aside and asked her to check

Katherine out.

When the EMT and I made it back to the couch, Katherine's face was pink as she tried to sit, a task made difficult by her stretched-out abdominal muscles.

"Lie down, Kate," I soothed, smoothing her hair.

"I…" Her face opened up like a storm shutter. "Oh no."

I frowned. Katherine shifted. Sparrow lit up.

"Katie," she said, "I think your water just broke."

The look Katherine and I shared was heavy with a thousand words in the span of a heartbeat.

And I held her hands and glanced at the paramedic.

"I think we're gonna need another ambulance."

PLATO SAYS

KATHERINE

"If your mom tries to light that sage one more time, I will have her permanently removed from the building," the nurse said, eyeing my mother, who held her hands up in surrender.

"It would help. I'm just saying."

The nurse rolled her eyes.

Commotion bustled around us as the nurses and a midwife broke down my hospital bed, converting it for delivery. I was a tangle of tubes and wires—from the IV in my arm and the epidural in my spine to the nodes stuck to my belly, monitoring my contractions, which had reached levels that my epidural could no longer mask.

Another one came, a wave of heat that slipped over my belly, tightening it against my will. I hunched forward, feeling the urge to bear down.

Push, my body said.

"Ah, ah, ah," the nurse warned. "Hang on, Katherine—your

doctor is on her way. She's here. Just hold on a few minutes."

Theo shot her a look. He had a hold of my hand, the leverage so solid and sure that it was almost enough to make me less afraid.

Almost.

It took everything I had to resist the urge, waiting impatiently through the contraction until it was gone. My mother was chanting something in a language that sounded Native American, shaking what looked like a maraca with turquoise and feathers dangling from the handle.

I gave Theo a look.

"Sparrow, could you get some more ice chips?" he asked.

"Sure, let me just finish this spell."

"We could really use it *now*."

She was close to pouting. "All right, but if I leave now, who knows *what* will happen," she warned.

"We'll take our chances," he said with a smirk as she left the room, shaking her head with the little pitcher and her maraca in her hands.

I sighed, leaning back in the bed with a weary thump. "Thank you."

He smoothed my hair from my face. "What do you need? What can I do?"

"I don't even know. My head hurts."

His big hand moved to my neck. "Here, let me."

His thumb pressed into the tight muscles where my neck and shoulder joined. A noisy groan slipped out of me.

He pulled my hair out of its bun, which was hours old and probably looked like a rat's nest. Another groan as his fingers slipped into my hair and massaged my scalp. I nearly wept at the pleasure.

Then another contraction came, and I nearly wept at that.

I curled forward, clamping his hand, putting my weight on it, which he bore without even moving. My chin pressed to my clavicle, and my eyes slammed shut. And the moment stretched out, the pain putting everything in the universe in a warp. Time didn't exist in that space.

When it passed, I flopped back on the bed, my awareness returning in tendrils. "It hurts," I moaned.

His face was dark with worry. "Can you turn this thing up?" he asked the nurse.

"Of course," she said, stepping to the epidural drip to fiddle with it. "There. That should help."

My hand darted out, snagging the nurse's wrist. "I don't want anyone in here but Theo."

Her face softened, and she patted my hand. "I'll go intercept your mom."

"Thank you," I said, relieved as she left.

Theo's hands were in my hair again, gathering it up, twisting it into a fresh bun with more ease than I'd figure a man of his stature and experience would possess.

"Lean up," he commanded, helping me to sit. He hitched a leg to half-sit so he could press his thumbs to the aching muscles low on my back.

I grabbed the empty stirrups with my hands and groaned.

He'd shucked off his coat, his tie gone. His shirtsleeves were rolled up to his elbows, that button at the top undone. And his face was cool and confident as always. But his dark eyes were laden with concern.

Dr. Stout rushed in, smiling. "Looks like we're having a baby," she said as she approached.

"Oh, thank God. Can I push now?" I asked pitifully.

She chuckled. "I think so. Let's see how we're looking. Come on, feet up, Katherine."

Theo moved out of the way so I could lie back just as another contraction came. I grabbed his hand, curling in on myself.

"Hold on, don't push yet," she said as she examined me. "She's ready. Next contraction, we're going to go for it, okay?"

"Mmhmm," I hummed through pursed lips.

"You're doing so good," he murmured.

"The epidural's not working," I half-sobbed.

"Don't worry," Dr. Stout said with a comforting smile. "You're almost there."

"That isn't really what I wanted to hear."

"I promise, when your baby's here in a few minutes, you'll forget all about it."

"Doubtful," I snarked.

"Trust me, if we didn't forget all this, we'd never have a second baby."

I looked up at Theo, and he looked down at me.

"A few minutes," he said. "A few more minutes, and she'll be here."

Tears surged out of nowhere. "I...Theo, I...I need to tell you..." The words died in my throat. It was too much all at once—the months of waiting, the depth of change, the realization of my feelings. The birth of our child. The look in his eyes. The ache of my heart.

But it was all cut short by that climbing sting of another contraction, my lungs locking.

"All right," Dr. Stout said, nodding to the nurses.

They abandoned their tasks of readying the incubator and supplies to come to her side.

"Theo, grab her leg. Show him how, Jenny."

Jenny wrapped her arm around the inside of my calf, offering cursory instructions as she took my hand with her free one. Theo mirrored her.

"Okay, Katherine. *Push*."

I bore down, my face pinching closed, my awareness shrinking to a pinpoint of pain as I flexed my abdomen from the top and pushed, bracing against the stirrups and the arms around my legs.

"Breathe," Dr. Stout directed, but I couldn't, not until I'd exhausted my strength.

I sucked in a breath and did it again, lips curling and chin tucking.

"She's got a full head of hair," the doctor said with a smile.

"I bet it's dark," Theo said to me. "I bet she looks just like you."

The contraction was over, but I couldn't speak, didn't lie back. My hospital gown was hitched up to the bend in my thighs, my vagina on display to the handful of people in the room, including Theo. I couldn't even find it in me to be embarrassed.

"Okay, here comes another one," she said. "Ready?"

I nodded, my vision dimming. I closed my eyes against it.

I knew when to push before she said it, the hyperawareness of every muscle engaged, the sensation of my body opening up overwhelming, the panic of knowing there was a human lodged in the exit maddening. I wanted her out. I wanted her out *now*.

So I pushed as hard and efficiently as I could.

"I've got her head!"

The panic rose higher, knowing I had another push but unable to swallow the logic. "Get her out!" I wailed, wild-eyed.

"One more push," she assured me. "Get ready."

I swiveled to look at Theo, who wore a peaceful expression.

"She's stuck," I choked.

"She's fine, Kate. She's perfect. Come on. One more, and she's here."

I sobbed, shifting to get myself ready, gripping their hands with slick palms, closing my eyes as the slow burn slipped over my aching belly once more.

And then I pushed.

I felt everything, felt her leave my body, felt the instant relief and alarming emptiness. Collapsed back on the bed. Heard her cry. My cheeks were cool. His lips were warm against them. His hands were strong and trembling as he touched my face. His words were soft and soothing as he whispered to me that I'd done it.

"Dad, want to come here and cut the cord?"

Dad. They'd called him dad. He was a father.

I was a mother.

I opened my eyes, and there she was.

She was both ashen and purple, her face smushed and eyes pinched shut. Her little mouth was red, opened wide with a wail that stopped my heart. Though I knew right then that organ wasn't mine anymore. It was hers.

Theo cut the cord with wonder in his eyes, and the nurses wiped her up, wrapped her in a blanket, and carried her over to me.

I reached for her, feeling the weight of her, the shape of her in my arms after carrying her in my body all this time. I cradled my baby to my chest, peering into her face.

And Theo leaned in, resting his hand on mine, cupped under her head.

"You did it," he breathed. "You did it, Kate."

"Hello, baby," I said to the tiny thing in my arms.

When I looked up at Theo, it was through a sheet of tears.

He smiled and pressed a kiss to my forehead.

And just like that, we were a family.

THE HOSPITAL ROOM WAS QUIET and still—as silent as hospitals could get at least. Nurses came in every couple of hours to check on Hope or me or the wind direction for all I knew or cared.

I was blissed out and exhausted and fascinated by the baby in my arms.

She slept soundly, swaddled in a scratchy blanket that didn't seem to bother her but smelled to me like bleach and nightmares. I untucked the corner of the swaddle, lifting it so I could see her tiny little hand again. I slipped my finger into her fist, and she squeezed it with strength that surprised and awed me.

She was smaller than average—surprising, given Theo's genetics—five pounds, twelve ounces, the result of being three weeks early, Dr. Stout had assured me. She was perfectly healthy, late enough that her lungs had fully developed, which had been the real concern.

But she'd scored perfectly on her APGAR test, which Theo stayed next to her for.

Didn't at all surprise me she'd already gotten her first A-plus.

I smiled over at Theo. He was all arms and legs, barely contained by the chair that was supposed to convert to a bed but really looked less useful than an old camping cot would have been. His face was slack with sleep, but he didn't look boyish or soft. His features were too strong, his jaw too square, his nose too Roman, his lips too luscious to be anything but a man. A man who was mine just as much as I was his.

The door opened, and my mother popped her head in, smiling. I waved her in.

She made her way over, sitting on the edge of the bed to peer into the bundle. "Katie, she's just so pretty," she whispered. "All that hair! I ordered her some bows. I hope you don't mind."

I chuckled. "I don't mind," I whispered back.

Mom glanced at Theo. "That looks comfortable."

A snicker. "That chair makes him look like a giant."

"Well, he kinda is."

"Yes, he kinda is," I echoed with a smile. "How's Sarah?"

"Still sleeping. I'm glad her surgery went well and that she's gonna be all right. Tommy and Amelia are in her room, the two of them somehow piled on one of those tiny chairs like Theo, sound asleep."

I laughed at the thought. "I'm sorry I kicked you out of the delivery room, Mom."

But she waved her hand, beaming down at the baby. "Oh, I don't care, honey. I just want you to be safe and happy. I know I don't go about it like you need, and I'm sorry. I feel like I always do the wrong thing." She met my eyes, hers sad. "I want to understand you, but I've never known how."

"To be fair, I've never given you much to go on but flak."

"Well, I can be a real wrecking ball. I don't blame you for getting upset. I just wish I knew what to do."

"If I start telling you, will you listen?"

"I can promise to try," she said.

"Then I will, too," I promised in return.

"I'm sorry for pushing you about Theo today, too. I just…I hate to see you sad, Katie. And he made you so happy. I want you to have that again."

"You weren't wrong."

She blinked her confusion. "Did you just say I was right?"

"No, I said you weren't wrong."

She laughed. "I'll take what I can get." She cast another look in Theo's direction when he shifted in sleep, unable to get comfortable in that godforsaken chair.

"So, are you and Dad getting back together?"

Her face was lined with exhaustion and bright with relief. "I know it doesn't make any sense, but yes. Sometimes, all you need is for the person you love to say the words you need to hear. I needed him to come here. I needed him to fight for me, for us. And he did. I know we're crazy." She shook her head, looking down at the baby to avoid my eyes. "This is just how it works for us. Our rules…well, they're not everyone else's rules. But that's the beauty of love. It can be whatever you need it to be. You can make your own rules."

A shock of understanding flashed through me. "We can make

our own rules," I whispered. "It doesn't have to be defined by anyone but me. But us."

She met my eyes. "Of course you can, honey."

"Theo only has one."

A chuckle. "Well, good thing. You have so many." She nudged me with her elbow playfully, but I was still in a blinking state of realization. "What are you gonna do?"

There was only one answer. "Tell him how much I love him," I answered simply. "And hope he'll take me back."

At that, she smiled. "Oh, he will. I promise, he will."

The door cracked open again, and this time, it was my dad's head that popped in. We waved him in too, and he moved to stand behind my mother, his hand on her shoulder as he peered into the baby's face.

"She looks just like you did on the day you were born, Katie-Bug. Best day of my life," he said quietly.

Unexpected tears nipped at the corners of my eyes and the tip of my nose. "Thanks, Dad."

"No, thank you. One of these days, we'll be able to show you what you mean to us. Just gotta learn your language. You'd think we'd have gotten the hang of it by now," he said on a chuckle.

"I think maybe it was me who didn't know how to speak. But I think I might finally understand how."

"Oh?" he asked.

I nodded. "With love."

He smiled. "*With love, Katie.* Sounds like a goodbye."

"No, it's a hello."

He pressed a kiss to my hair. "Come on, Sparrow. The cafeteria's about to open, and there's a cream cheese scone in the window I want for mine."

Mom frowned. "Is it organic?"

"Sure," he lied.

She sighed, smiling as she slid off my bed and into his arms. And with a wave and a quiet goodbye, they were gone.

And I held my baby, watching Theo sleep, waiting for the moment he woke so I could tell him what he meant to me.

THEO

The hospital room was mostly dark when I woke not knowing what time it was, my neck stiff and back aching from the too-small convertible bed. Katherine smiled at me from her bed, gently bouncing the baby in her arms.

I checked my watch. Four thirty.

"When did she wake?" I asked, blinking the sleep from my eyes.

"Just a little bit ago. I changed her diaper, but I think she just wanted to be held."

I smiled, hauling myself out of the makeshift bed to stride over to her. She shifted, making room for me to stretch out next to her. I slipped my arm around her as we looked down at our baby.

"How are you feeling?" I asked.

"I think I'm high on oxytocin."

I chuckled. "It's intense, isn't it?"

"I can only compare it to one other thing."

"What's that?"

"Falling in love with you."

Everything stilled. My heart. My lungs. Time. I looked down at her, my Kate, her face soft and open.

"I realized it yesterday," she said quietly, "something I'd known all along. But I was caught up in the word and what I thought it meant. I never thought how I felt about you could be the thing itself, that I'd felt it all along. I think I might have loved you the first moment I met you. Is that crazy?"

"No." A single syllable, tight with emotion.

"I've put you through so much, Theo. And you've endured it all with patience and grace and understanding. I don't deserve this. I don't deserve you. And I understand if I've hurt you too bad to get you back, but—"

I stopped her—answered her—with a kiss.

I'd waited for months for that kiss.

I'd waited my whole life for that kiss.

It was laden with relief, deep with emotion, whispering promises and gratitude and absolute adoration.

When I broke the kiss, it was to look into her eyes. "Kate, I'm yours. I've been yours since the first. And I'll love you until I die."

"Good," she said with a smile. "You'll have to if we're going to get married. I don't want to end up like my mother."

I blinked at her. "Married?" I said stupidly.

She nodded. "Married. Unless you've changed your mind." She watched me for a moment. "Will you marry me, Theo? Because I don't want anyone else but you."

"That's my line."

She chuckled.

"Are you sure you don't want to wait to decide? You're all pumped full of happy hormones right now. Are you sure you're being rational? What happens later if you change your mind?"

"I won't because I can't. And love, I've realized, isn't rational in any form." She paused, searching for the words to explain. "Plato said that humans originally had four arms and four legs and were so powerful that Zeus worried for his safety. So he cleaved the humans in half, split them in two. And the only way they could be strong again was to find their other half. It was the only way they could find peace and strength—to become whole again. And love was the only thing that could bind the wound."

She looked down at our baby for a long moment. I didn't dare speak for fear I'd break the spell.

"I knew there was power in whatever was between us from that first night—it's why I stayed away—but I thought that power was destructive. Depleting. I thought that power would take. But Theo, I was wrong. Your love bound the wound in my heart I hadn't known I had. I'm sorry I didn't know. I'm so sorry for putting you through this. I'm so sorry for resisting when all you've done is love me. I've been trying to find a way to repay you, a way to show you my love the way you show me every day, in every little thing you do. And I've finally found it. Let me love you forever. Marry me."

The answer lodged in my throat, the words waiting unspoken. Because I couldn't speak.

So I kissed her instead, kissed her until my throat eased and my heart ached. Felt her life and mine click into place, felt our hearts thread together, healed by love like Plato had said.

When I broke away, I gazed on the face I'd love my whole life.

"Was that a yes?" she said with a husky voice and a sideways smile.

"That was a hell yes."

And I kissed her laughing lips again, the first of millions I'd collect.

EPILOGUE(S)

KATHERINE

HOPE: 2 DAYS OLD

I blinked through a trail of sage smoke.

My mother led the train down the hall, first her, then Theo carrying the car seat with Hope nestled inside. I followed behind, smiling at the tiny, sleeping baby's face, and my father brought up the rear, hands in his pockets and smile on his face.

Mom circled the room, sage in the air like the Olympic torch, and I sighed, too happy to be bothered.

I had a sneaking suspicion this would be my new state of mind, and I didn't hate it one bit.

Theo set down the car seat as Mom finished cleansing the room, handing me her blanket so he could reach her seatbelt.

Hope's eyes blinked open, and she sneezed the tiniest sneeze I

"All right," Dad said, reaching for my mother. "I think that's enough sage."

"Oh!" she gasped, rolling her eyes. "Silly me. Come on, Dave. Let's go do the rest of the house."

"Sure thing, baby." He ushered her out, winking at me along the way. "You did good, Katie."

My smile widened. "Thanks, Dad."

By the time they were gone, Theo was lifting Hope out of her car seat like he'd done it a thousand times, the picture of confidence. She was so small in his big, square hands, I found myself absorbed in the sight. He cradled her for a moment as he stepped to the crib and laid her inside.

I moved to his side, my hand resting on the rail, watching him swaddle her with tender care. She was asleep again before he was finished.

For a still moment, we watched her without tangible thought, standing in her quiet room. When Theo moved, it was to slip an arm around my waist and tuck me into his side. With another sigh, I leaned into him, resting my head on his broad chest.

"So," he started, the word rumbling through me, "when are we getting married?"

"Already trying to lock me down?"

"Since day one, Kate."

I chuckled, my cheeks warm and heart fit to burst. "Well, we can go to the courthouse next week, if you want."

When he didn't speak, I shifted to look up at him. He was giving me a look, a sideways, amused, hopeful look.

"You want the whole white dress, centerpiece, first dance thing, don't you?"

"I really do," he answered.

With a laugh, I rolled my eyes. "Anything you want, Theo."

"God, I love when you call me that."

I turned in his arm, gazing up into his bottomless eyes. "Well, we're even. I love when you call me Kate."

"Who knew?" he said on a laugh.

"You did. You always do. It's one of the many, many reasons I love you like I do."

"That reminds me," he said gently, letting me go.

In what seemed like one motion, he reached into his pocket and dropped to one knee, just like he had once before. Though instead of a garden in the moonlight, it was in our baby's nursery, next to the occupied crib. And this time, instead of fear, I only felt a rush of emotions. They welled in me like a plume of smoke.

"I love you, Kate, and I'll love you forever. Marry me."

I smiled down at him, extending my left hand. "I already asked you to marry me."

"I know, but I wanted to hear you say yes."

With my free hand, I cupped his cheek. "Yes. You have all of my yeses, forever."

"Forever," he said, slipping the ring onto my third finger.

"Forever," I echoed.

Before I could speak again, I was in his arms. And that promise was made into truth with a kiss.

THEO
HOPE: 1 YEAR, 2 MONTHS, 12 DAYS OLD

Fireworks.

From the beginning, she was fireworks—a burst of light against the black of night. And here, in the end, our world was fireworks.

We ran down the paved path in what felt like slow motion. The golden glow and smoke of sparklers illuminated the smiling faces of everyone we loved. Those faces were soft with joy, some bright with tears. And those faces lit us up even more than the fireworks they held.

They lit Katherine up like a beacon. Her dark hair uncontained and brushing the pale skin of her back. Her cheeks high as she laughed. Her eyes shining with unshed tears. Her snowy dress cast in gold.

I saw my mother, waving and crying, tucked under my brother's arm. Tommy, tall and dark and smiling with Amelia under his other arm. Amelia, small and delicate, her face flushed and happy and tearful. Their son was hooked on Amelia's hip, dark as Tommy but with Amelia's bright eyes, opening and closing his fist in his version of goodbye. Rin, elegant and beautiful, her arm around Court and swollen belly nestled into his side. Val and Sam, who had just gotten married the month before—our concession to everyone's double wedding request.

And Katherine's mother, waving with one hand and holding Hope on her hip with the other. My baby smiled at me, her little lips shaping the word *daddy* as she waved like her Nana had shown her, her tiny hand swiveling at the wrist and elbow. Her dress was white as snow, just like her mama's, and she'd toddled down the aisle with a basket of rose petals she forgot beyond a cursory handful and a solid tumping of the basket at the foot of the vined arch where I made Katherine my wife.

Forever and ever, amen.

The smoky tang in the air. The feel of her hand in mine. The sight of her, dress gathered in her other hand, the tips of her shoes darting out as we ran for the Mercedes waiting at the end of the path. In she went, and I paused, looking back at every face, at the path we'd been on, all things leading us right here, to this moment.

It was an end. And a beginning.

I waved goodbye, and their hands rose together to wave back.

Into the car I went. Into her arms I went.

I gathered her up, collected her delicately, and kissed the lips I loved so well.

"Mrs. Bane," I said when I released her lips.

"Mr. Bane," she said with a smile. "Was the wedding to your liking?"

My brow rose. "Was it to yours?"

With an exhale, she melted. "Oh, it was. I'm glad you insisted. A courthouse wouldn't have been nearly this lovely."

"No. And I would have missed you in this dress. I love you in this dress." I pulled her into my lap. "I'd love you out of this dress."

Her laughter filled the air, her arms winding around my neck. "You'd love me anyway."

"You sound so sure of yourself."

"Because I am. You love me in equal measure to my love for you. It's why we're so well suited."

"And here I thought it was because I was so clever to have tricked you into marrying me."

Another laugh, a tilt of her head. "Well, you *are* very clever. But I didn't need tricking, only patience while I figured out that I'd loved you all along."

"Maybe that *was* the trick."

"Then you, husband, are a magician."

"And you, wife, are mine."

Her arms tightened, her lips angling for mine, but our gazes were locked. "I was always yours, and I always will be."

The kiss was heavy with the promise, the depth of the truth, the weight of our love.

And forever was sealed with that kiss.

And it was fireworks.

ACKNOWLEDGMENTS

There are always so many people to thank, and I feel like there are never enough words.

As always, my husband Jeff comes first. This time, there's a special thanks for giving me three smart, funny, beautiful girls, and three pregnancies to combine in order to write this book. And thanks for not making me have a fourth.

Thank you to my daughters, for making me a mom and testing my patience and will and the bounds of my heart daily.

Kandi Steiner—You are my sunshine, my only sunshine. Thank you for the constant petting and loving and support. For the laughs and the warmth and the tears and the love. Can't do this without you, babe.

Jana and Kayti—To the group text to rule them all, to the Enyalightened bitches, to getting shit done on the daily. Cheers to you both!

Jacqueline Mellow—Your daily love gives me so much life. Thank you for always lifting me up, for always lending an ear, for always inspiring me. And thanks for saying "I Do" and becoming my forever work wife. #putaringonit

Sasha Erramouspe—You deserve a private island. I'll get you one next to mine when I retire. Thank you for reading this book 8392 times, for the marathon phone calls, for always making time for me, even when your life is crazy. I cannot ever thank you enough for all you do!

Abbey Byers—If it wasn't for you, I never would have had the thought to knock up our poor, robotic Katherine. If it wasn't for you, I wouldn't enjoy this process so much. If it wasn't for you, I'd probably shrivel up and die, so thank you for keeping me fed and watered and near the sunshine.

Kerrigan Byrne—WE DID THE DAMN THING OH MY GOD! Now, let's do it again.

Karla Sorensen—Just thank you. Every day, thank you. Thank you for holding my emotional bucket and petting my hair while I empty the contents of my heart into it. For your beta feedback, which I cannot survive without. I love you!

BB Easton—You are my favorite. Every day, talking with you just refills me, recharges me, makes me feel less alone. And you're a great bedmate. I'd share sheets with you any day of the week, Beastie!

Kyla Linde—Every. Damn. Day. Thank you. I don't know what I'd do without you!

Sierra Simone—Thank you for the best half hour of voice messages I've ever received. Your experience as a librarian was invaluable to me, and I am so grateful that you shared it! Thank you so, so much for taking the time to advise me.

Tina Lynne—As always, you are my rock, my right hand, my favorite. Thank you for everything you do!!

Carrie Ann Ryan—Your advice in the cover redesigns was beyond instrumental. In fact, YOU are instrumental to my life, my success, my confidence. Thank you!

Sarah Green—You are one of the kindest, smartest, most supportive women I know. Thank you for always being here for me, and thank you for your thoughts, your time, your heart and energy!

Ace Grey—Thank you for reading my manuscript when you had no time or energy to do it! I love you, babe.

Danielle Legasse—You are a gem!! Thank you for always dropping everything to read for me. You are a SUPERBETA!

Kris Duplantier—Your notes are always my favorite. ALWAYS. Thank you for reading for me!

Jenn Watson—Thank you for your time and brainwork on the redesign of the RLC covers! WE DID IT!! I am so thankful for you!

Sarah Ferguson—Thank you for always being there, for your positive attitude and your snark. You are amazing!

Jovana Shirley—Sorry I made you cry while you were editing my RomCom! Okay, that's a lie. I'm not sorry at all.

Ellie McLove—Thank you for polishing up my baby! Here's to another dozen books together.

Nadege Richards—Thank you for the brilliant formatting! You're a damn genius, and I'm so grateful to work with you!

ABOUT STACI

Staci has been a lot of things up to this point in her life: a graphic designer, an entrepreneur, a seamstress, a clothing and handbag designer, a waitress. Can't forget that. She's also been a mom to three little girls who are sure to grow up to break a number of hearts. She's been a wife, even though she's certainly not the cleanest, or the best cook. She's also super, duper fun at a party, especially if she's been drinking whiskey, and her favorite word starts with f, ends with k.

From roots in Houston, to a seven year stint in Southern California, Staci and her family ended up settling somewhere in between and equally north, in Denver. They are new enough that snow is still magical. When she's not writing, she's gaming, cleaning, or designing graphics.

CPSIA information can be obtained
at www.ICGtesting.com
Printed in the USA
LVHW111734130521
687356LV00006B/734